Congratulations on your giveaway win!

[illegible signature]

x

Charlotte E Hart

THE SPIRAL

****

THE SPIRAL

A Dark Romance

Cover Design by MAD
Formatting by MAD

****

Charlotte E Hart

THE SPIRAL

ISBN: 9781723978968

Charlotte E Hart
THE SPIRAL

License Notes

Charlotte E Hart

THE SPIRAL

****

"An idea, like a ghost, must be spoken to a little before it will explain itself."

Charles Dickens

Charlotte E Hart

THE SPIRAL

Chapter 1

Jack

The pad vibrates in my fingers, an enthusiastic yelp coming at me from the distance because of it. I scowl, enough energy left in the sound to make me wander through the woods towards it. I don't need to. Two more presses against this pad and they'll be rushing back to my feet anyway, but there's still that obstinate element in me that enjoys the sound of their pained howls. Likes to see it.

Dogs.

There are three of them. I've let them out for their weekly run. One is bulky and stout. He's the fighter, the one who pushes the other two off the food. The leaner one is crafty, forever hovering behind the stout one's feet, waiting for his chance. And the last one is near starving, scavenging for any small scrap he's left with, constantly whining. They're hunting for rabbit now, foraging through ditches and headlands, hoping for something to eat. It's their chance to open up and stretch, my offer of normality. Although, they won't get any more freedom anytime soon.

I stare around the parkland, letting the warmth of the sun bask down on me in the hope I'll feel it. I don't. It may as well be the depths of winter for me. Everything is cold, pointless. It's only these three dogs that keep me going. Feed them. Walk them. Train them. Remind them. That's it. Nothing else exists for me other than those four disciplines.

My phone rings somewhere on my body. I ignore it, not caring for whatever irrelevant topic the caller wishes to discuss. I have no reason to talk to anyone now apart from these dogs and one member of staff, and he barely gets conversation. It beeps a message at me, one I'll ignore further until I can be bothered to look at it later. The last message was from my brother, some counter topic about selling up soon. I ended the call before the message got a chance to finish. I'm not selling anything. Ever. It belongs to me and me alone now. No one is forcing anything from me, even if it is with the best intentions.

Another yelp sounds out as I turn into the ditch, my finger pressing the button in my hand so one of them shows themselves to me. A flash of brown darts around the corner, mud being kicked up as it runs and tries to hunt for rabbits again. I chuckle at the sight of it, and move branches out of my way as I clamber out the other side of the boggy ground. This one's fast. He likes to play games with me, testing my patience with every break for escape. The others are slower, easier to keep up with, but I haven't seen either of them since we made it past the border of the headland. They've probably turned back, given up the chase in the hope that this one will bring home the bacon. Either way, I don't care. The buttons I'm holding will do the work for me when I need to call them all back.

I stroll my way through the marshy ground, picking my route carefully, and stare back at the house to look at its grandeur. It's still as striking as it was the day we first saw it, imposing its presence on the parkland around it with little care for competition. It sits tall, casting a now ominous glow over the area and warning intruders to stay away. It never did at first. It was beautiful then, a perfect pretence of modern fairy-tales waiting for happy families and a king and queen to rule over their land, children in tow. Now it's a mausoleum, one I create and allow myself to weep within. Happily.

A shriek of sound splits the air's quiet meander, growls and snarls floating through the trees back at me. I turn and hurry along the paths, wanting to see the kill and watch the throttle of fur as he takes his meal. It feeds me somehow, gives me a sense of purpose or pride. Maybe it just gives me something to live for, something to witness and cling onto. They've become like my children somehow now. My purpose.

The trees clear as I round the corners, only the small bushes hindering my view of the cacophonous sound. I climb the bank, heaving my feet through the wet ground to get a clear line of sight, but I'm already too late. There's nothing left but traces of blood surrounding his muzzle, and fur hanging from the carcass at his feet. I sneer at it, annoyed with myself for missing the entertainment, and press the buttons six times just to watch the fucking thing yelp in quick succession. His body quivers and thrashes under the shock that rides him, legs giving up bothering to stand.

Fucking dog. I should have moved quicker, kept up with it.

The thought's annoying enough that I press the other buttons, too, listening for more yelps in the distance so I can punish them for this one's indiscretion. He knows he should wait; they all do. They fucking wait until they're told to do anything, eating included.

Howls sound off to the left somewhere, both of them agonised and tormented. I smile at that as I look down at this one still bucking about, some element of me feeling amused with the thought, and then release the buttons and turn for home. Their run is done now, called short by this one forgetting his training. Maybe they'll get another one next week. Maybe they won't.

Hard ground eventually crunches underfoot. I keep moving with little care for the continued whimpers that come from behind, and stare into a mist that's come down. He can suffer the pain. It might make him think faster next time and remember his place. This is a partial freedom I allow them, not a chance at proving some attempt at superiority. Starving or not, they will not eat until they're told to. They won't do a fucking thing until they're given permission.

They can all go back to their damn cages and wallow in their misfortune again. Wait until I give them another chance at escape, just so I can force them back to where they dared to once wreak havoc. They can sit in their place, staring at her photographs and learn some more about what it means to destroy something I love. They'll rot in the poison I let them drink, eat the pungent meat I charitably offer them. Beg and whinge for decency as I hurt them for their rashness, all the time staring at the faces of those they destroyed. They'll putrefy in their mistake, dealing with whatever fate I choose to deliver for as long as I deem necessary.

Charlotte E Hart
THE SPIRAL

Damn dogs. Vile, insipid, treacherous fucking dogs.

If she were alive now, they'd know the benefits of protecting her at all costs, know how much more pleasurable life is with her around.

They'd know their manners now.

They'd kill *for* her rather than take liberties they never should have damn well taken.

Chapter 2

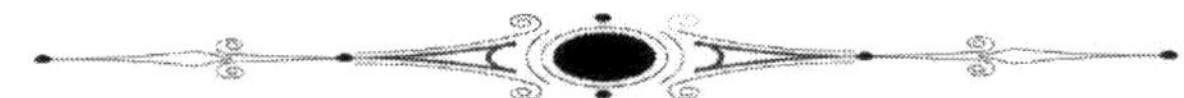

Maddy

Fifteen minutes I've been standing here looking out into the garden. Fifteen minutes digesting the last hour and trying to find another way for us, but there's nothing left anymore.

It's hopeless.

I stare out into perfected grounds and manicured lawns. There should be nothing like the spring to remind me how life should be—warm, carefree, happy. The ground beneath me dry. The skies above me blue. But life isn't carefree here; it isn't happy, and nothing here is warm. This world I live in is dead. A lie. A jail, if truth be told. Nothing but fragmented dreams and shattered skin. That's all there is now. Shattered skin.

Charlotte E Hart

THE SPIRAL

Cradling my face and trying to find another rag to soak in ice, I eventually shuffle my way out to the garage, clinging to the wall as I go. It's not that far from the house, and thankfully I can get to it from the back door, meaning I don't have to go around the front. I'm not ready for that yet.

Not yet.

I've managed to cover it for years. Sometimes with foundation, other times with hats and scarves if its winter, but this time it's so bad I know nothing's going to mask the bruising when it comes. And summer is coming, anyway, that lovely time of year when everyone should be leaping about in close to nothing. Enjoying the sun on their skin and appreciating all that life is, perhaps getting in the pool at the bottom of this garden and having some fun, a barbeque even. That's not going to happen this summer. Not that it's happened for any other summer in the last two years with any plausible admittance of contentment.

The door creaks as I shove my weary frame against it and flick the light on, hoping it will help me see through the swelling that's beginning to worsen on my left eye, but the fluorescent light is so bright it actually makes it harder to see rather than easier so I switch it off again and rest in the dark instead. Maybe I should just stay in here, lock the door and stay where he can't get to me. I chuckle at myself as I turn to the freezer and pull on the handle. He'll get to me anywhere, won't he? Always has. Always will.

Charlotte E Hart

THE SPIRAL

I tried getting away from him the second time it happened with any real brutality. I went to Callie's house and told her he'd gone away to mull his actions over. I told her that he'd apologized and said it was just stress, that he didn't mean it. She'd snorted and slapped my non bruised cheek immediately, a sharp reminder that once they hit, they always hit. Once they beat, they always beat. Once in fear, always in fear. She was right. I may not have believed her at the time, and I certainly didn't listen to her when he came and picked me up to take us back home, but she was right.

I've been scared ever since.

Nothing's changed. Maybe he was better for a while. He didn't hit me, anyway. But the aggression's always been there, lurking in his hands and waiting to come out. He wasn't like this when we originally met. I couldn't have asked for a better man than the Lewis I met in Paris as I placed my crepe order. He was kind, thoughtful, and extremely attractive with his relaxed sense of style. He paid for my crepe as I shyly smiled back, and then we sat by the Seine all afternoon and chuckled about anything and everything.

He was slightly older than me, but that didn't matter. I was nineteen and in a French college studying French and biology. What did I care? He was nice, seemed happy enough and laughed all the time. *We* laughed all the time. And attentive, he was always so attentive. He'd pamper me with all sorts of things, taking me to high end shops and expensive restaurants. I guess I never questioned where it all came from. I just enjoyed it. I enjoyed him.

It wasn't until about a month or so of dating that I found out about his family and their wealth. Fourth son of Phillipe Blisedy—France's answer to the millionaire club. Bankers. Not that Lewis showed any interest in either the money or the industry. He seemed to not give a damn. He took me out after college, showed me all the sights he'd grown up with. He even got me into appreciating art and literature as he talked endlessly about sculpture and design, something I'd never been interested in before him. But the moment we moved to America, it all stopped. Everything changed after that job offer of his, the one his father made him take.

Life was never the same again.

The ice stings as I tentatively hold it over my eye and let my body sink down to the floor in exhaustion. One hour fighting for my life again. One hour trying to curl myself up as tightly as possible so he couldn't get to my face. One hour just hoping that if he didn't get to my face then at least I'd be able to leave the house and go to work. One hour I shouldn't have bothered trying for. I should have just let him do it straight away. Stood there, opened my arms, and let him get the death punch in instantly. Taken it and let him have his ego helped on its way before his meeting.

Maybe I wouldn't have the split skin on my calf from his shoe then, or the grip marks on my arms, or the hair ripped from my scalp. Instead, I'm a walking disaster again. One who's going to have to cancel all my appointments and rearrange, tell the museums they will just have to look after themselves, and somehow put off the Blandenhyme deal for a while.

I find myself staring into space as I dab at my eye continuously and gently feel for where my hair used to be, foolishly wishing the bruising away. This couldn't have come at a worse time. Not that any time is a good time for being beaten, but one week before the biggest deal of my life isn't great. If I wasn't so furious with just that thought, I'd be crying I'm sure. I'd probably be screaming silently into this gloomy garage and asking 'why me?' constantly like I have done all the other times, but I've got no questions left anymore. No tears either. There's just anger and frustration in me now. Hatred, if I'm honest.

I don't *love* him anymore. I don't *like* him anymore, and I can't put up with his self-serving attitude anymore. In fact, I can't remember one damn thing to make me want to stay anymore, regardless of the enormous attempt at a home we've built. It's time to get on with the plan. Madeline's plan. Money, most definitely, is not everything.

Some time passes as I look at my bare legs and wonder which trousers to wear tomorrow instead of a skirt. That's all I've got. Which Prada or Gucci trousers to put on next. Any of the hundreds of pairs will do, I suppose. They'll all cover the broken skin, or the scars left from the other beatings I've taken. He's always liked the legs; he knows they can be covered easily.

I still don't know why he did it. I've asked a thousand times, pleaded for some semblance of apology in the aftermath of the event, but there's never an answer, just the threat of another bruise and a sneer. So now I don't care either. I'm done with this, with him. There's nothing left for us.

I just need to leave.

Slowly pulling myself back up the wall, I walk back to the house with little concern for him coming home. He won't be back until later tonight or early tomorrow morning. He'll go to his high-powered meeting, win whatever battle he's currently in, and demolish his opponent, undoubtedly racking up our bank account another few million as he does. And then he'll go out and get drunk with his colleagues, celebrating his outstanding achievements in the only way he knows how—drinking. After that, he'll roll in around two am with a bunch of flowers in his hands, stinking of some spicy perfume as he apologises again and tries to get me to have sex.

The thought's almost pitiful. It's exactly the same procedure every time this happens. I can set my watch by it, and I can already hear the words as they leave his lips.

"Mads, I'm sorry. It won't happen again. It was the stress. I'm trying. Please forgive me."

My lip scoffs at the tone of his voice. *Mads*. I hate that nickname now. He only ever uses it when he's sorry for something. It used to be sweet, loving and full of kind thoughts. It used to fill me with joy and make me laugh. Now, the sound of it repulses me, almost to the point of wanting to be sick. Mads. Cute little Mads. Mads who rolls over and takes it. Mads who lets him get away with it. Mads who, for some godforsaken reason, loved him in spite of it. Mads Blisdey needs to die along with every other dream the stupid cow had. Madeline Cavannagh is the one who's going to make it out of this now and find her way. Madeline is the one who will stop this unending control he has over me. And Madeline will make sure he doesn't do it again.

My bare feet hit the kitchen floor and I head into the dining room where the remnants of his attack still lie scattered around. Crystal ornaments, shattered. Chairs upturned. A small spray of my blood on the glass table and up the cream curtains. I pick up a silver photo frame from the floor and place it gently on the fireplace, hardly able to smile at the image of our wedding. There's nothing to smile for anymore, no matter how happy we might appear to be in this photo. I can still remember the limp I covered by hanging onto him that day, grinning idiot that I was at the time, pretending we were fine.

What might have once held hope is lost.

We're done.

Turning the photo down and sliding the diamond rings off my finger, I place them beside the frame then turn to leave the room. I don't bother with tidying like I normally do. Instead, I head straight to the lounge for my bag and keys, knowing this will only end when I make it end.

I've been clever about it, organised myself to some degree. Bank accounts in my maiden name, enough to keep me going when he freezes everything. A house bought and paid for, which is nowhere near here. I've got my own business, my own car, my own everything really. Just not my own life.

That's about to change.

It doesn't take long for me to pack my bags and haul them out to the Range Rover. Apart from a few clothes, shoes and toiletries, I don't want anything from here. No furniture, no paintings, no reminders. I'll do it all again in my new place. I haven't showered or changed. I need the evidence fresh under my nails and the blood still clotting around my skin. I wish I could remove his semen from inside me, but I can't even do that yet.

They'll have to do that for me when I get there.

I slam the door none to quietly and head for the car. I've timed this run before. Twenty-one minutes at a decent time of day. And that's exactly what it takes me to get through downtown traffic, drive by his building with my finger held high, and then park outside the police station. Twenty-one minutes, thirty-five minutes floundering in my pain, plus one hour of being beaten and raped. That's how long it's taken me to get my act together. Why I haven't done it before now, I don't know. Why I didn't listen to Callie after the first time, I don't know. And why I've put up with it every time since, I don't know. I loved him, I guess. Maybe I thought that each new time he said he wouldn't do it again, he wouldn't. I believed him.

I don't anymore.

A police car passes behind mine as I stare through the tinted windows at the building, getting ready for my ordeal. It's almost easier to think about Lewis doing his worst than going in here and having them prod and poke at me. I'll have to explain it all to someone, be honest about the last few years. These people will be the first to know, the first ones to hear the words out loud. I don't even speak out loud to myself about it. It all stays inside my mind where I can contain it and put it into logical thought, even if none of it's been rational in any way.

The thought suddenly scares the life out of me as I squint at the doors and wonder who'll be the one who asks me questions first. A man, woman? Who goes in between my legs? How many photos will they take? And when they've taken them, where do those photos go? Who gets to see them? And what about the papers? Will this be news tomorrow morning? Will my name be plastered across the papers with photos of the evidence available for the world to dig into and paw over?

My fingers refuse to let go of the steering wheel as I try to turn my body and open the door. They just stick to it like glue, telling me not to move. To stop and think a little more about this. I could just disappear instead without all this drama, couldn't I? Go to my new house, have a shower, stay inside for the next week or so and then get on with my life. We don't have children. I don't want the house, and he can keep his money. There's nothing else to fight about. Just the fact that he'll want me back where I belong, or his father will. But if I don't go inside this place and do this, I've got nothing. No proof, nothing to threaten him with, no ability to ask for a restraining order, nothing.

I have to do this. I have to.

Have to.

I don't have to, and this is proved by me reversing out of the parking area and turning back towards the traffic. I can't. I don't want to. I just want out. I want to move on and forget, put it behind me somehow. I'll deal with divorce if I have to. I can see the papers now as they dirty and drag up our lives. The moment they get involved, the great Blisedy family will get involved. His father will drag my dad into it, say I came from an insane background and probably try saying Lewis was only defending himself against the crazy Cavannagh family. No one is insane in my family, certainly not me, but my dad has been in a mental institution for the last ten years. Anxiety and depression, certified. So much so that they came and took him away the day before I started my GCSE's. After that, Mum finally got a chance to live again, and she told me to go get on with my life. To make something of myself. To go abroad if I wanted to and to never live in fear of anything.

Fine job I've done of that, not that she knows.

The streets of Atlanta all blur into one another as I cross town again and head for my new place. I can hardly see out of my left eye, but at least the pain is wearing off a little now all thanks to the extra strong pain killers. The blood on my leg has dried up, and the ache in my head seems to be dulling down. Hopefully, the ice did some good to my eye and it won't be long until it's coverable. With any luck that will mean I can deal with the Blandenhyme estate properly.

You wouldn't think antiques were so hard to deal with, but valuing, supervising, cataloguing, categorising, transporting, and correctly placing objects, are significant tasks. I get paid a lot of money for doing it. I spend most of my time travelling to one museum or another, or picking up an artefact for someone and taking it to another country. It started when Lewis' father had an old Rembrandt hanging that he hated, so Lewis asked me to take it to Scotland because he couldn't. An old Laird had bought it from the Blisedy family. I've been doing the same sort of thing ever since. It's the one thing I do have Lewis to thank for—my job.

It's a detailed career, one I sort of fell into I guess, but it's one I love. It responds to my sense of organisation. It's chaotic sometimes—I'm forever panicking last minute and worried about what could go wrong with the next million pound thing I'm categorising or moving—but it's all mine. And now it really is just me. No help from Lewis. No back up. I'm alone.

It's a revelation I hadn't really thought about, not enough to consider the feeling of actually being alone, anyway. It confuses me, as I turn back onto the highway and travel south towards my new home, making me question what I'm doing for a minute even though I know I've done the right thing. Of course I have. I'll be fine on my own. Fine.

Opening the window, I let the fresh summer air cascade in and blow my hair about. It soothes the aches that still remain, filling me with a new sense of hope that everything's going to be okay. I mean, what can he do other than scream and shout about things? The new place is like Fort Knox with its state of the art security system and lockable everything. He might be able to find me—I doubt that will take long at all—but he won't be able to get in. I've made sure of that at least.

My hand turns the radio on of its own accord, ready to listen to something brighter than the constancy of dramatic dark strings I've been made to endure for too many years. I need light and happiness now, pop, maybe some graceful classical to help bring on visons of breezes and hope. There will be no more darkness for me. I want light and airy, uncomplicated cheerful and joyful notes that uplift and bring euphoria rather than shadows of doom. Lewis can decompose in that if he wants. In fact, Lewis can submerge himself in whatever hate he wants to for the rest of his life. I hope he enjoys it, languishes in it even, and buries himself. He won't be doing it to me anymore.

It seems to take no time at all to arrive, regardless of the two hour drive. A new home, new life, new chance. Cherry trees line the road, their pretty pink petals fluttering to the ground as cars slowly drive by. It's enchanting, much prettier than the road we lived on where tall imposing buildings looked like eyesores and made all who dared enter cower in fear. No, this is beautiful, welcoming. It makes me think of grandmas and apple pies. Not that I care for baking in the slightest, but the thought's lovely nonetheless.

Slowly creeping along, I peer in other people's windows, noting all the architecture and quaint Victorian frontages. They're not small houses, most four bedroom I suppose. Mine certainly is, but compared to the ten bedroom mansion I've come from, they're beautiful in their size. Perfect for families of a middle class predilection who try to attain more. I laugh lightly at the thought. They shouldn't bother. These people should just relax in their homes, enjoying the time they have and loving each other wholeheartedly. Have children, play in parks, go shopping and on holiday frequently. I can most definitely tell them the wealth they want is worth nothing.

Not one thing.

Eventually, I pull up outside my new place and breathe in a long, full breath. Home. The light blue door hangs gracefully within the white panelled exterior. Five windows balanced perfectly and all sitting snugly beneath a tall red pitched roof. Roses grow up around the door, climbing towards the first floor, and just to top it off, the quintessential white picket fence cages the whole property in and reminds me of the English Surrey countryside I grew up in.

There isn't much furniture here, but it's enough to get by with until I find the time or energy to go out and get more. Perhaps once I truly feel like I'm at home the right furniture will present itself, but at the moment what I have is minimal—a few things dotted about and a kitchen ready for use. Two of the bedrooms are fully furnished I don't know why. I thought perhaps, if I was lucky, maybe Callie would come and visit.

I miss her. I miss the giggles and the fun we used to have. I miss going out with her, and the way she just knew me so well. And that's all my own fault. If I'd just listened to her I might have had a chance at getting away earlier, but I didn't. So instead, I've spent the last year or so socialising with Lewis' friend's wives and girlfriends. None of them have been real people. In fact, the entirety of the social scene we've been a part of is pretentious and fake.

Thankfully, I can choose my own everything now, including friends. I'll learn to become who I was before Lewis again. Learn not to jump at every shadow that creeps up on me, fear of the next blow heading my way ruling my every waking second.

Just me and my new life.

I turn back for the door and close it. I'll just get myself settled in and have a coffee, and perhaps then I can go get some groceries in, rent a film on Netflix, have a bath and wipe the last of my husband off of me. That's my choice now. No ordering. No comments on what I should or should not be doing.

Just me. Alone.

I walk back into the kitchen and dig around in cupboard, flicking the boiler on for hot water and then drawing out the first aid box I prepared. Sadly, I knew the day I arrived it would be because of a beating I'd taken. It makes me frown at my own mindlessness, causing a wince of pain as I begin strapping an eye-pad into place gently and sealing the corners securely. It's funny how I could prepare for this but not just get myself away before it happened. Pathetic of me really. It won't be happening again. Nothing like that will happen again. These bruises will be the last ones I take from anyone. They'll heal, I'm sure, and then my skin will finally be free of torment. My life, too.

I stare back at the cupboards, travelling my eyes down to the one below that hides the gun safe I had installed. I'm going to get that gun he wouldn't let me have, and I'm going to use it. I'll prove myself safe somehow. I have to learn to be free again. Be without him.

Because nothing is getting to Madeline Cavannagh again.

Chapter 3

Jack

My fingers grate against the tartan fabric of the chair, picking at the loosening threads to remind me of little fingers and their mischievous habits. Sounds of sweet laughter attack my mind instantly, followed by the pattering of tiny feet and crashing objects as he ran by. I wallow in that, closing my eyes and allowing my frame of mind to torment every inch of me. Her voice joins in, too, calling from the kitchen garden and telling me to come grab a basket for her. It's so clear—clear enough that I can almost smell her perfume and feel her hair between my fingers.

I open my eyes, leaning my head back to stare at anything but the spiral in hope that I'll see her. I won't. I never will again. And yet not one fucking thing, person, object or image makes their faces disperse to the shadows I need. Time is static, filled with nothing but dark corners and visions of crimson stains against sepia walls. There's just white ceiling above me, faintly lit by the gold lampshades she chose that dimly light the ornate cornicing above. Darkness and shadows, just the way I like it. Heavy dark blue velvet curtains. The blinds drawn. The doors closed again after my fucking dogs have been walked. Never locked, though. I leave them open, inviting anyone who dares come in to attempt at decadence again.

Their voices subside after a while, leaving me with silence and emptiness again, so I tip my head back to the spiral, snarling at the bottom step that taunts me with its worn surface. It took a little over a month for me to step on that one, then another to try a few more out for size. After drinking myself into a near coma, I managed to pull myself quarter of the way up, and there I slept all night, desperate to hear her voice berating me for being a drunkard.

The toe of my shoe scuffs the step I didn't realise I'd made my way to, halting before it plants down. Fuck these steps and their climb. I glare at them, willing my feet to move, but they won't. Not one fucking inch. I know why. It's too soon. They're not ready for me yet after yesterday's misdemeanour. The sole of my shoe buffers itself around on the black material instead, wearing the tread away some more before returning to the wooden floor below.

Fucking steps to my hell.

I turn and head for the poolroom, choosing one of the only things I take any pleasure in other than my purpose here. What little civility I had for the outside world is long gone. It died its fucking death along with them. I've left that side of life to Toby. My sibling is less dulled by hatred than me. He's still ruthless as a shark in the boardroom, but more inclined to take a lenient route if required. There is nothing lenient about me. Not anymore. The small part that was once content to engage frivolities and happiness was lost the moment I came home and found their brutalised bodies. Selma—raped, tortured and split open like a pig on the bathroom floor, and Lenon, my son, shot and left to die in his toddler bed, bleeding and alone.

Most humans deserve nothing but contempt and loathing now.

Knocking on the lights in the poolroom, I cross to the cabinet and begin fastening together the cue, slowly grinding the screw together. The solid beech feels familiar in my grasp, like an old shirt that eases woes. It gives me a sense of security, or simply the unhindered feel of something dense in my hand to remind me. I smile as the wood accidently bounces off the side of the table, enjoying the weighty sound that ricochets off the cloth's surface. It's a sound I know well, like the swift strike of wood against boned extremities, or the sound of agonised howls.

My guts coil as visions crash through me again, causing me to brace a hand on the table. Selma's body was like a massacre—prone, exposed, drenched in her own blood and splattered with semen. She wasn't bound; she was just there, her glassy eyes staring up into me and her body spread open and left to bleed out on the tiled floor. No bullet holes, just a large impact wound to the head and a mutilated frame. It's a sight that preoccupies every fucking step I take since that night, especially the ones up the spiral.

I sigh and rack up the balls then wander to the other end of the table, dragging my fingers along the cloth as I go to imagine her skin beneath them, soft as silk and olive tanned as the night. She was my reason for life—her and Lenon. Nothing mattered before her. No woman of consequence ever found a way to interest me for longer than a few weeks, but with her, I learned to breathe more deeply than ever before. I learned love and compassion, and a depth of feeling I'd never experienced previously.

Not anymore, though.

All I have left now are the spaces within this fucking crypt of a once held life. It's sacred to me, honoured for the beauty she bestowed on it and left to decay in her wake around me. Sell up? I glower at the thought, ready to give Toby more of my mind than he's already had. I'll do what I want with her perfectly created spaces, no matter how they rot without her in them. Lounges and dining rooms.

Two studies, nine bedrooms, sun terraces and conservatories. Manicured fucking gardens becoming ruins with each passing day she doesn't tend to them. They're mine now. My memories.

All mine.

The crash of the cue breaking against the fireplace causes shivers of hatred to rear up and remind me of where I need to go, of the fucking dogs. My muscles tense instantly, my own hackles rising on the back of my neck, ready and willing to rage all the hatred I have. I snarl at the broken cue and walk for the door, throwing one snapped end onto the table and watching the balls bounce off each other. Fucking balls. There's only one place to alleviate this need. It's up that spiral, waiting for me, but the splitting skin is less avenging than it was at first. It no longer masks the pain inside. It increases the hunger for more odium to be reigned down. More animosity to be bestowed.

More fucking insanity to come.

Doors slam behind me as I grab my coat to give the pretence of respectability. Suits and expensive shirts still clothe me, all things chosen by her. It glamourizes the impression of society's needs, shielding others from the actual truth of what this mind now holds inside. Hate. Revenge. A fury so engrained it doesn't want absolution or alleviation. It desires nothing more than to ruin those who derived pleasure from their acts. It bleeds from me as I bleed it from them, the crimson droplets and stripes moulding sins into something tangible that I can feel beneath my hands rather than the hollowness of life. Those dogs revitalise her memory, keep it vibrant and alive inside my mind so I can continue seeing them both. Brown hair, green eyes, smiling mouths and fluid limbs. Limbs that ran and lived. Limbs that were still alive.

The cool night air causes another shiver as I step outside and scan the yard. There's nothing but the few servants' houses dotted about on the park's grounds. Nothing has happened here since that evening. Police reports were filed. Officers with tracker dogs and crime scene investigators did their work while I sat and watched them. Another officer asked me questions, ones I nodded and shook my head at in response. And then I stared blankly as two body bags were taken from my home, Lenon's small hand still visible where the fastening hadn't been zipped correctly.

My life left that night. All of it. But it was five months after that when I changed. Those five months turned up nothing. Perhaps previous to that I believed in justice, trusted the system and expected that criminals were found so they could pay for their atrocities, but they weren't found. Nothing was found. The case was closed. But money made things work more successfully—money and criminals who knew their own kind. I found the fuckers then thanks to my wealth. I found them and had them brought here.

And here they still are, paying for their crimes.

Lights flicker around the drive leading down to the house, illuminating the gravel underneath and lighting up the area. I gaze at the drive and sweep my eyes over the grounds surrounding it, fields upon fields of grassland. All bought for our children to eventually run around in and play, to grow up on, to enjoy and be free to feel safe in as they roamed aimlessly. It's all useless now, just barren grassland wasting away and lacking any reason at all.

I wander towards the garages, still taking in the night air, and fish around on the wall through the selection of car keys. A drive is needed to calm down. They won't survive another attack from me. Not yet. They need time to repair their grotesque little selves so I can do it again. I lost control, lost the order of beatings when that fucker disobeyed me. Now I've not rested one of them long enough. It fucking infuriates me again as I snatch at the Merc keys and search the room for the car amongst too many other fucking cars, then eventually find it at the back.

I close the front door and open the back section instead to pull out onto the back driveway rounding the estate. I haven't been this way for a while. It's the way she used to come in, saying it was prettier, so I follow the curvature of the road as it swings its way, barely noting all the small servant houses and barns along the route. They're empty now and of little interest. I fired the majority of them that night, hardly containing the need to kill the lot of them for not doing something, or at least noticing something was wrong. It didn't matter that they'd been in the house on their own that night. It also didn't matter that all the servants had been out at the cook's daughter's christening. Someone should have checked in on them. No one did. Not one of them.

The only one who remains on site now is old Bob Ritters, the gardener-come-handyman. For whatever reason I've kept him on, perhaps as a nod to the fact that he's been here for thirty-two years, long before we arrived. Bob worked on the estate for the previous occupants. He knows the old house like the back of his hand and keeps it standing regardless of the fact that he can hardly see anymore. Or maybe it's just the fact that the old man once carried Lenon across the brook on his shoulders and the image still mingles with the other more disturbing ones. But he never goes upstairs.

No one goes up the stairs but me.

And he never questions what he damn well sees either.

My foot flattens on the accelerator as I hit the top road, increasing my speed and swerving the corners to drown out the screams I never heard.

Charlotte E Hart

THE SPIRAL

"Selma."

It blows from my mouth, aggravation numbing the volume to nothing but tormented woes. One more time? A thousand more times? Perhaps the next time I tear flesh apart I won't see Lenon's face as I pound into one of them. Or better yet, perhaps I will again and I can let that rage fill me with absolute vacancy as I deliver another blow, the fury intended to either diminish or relight the fire for more. Just pain—that's all I want to provide. I want to sweat and rip at them, punishing them and making them feel the hate that courses through me. I want expulsion, discharge, so I can see her face smiling and forgiving me for letting them down. I want that wrapped all around me, reminding me of Sunday drives in the country, of relaxed afternoons and wicked evenings in the arms of warmth. Fuck this life and moving on. There is no moving on. I am stagnant, and desperate to stay motionless. The thought of anything gaining momentum, other than hatred, is enervating.

Life is safe in this unending hole I've created. In stasis maybe, but predictable in its regularity at least. Dark and foreboding is comfortable. There is solace in its arms around me. I am in control in that house, delivering revenge and justice. Out here I'm lost and alone again.

I slam on the brakes and haul the car to the side of the road, disordered about whether to go forward or travel home to the fuckers. What does it matter if they're half dead already? I could do it this time. Finish it all.

Cars scream past me, blaring their horns at my untimely halt mid-swerve. I hardly hear them, couldn't fucking care less. Her name is out there now, loud and clear in the air. I can hear it still.

My forehead rubs into the wheel, trying to see her more clearly, but nothing materializes. Only blood and disgraced skin.

I sigh and lift my head again, resting it back and considering turning the car around, but something catches my eye outside, something consuming to the point of irrationality. Her smile and hands seem to be beckoning me outside the car for some reason. She's there, hovering in sight, almost real in the headlights and trying to suggest something as a mist rolls in from nowhere.

"Selma?" I whisper the name into the car and watch her mouth broaden in the lights.

The ghostly apparition just continues smiling, her clean, white dress floating around her feet as she slowly begins to disappear again. "No, Selma, don't…"

My hand reaches forward, my fingers knocking against the windscreen as I try to touch her, but it's too late. She's gone. Lost into whatever cloud of light she came from as it disperses back into the trees. Only a slight fog remains to confuse me further. I stare at it then open the door and walk towards it. There's nothing but the bright shine of my main beam against the forest lying ahead, nothing but the black of night, more screeching tyres running by, and dense thickets of hedgerows.

I turn within the space, searching for anything to show me I've actually seen a ghost of my dead wife, but still nothing highlights anything odd. All I have is memory of the vision I've seen, and an unusually frigid chill in the air for the time of year.

"Selma?" I call out again, louder this time, perhaps hoping she will reappear. She doesn't, but the faintest sound of laughter comes from somewhere, causing me to spin on my heel and move forward into the undergrowth. "Selma?" I call again, even louder.

There isn't a response, but I can hear the laughter still echoing. It's her laugh, full and bold, happy, gregarious. It initiates a smile, the first real one in months to break out on my face, as memories of happy times come flooding back. And I chase it. I chase deeper and deeper into the woods, desperately searching for her image and not caring for the fact it's ghostly. Any image of her not sprayed with blood is better than the only one I have left. I want this new one, want it like my life depends on it.

Trees blur as I dodge the branches and follow the sound of her voice, owls calling out a night chorus as I hurry further on. The dense floor beneath me crunches and clatters, cracking twigs and knocking stones out of my way as I run on and finally arrive in a clearing.

I eventually stop and brace my hands on my knees, sucking in rapid breaths for oxygen as I hunt for her voice again. Nothing comes back. No sound at all other than the groan of trees in the breeze. I peer into the dark depths, examining it for any sign of light or fog, but still only shadows reflect back at me, shadows and gloomy offerings of ancient parkland trees casting their branches under the moonlight. My eyes narrow, my lips chuckling at my own futility. Ghosts? What am I thinking? But she was so clear in those lights. And her voice was crystalline. It was hers; I know it so well, still. I hear it daily, calling me, shouting at me, her moans, her screams of pain or pleasure.

"Selma?"

Nothing again. No white lights. No fog. No guidance to what the fuck just happened.

I glare into the night again with one last hope that she will materialise and explain, or just hover again so I can look at her for hours and remember the way she moves, the way her cheeks glow. The way her body sways even, and the effortless way her eyes sparkle and make everything dull in comparison. I just want five more minutes, an hour, twenty fucking seconds, anything more than this empty oblivion again. But nothing happens as I keep looking around.

Not one thing.

Eventually, I huff and turn from the clearing, heading back towards the dense tree filled forest and wondering how the hell to get back to the road. Where did I come from? I can't remember. I track as best I can, following the uneven surface and checking for footprints within the damp ground. It's good enough, because some time later I see the headlights of my car glinting in the distance, enough that I fight my way back through the undergrowth to get to them.

I pull my coat tighter around me as I get to the Merc, sensing the frigid chill in the air again and turning back to face the forest. The fog's behind me again now, drifting through the undergrowth and offering some resemblance of the image I saw earlier. Is she still there?

"Selma? Please, if you're there…"

The mist disperses instantly, evaporating back into the woodland and tumbling away from me through the brambles and thickets. Gone again.

I frown at the thought, chastising myself for my folly and shaking my head back into order. It's time to get going, to continue on with whatever I was fucking doing before this interruption took hold. I get into the car with one final glance back at the woods, hoping she appears, but she doesn't, so I slam the door and buckle up.

Pulling out onto the highway slowly, I stare into the oncoming lights and shake my head again. Irrationality and foolishness. Ghost stories? Perhaps I'm going mad. My brow rises as I let the thought wash over me. Madness isn't an unfathomable thought. I could be. I hardly socialise anymore, taking little interest in normal activities. I chuckle, amused by the image of myself going mad.

Jack.

I slam on the brakes again at the sound of her voice, not bothering to pull to the side this time. It's so clear, so profound that I nearly get out of the car before it stops, wrenching at my belt for escape as I open the door again.

"WHAT?" I call out into the air, tripping over my own feet and trying to avoid the oncoming car as it swerves around me. "JESUS, WHAT? SELMA? Please…" I fling my head around, wildly searching for the source of her voice, but there isn't anything, only more cars blaring and screeching around me. "Please, Selma," I mutter, chasing my own feet to get me off the road and onto the path. "What do you want?"

And more nothing. Nothing but the sound of cars hurtling by, narrowly missing the Merc every single time as I shake at the side and wonder what the fuck is happening to me. Madness. This is fucking madness. I scrub my face, scratching at my hairline to wake myself up. I'm damn well dreaming. I must be.

I kick out at the car, furious with my own lack of understanding and irritated by the loss of her voice again, then rip my coat off and fling it to the ground in rage.

More fucking mist rolls in from somewhere. I back away from it and stumble into a ditch, falling down the slope until I bottom out on my backside. "What the fuck is happening?" I shout into the fog, anger and confusion wracking my every thought. "What do you want?"

Home, Jack.

Chapter 4

Madeline

"So what's the plan?"

"What do you mean?"

"The plan, you know, a new man to play with?" I smirk, shaking my head at Callie and turning around to face anything but her in the restaurant. I haven't played with a man for a long time. Lewis became anything but playful. But if ever there was someone to not beat around the bush, Callie's it.

Eventually, having searched for an escape from the conversation only to find there still isn't one, I look back at my food. Salad appears to have become standard eating material over the past week. Salad and anything that could be deemed easy to digest. I've got no appetite at all. I don't know what's happened. I expected to be full of energy and life after leaving Lewis, but I'm not. I'm sad, feeling sorry for myself for some unquantifiable reason.

"Because you're moving on, right?" I snap my head up to her. Of course I'm moving on. What does she think, that I'm still pining for my old life and its violence?

"What's that supposed to mean?"

"Well, I've been here a while now and you're still eating salad. You're moping and pathetic." She dabs her mouth and puts her cutlery together neatly, leaning back and crossing her arms at me. "It's getting a bit old, Maddy. I thought I was coming here to party, wake you back up so you could get on with life, but you still love him, don't you?" No. Not at all. Perhaps a little bit in some way, but not enough to give a damn. "Either that or you don't know what to do without him. Which one is it? Are you still hopelessly in love with the bastard? Or are you just weak?"

"May I remind you that I did actually leave him last week, and that I have a house without him in it. I'm over it, Callie. It's just, I don't know, I feel like my left arm's been cut off. That's all. It's odd being on my own."

"Even though he beat the shit out of you constantly?" A shushing noise comes out of my mouth quickly as I scan the room surreptitiously. I could have clients in here. "Yeah, whatever. You're not over him at all. I don't know why. He's an asshole. I told you, but you wouldn't listen, would you? How often did it happen?

Weekly? Daily?" Oh bugger this. In the middle of a restaurant, really? She's been here two days and she chooses this place for *the* conversation?

I'm leaving the chair and walking over to the paying booth before I've thought about it. It's been great having her around, just like old times in some respects, but as always with Callie, mouth moves before brain thinks.

"I'm not letting you walk away from this, Maddy. You need to speak about it, you know? Get it all out there in the open. Just because the bruising's about left your skin doesn't mean it's gone from your mind, does it?"

She's right. I know that. I do. But not here, and certainly not until I'm consciously ready for that sort of discussion. I didn't ask her here to railroad me into this. I just wanted some laughs, like the old days, something to get my mind over being on my own.

I pay the waiter who happily offers me the stupidly high bill considering the nine scraps of lettuce I've eaten, and I swing myself towards the door hoping she doesn't follow. She does.

"And what is it that he had anyway? He wasn't even that good looking with his floppy hair all on display," she says, hurrying to catch up and linking her arm through mine. "I really can't see it at all. I know it wasn't the money. That shit's never interested you, so what? The lifestyle? Did you enjoy the beatings or something? Was it sexual?" God no. My scowl lands directly in her direction as I shrug my arm from her and quicken my pace. What the hell does she think I am? "Don't look at me like that. I mean, there's stuff like that about or so I hear. Apparently people get off on it. And you did stay with him, so…"

"Well, I'm not one of them," I mumble in reply, opening the car door. "And I don't know why I stayed, but I've left now so it doesn't matter anyway. I'm not ready for this, Callie. I just need to work more and find my way out the other side. I'm happy right now. It's okay. Just leave it, will you?"

She buckles up and shunts herself about in the seat until she's got her booted feet up on my pristine dashboard and is fully facing me. My look of horror at her blatant disregard for cleanliness clearly goes unnoticed.

"I call bullshit. You're not okay. You're still all screwed up about it." I huff out at her continued interrogation and start the car, trying my best to ignore her irritating feet and her irritating mouth as I slam on the power and rev out into traffic. "Nope. That's why you asked me to come stay. So I'm here, right? Doing my thang. Winding you up and causing chaos. You should thank me really. By the time I'm gone, dickheads will be a thing of the past." I can't help but snort at her as I round the corners and see her eyebrows shunting up and down out of the corner of my eye. "We'll have you fucking someone new in no time—a nice boy with a little cock so it doesn't hurt too much." That causes a splutter of laughter to come out of me. "Not too little mind, no fucking point if ya can't feel something going in and out. Unless his hands are handy, you know?" And now I can't keep a straight face. "Poking without substance is actually highly nauseating. Gotta have a bit of girth, right? I mean, this last guy I was fucking was all at it. Big, broody, the works. And then, tiny fucking wiener." There's another snort from me, followed by me still trying to appear irritated with her and failing. "It was like puny. Fucking useless with it, too, by the time he found the fucking hole." She's waggling her hips around now, pretending to have sex badly. "And how do they get that big without their cock growing, too? How does that fucking happen? Wasteful. Their mama should've fed it better." I think snot just came out of my nose. I quickly delve around for a tissue, attempting to cover my accident. "Did you just snot out your nose 'cause I was talking dick?" Oh my god. "Dick, cock, shoving and grinding. You knoooow you want it again. You do. Say you do. Go on, say it. We'll find you a nice one. You just leave it to Aunty Callie. You'll be having that pussy licked out before—"

"Will you stop?" I spit out through my still snorting nose. "Jesus, Callie."

I continue with my coughing and spluttering for a while as she carries on and does not stop. In fact, she carries on with her amusing tales of sex for about fifteen minutes as I try to drive in a straight line, aiming for home. So much so that by the time we actually arrive home, I'm crying, full on tears of proper hilarity pouring down my face as she keeps talking. "And so, yeah. He's going at it like a trooper and I'm like, 'You finished? 'Cause I've got a shift in ten and someone better at fucking to find after it.' He got a bit fucking pissed at that, started going hell for leather, fucking lubing up and sticking his thumb in my ass, which was getting somewhere, you know…" She's shoving her crotch about again, boots scuffing my dash and grunting out, ungodly sounds coming from her mouth. "Yeah, then he revved the fuck up. Dick grew, too. I was like, 'yeah, baby, ride that ass'" I'm crying hard as I slide the car up to the drive, shoulders shaking as I desperately try to park.

"STOP! Oh, for god's sake. Please, I can't breathe"

Silence descends, thankfully, and I eventually turn to her hoping she's not going to carry on any further. I seriously can't cope. My guts hurt from laughing so hard. She's smirking at me, finger pointing at my face and her brows up.

"And that, Maddy, is the first time I've seen a real smile from you since I got here." I roll my eyes at her and get out, still snorting back tears and checking my watch for the time. Eleven am, plenty of time to get this show on the road and head for the Blandenhyme meeting. I just need to get changed and get my serious head back on. “See, that’s why I came.” My breathing slows to something close to harmonious as I open the door and switch the alarm off. “Gotta get you out of whatever the fuck this past few years has been, right? Find the old Maddy again? Talk about shit and clear the route forward, yeah?” Maddy’s gone. Madeline finds her way through this. Perhaps then Maddy can come back, but not until then.

I throw the keys on the kitchen table and shrug out of my denim lightweight jacket as Callie goes straight for a beer from the fridge then sits on my table and waits for my conversation.

“Okay, okay,” I say, throwing my hands up in the air at her relentless attack. “So I’m still a bit preoccupied with it all, but I’m moving on. Okay? I am. I don’t want him back. I’ve left. Done. Maybe I’m just not quite ready to acknowledge it all yet. It’s hard to think about. I feel alone, Callie. Like a part of me is missing and I’m lost without it. You wouldn’t know how it feels…” I trail off and sit on the chair in front of her, not quite knowing how to get the words out, and probably not wanting to anyway. She puts her hand on mine and squeezes.

“No one expects it to be easy. You just gotta talk it out, yeah? I got a few more days here, that’s all. We talk as much as you can ‘til then, okay?” I nod, at least acknowledging in some way that I get it. She's right. As she always bloody is.

"Tonight then. We'll start tonight. I've got to meet this guy first and deal with that. It could be worth a fortune to me so I don't want to be all bleary eyed when I meet him."

"Guy? Like hot guy?"

"I don't know. He owns the Blandenhyme estate about fifty miles from here. They're selling off some antiques and paintings. His name's Mr. Caldwell. Other than that I don't know anything about him."

"Married?"

"Don't know. And It's none of my business whether he's married or not. He could be a grandad for all I know."

"Mr. Caldwell. Sounds like a headmaster. Could be kinky."

"Stop, will you? It's business. I just hope he's got things he wants me to remove for him."

"Like your clothes."

"STOP!"

"What? You're still hot as fuck, you know that, right? It's that dark tumbling thing you've got going on. You could get all down and dirty in 'The Estate'." She's doing inverted commas with her fingers, and shoving her crotch around again, this time all over my table with her open legs forging in my direction. "Wear the hair down, flick it around a bit. You're not doing a boring suit, are you?"

"Yes, Callie. Business meeting. You do understand the concept?" Clearly not with the grinding still happening and the banana she's pretending to give a blowjob to.

"Fuck business. You don't need the money. You've got loads of it. You need fucking," she snaps out, driving her teeth through the banana and widening her eyes at me.

"Oh My God. I cannot listen to this anymore. I'm going to change."

"TITS OUT!" she shouts far too loudly at me as I get up and head for the stairs.

Tits will not be out. My C cups will be demurely held precisely behind my bespoke Richmond shirts, and well covered beneath whichever designer suit I choose to put on. Tits out? It's no wonder the woman's never held a job down for longer than three months.

I stare at myself in the mirror for a while, trying to find rational thought again amidst the rowdiness that is Callie. She might be amazing in her own right as she crashes through life not giving two hoots for basically anything, but I need professional again.

Thankfully, most of my bruising has gone now. There's only a small green-yellow dusting under and around my eye, which is mostly coverable. And the damage to my leg is now only a small scrape, which again can be covered over in minutes with the specialist creams I have. It's not really makeup as such; it's high end scar concealer, something I found on the internet after the first real beating happened.

We had a party that weekend at our house, not that Lewis had thought about that when he threw a bottle of Jack Daniels at me, knocking me to the floor in the process. The purple had grown gradually to the point where no amount of concealer could do anything to help. So I searched for something better, and this little brown bottle I'm currently shaking was it.

I top up the small area of colour left, smearing it gently into the corners of my eye, and then carry on with mascara and eyeliner again. There's nothing I can do about the bloodshot bit that still hasn't left, but at least it no longer looks like I've been in a fight. I'll have to pretend I've got an eye infection, or make something up if asked and hope there are no more questions on the matter. It's not like it's any of Mr. Caldwell's business anyway.

I've dealt with his secretary rather than him. She's sent all the relevant files to me without me once having to go to his office. It's been a bonus given the bruising, and I managed to put off the meeting at the house citing a family emergency. They didn't seem too bothered by it, thankfully.

Half an hour later and I walk downstairs to find Callie stretched out on the sofa, her boots up on the end of it with half the contents of my fridge and cupboards scattered around the place.

"What the bloody hell?" Is all I've got to say about the state of my, once beautifully calm, room.

"What?"

"What do you mean, what? Look at the place." She surveys her damage, flicking crumbs off her t-shirt and then brushing a crisp packet off, too.

"Yeah, yeah. Whatever. Go do businessy stuff while I chill and find you someone to fuck."

I have nothing to answer that with as I stare in shock, although why I don't know, and what's the point anyway? I'll just clean when she's gone home.

"Right," I spit out as she turns away from me, staring back at the television and popping another one of my peanut M&M's in her mouth. Mine.

"Right. Bye then. Hot ass by the way."

There's another exasperated huff from me, which only rewards me with her flicking up one finger and then proceeding to shove more of my M&M's in, so I don't bother anymore. I'll just go, do what I've got to do, and then come back here and drink. Hopefully that'll give me the ability to ignore the festering cesspit my lovely new sparkly home will turn into. Presumably this will also make my face hurt through smiling too much. Something that has, she's right, been sadly lacking in my life.

I end up snorting out a giggle and making my way for the car, grabbing my bag on the way and throwing a pair of her socks at her, which have somehow ended up discarded in the hall. Not unlike half a dozen other things that shouldn't be there.

The drive gives me a bit of time to think, something I also haven't done a lot of on my own since Callie arrived. I called her the week after I arrived in the new place and she turned up that night stating, *"This better be good, 'cause I left a rock hard dick for you."* Nice. But she smiled as she said it, and then we hugged. We hugged so hard for so long that we ended up on the floor at the bottom of the stairs with me crying into her shoulder. But then that was it. She's not given me five minutes to think, talk, react, cry or release any other emotion I might have needed to get rid of. Even after she saw all the texts and calls I've been ignoring from Lewis, some of which are truly nasty.

At first he tried for sweet, begging and pleading. That soon developed into the underlying rage I know so well. Then the voicemails started becoming verbally abusive, threatening me with ruination and that he'd find me and show me what real violence was. He never said it directly, but I understood the implication nevertheless. I spent all that week jumping at every shadow, dodging phone calls and hiding inside. Still, though, when she arrived Callie didn't let me cling onto the fear I was beginning to feel. She's kept me busy or laughing, and hasn't allowed one part of me to wallow. Perhaps that's why I'm not quite there yet. Maybe she's right and I do need to talk it out. I don't know. I am lost, though. I feel alone, and very much like this won't be over until I make it that way somehow.

I snort lightly. Dead is the only way he'll ever stop. Not that I've got the gumption to pull that one off any time soon. I'm no murderer.

By the time I've finished daydreaming about times gone by, I end up realising I've missed a turning I needed to take, so I try to make the Sat Nav redirect me. It does, straight into the middle of God knows where, until I'm driving along a stupidly bumpy road and thanking the heavens for the Range Rover beneath my bottom.

Where the hell am I?

I pull over and survey the area, checking out the large expanse of nothing but grassland for any sign of a landmark or even a signpost. There's nothing but an extremely rickety looking bridge with a small brook running underneath it in the vicinity. And because of the post and rail fencing all along the side of me, there's no way for me to turn around either. I start on the road again, checking the time and hoping that being twenty minutes or so late won't matter too much. It's not my fault this place is in the middle of nowhere, is it? Although it is my fault I'm lost.

On further examination of the road ahead, I see there's a gate before the bridge, one I'm rather thankful for because there's no way this car is going over that safely. I pull over again and trip round the dusty ground to open it, then wonder how I'm going to get back on the road on the other side. So now I'm just standing here, hand perched over my eyes to try to see along the road for another gate somewhere. There isn't one, but as I keep peering I do see the top of a house in the distance. It's hiding behind some trees, all grey stonework, and bloody huge by the look of it.

It can't be, can it?

I go back to the car, digging through my paperwork to find the picture of Blandenhyme. Grey building, elaborate finials. I peer back again, and yes, grey gravel driveway. Okay, go me. I must have found a back entrance somehow, though I'm still not going over that bridge. But if that's the house, then surely it wouldn't matter if I just followed the grassland down. This is an off roader after all. That's what it was built for. Not that it's ever set wheel on grass that I know of.

Before I think too much of it, I pull through the gate and pop back out to close it again, then tentatively start my off road journey. Seems Range Rovers are quite adept at traversing fields because nothing feels any different for a while. The ride stays smooth, the ground beneath me passing with no trouble at all, and then something happens I'm not quite sure about. The steering wheel seems to turn of its own accord, sliding through my fingers as if the car thinks another direction is a better idea. I peer over the top of the bonnet, looking for what might have caused the issue, and find the ground undulating away from the flat I was on. This steadily increases to rolling bumps, which in turn, rapidly descends into me being flung around in my seat as the bumps increase in size.

I grip on tight, trying to keep the car straight and heading for my target, which doesn't seem too far away now, but the flinging about becomes wilder and wilder as the car lurches and rebounds again. I don't know how I've managed it, but I appear to be navigating a bloody minefield all of a sudden as I heave and pull on the wheel trying to steady the jolts. And then I hear a whirring noise, followed by an almighty rattle and clank as the car slides to a stop. What the hell? I rev again. Nothing. Then again. Still nothing.

My fingers push the door open to look downwards and back as I rev again, and I see the rear wheel spinning away in a deep wet patch. Great. Some off roader. Mud sprays constantly as I keep revving, hoping something of use will happen. Nothing does. If anything, the spin just seems to make the hole bottomless in the ground as the car rolls back and forth a bit. I slam the door again and put my forehead on the wheel, shaking it repeatedly and then knocking my head on it. Stupid. Jesus, of all the days to screw something up, this was not the day to do it. Why? I just want to get on with my life for God's sake. It's a bloody Range Rover. Aren't they supposed to get over anything? I might as well have the Porsche I wanted for all the good this thing has achieved.

Huffing out yet more irritation, I lay my head back against the rest and stare down to the mansion ahead of me. I suppose I'll have to walk down and see if anyone can tow me out, apologize profusely for my foolishness and hope it doesn't blow any chance I have of making this deal. I need this—not for the money, Callie's right. I need it for me. At the moment I just want to know I can do all this on my own. That I don't need Lewis' backing or support. That I can weather my own storm and rebuild my life on my own. This unreasonable position I've gotten myself into is not how things are going to get me forward, literally.

My patent blue heels sink as I cautiously step out onto the ground. I try to search for better footing, but there isn't any. It's like a bloody bog beneath me, and as I reach for my bag, I notice the front wheel, too, is sunken into the wetness engulfing it. Great. Properly stuck. Well, let's hope Mr. Caldwell is a decent sort who can help me out of the hole I've plainly dug myself into. If not, I'll have to call the recovery people who will take all bloody night to arrive because I'm not exactly at risk in someone's field.

It only takes a ten minute struggle to get myself over to reasonably solid ground, but by the time I've gotten to it I no longer have stylish blue heels on. They've been replaced with mud caked apparitions of style. And my bloody legs are also caked, giving me the appearance of an idiot.

I throw my bag on the road I eventually get back to, digging around in it for tissues or napkins. There's only a small pack but I have to at least try to make me feet resemble elegant again. It's not perfect by a long shot, but it's all I've got until I get to the house. Bloody Range Rovers. I'm selling the damn thing. The moment I get done with this I'm getting my Porsche. I only got this thing because Lewis said it would be better and we already had a sports car. It's not better. In fact, as I keep trudging along, I remind myself that I never really liked the bulky monstrosity anyway. We didn't have dogs, or children. No horses to tow about. It's not even like I use it for moving antiques about. I wouldn't dare. I leave that to the professionals who have insurance and the like.

A noise alerts me to something happening in the distance, so I stop my internal ramblings and look up to see a small red truck coming down the drive in my direction. Oh good, help. At least something's going right. I take another swipe at my ankles and feet, attempting to clean some of the drying mud a little more so I can try to appear in control when it arrives.

"You alright?" a wrinkly sixty-something man says as he pulls up beside me.

"No, well yes I'm fine, but I'm afraid I've got my car stuck in your field, Mr. Caldwell. I'm terribly sorry. It's just the bridge didn't look very safe," I reply, mortified by my own stupidity and assuming this is him. He smiles, crinkling his weathered face up, and hops out of the truck to stand beside me.

"Stuck in the bog, is it?"

"Seems so."

"These bogs have been the bane of my life for thirty-five years," he says, as I stare at his dirty overalls and wonder what it is that Mr. Caldwell does for a living given this building he lives in. "Can't drain them, can't dig 'em out. Horses been stuck in 'em, cows, sheep. Ain't nothing fixed 'em yet. It's the brook, see?" Yes, well quite. I suppose it must be, but chatting about the reasoning isn't going to get my car out regardless of his nice grandad appearance. "They're worse on the other side of the headland. Good job you didn't drive up there, lassy."

"I'm sure you're right, Mr. Caldwell. I'm Madeline Blise.." I stop myself, annoyed at the name that comes too quickly. "Cavannagh. Madeline Cavannagh. I'm here to see about the artefacts and antiques you want to sell?" He nods his head and takes a few steps towards my car, looking it over, or sizing it up. I'm not sure. "Should we do that first? Or I could call the recovery company first if you don't think you can—"

"We'll get you out. Not a worry," he says, cutting in and then walking back towards his truck with a smile. "Just need the tractor to pull your beasty out. Hop in and I'll drop you off to the house so you can clean up."

"Right, good news. Thank you." He smiles some more as I hitch my skirt up to get in the truck, trying not to expose too much of myself. "I really am very sorry. I'm not quite sure how I got on this road in the first place." He pulls away sharply, causing me to ricochet off the seat and grab onto the handrail. "It's just, your bridge seems a little dilapidated, and—"

"That bridge has had tractors over it for thirty years. There's nothing wrong with it."

"Oh, sorry, I don't mean it's not capable. It's just it seemed … Well, and I didn't want to damage it any further because it looks a bit... old." Christ, I'll shut up, shall I?

He smirks, clearly enjoying his torment of me, and begins chuckling away to himself as we potter back down towards the house.

Charlotte E Hart

THE SPIRAL

"Sometimes, you gotta rely on faith to get you through. You remember that, lassy. Just like the old girl up here. She keeps holding on, weathering storms."

He points up to the mansion we're steadily travelling towards as the trees seem to part around it. It's stunning, in a slightly eerie fashion. Its grey façade is covered with a blackening edge, as if years of smoke and the elements have engrained themselves into the fabric of the place. And it's vast, much bigger than I thought from the top of the hill I was on. The long drive sweeps away from it into the woods, enhancing its ghostly appearance as tall redwoods dominate the area behind and around it, somehow caging it in like a fortress of protection.

"It's... Wow."

He chuckles again, changing his gears and slowly trundling us down into the main forecourt. "We've not had many visitors here for a while. Shame really. The old girl deserves to be seen more often, lived in."

"She does indeed," I reply as I stare up at the building's magnificence and feel dwarfed by its scale. "How old is she?"

"1872. She's a beauty." She is. If one calls a building a she. I'm not actually sure I've got words for how the building looks, especially at this time of day with the light cascading over the roof. The whole frontage is dappled with flecks of sunshine, almost ridding it of its darkness, and somehow oozing power and luminescence in the dark covering of the trees.

"I guess the redwoods are nearly as old?"

"The books have all the details. Mr. Caldwell will know."

"You're not Mr. Caldwell?" I snap out, shocked and also mortified once again at my stupidity as I gawp at his face. Why didn't he say? Oh my god, could this day get any worse? He just chuckles and nods as he pulls us to a stop outside the main doors.

"Go on out. I'll get to pullin' that Range Rover out for ya, and then get it cleaned up before I bring it back."

"No, no, you don't have to do that," I reply, sliding as best I can from the rickety old truck and dropping my feet to the floor. "Just out is fine, really. Thank you."

He hands me my bag and nods again, so I close the door and repeat my thanks over and over again until I feel utterly inane and stop my mouth moving. And then he just leaves me standing here as I watch the truck disappear up another small dirt track to somewhere.

Guess I'll go fine Mr. Caldwell then.

Chapter 5

Jack

Selma?

I mutter her name, not daring to believe she's here but still feeling her aura in the old building nonetheless. It followed me back last night, or maybe it was already here when I got back. There isn't a reply, but the fabric of the place creaks and groans with her voice's harmonic tone. It whispers memories at me, reminding me of love and niceties I no longer believe true or worth thought.

I drove on last night, ready to floor the damn thing and release pent up aggression, but the mist kept getting in the damn way, slowing my route and eventually halting my progress entirely. I just sat there in the middle of a dark and dismal road, letting the gentle rain patter the window as I stared into thick fog. No more ethereal words had come from her, no orders or directions, and I didn't see the apparition again, but she was there. I felt her—felt her warmth on my skin amidst the frigid chill, just as I do now.

"What do you want from me?" I ask, walking along the deep red hall and glancing in every room I pass in case she appears again.

The dining room is blank apart from the exquisitely dressed memory of Christmas dinners and champagne. The formal lounge is nothing but a charade of tartan, velvet, and roaring log fires now. The snug, one of the only rooms I still entertain entering, is lifeless without her in it, but memories of Lenon playing with his fire trucks continue to make me smile every now and then. The study is a place of work and nothing else, certainly not somewhere she ever enjoyed unless she was bent over my desk. I stop and smile, remembering the sound of her moans, as I push on the door to widen it. The desk is clear, no papers or clutter, and the floor is still clear of obstacles due to the lack of Lenon crashing through and leaving Lego scattered around.

I finger the door's surface gently, remembering the feel of the boy's tawny hair in my hands. So fine. Nothing like his mother's thick, dark curls.

Sighing, I run my hands over my face and brush the image away as I carry on to the drawing room, once one of our favourites. A place where we would all eat breakfast from our laps and drink coffee. It's as vapid as the last room now, vacant of life or hope. It just sits, stagnating along with me, happily gathering dust and slowly disintegrating further into emptiness.

Jack.

My head swings at the sound of her again, and I hurry back along the hall in the direction of the voice. There isn't a vision of her, but the light of the mid afternoon sun filters in around the main door, highlighting the stained-glass window's greens and yellows. They cascade into the hall, throwing aquamarine tones onto the dark flooring beneath my feet.

I stare at them as the light bounces around on my tan shoes, watching the vivid spots and mixing colours dance with each other. Turquoise—her favourite colour. It reminded her of our honeymoon, and me of her eyes, sun drenched beaches and blue lagoons. Leisurely days. Long, long nights. Lazy mornings fucking anywhere that was acceptable. Making love. I smirk at my own thoughts, imagining her slapping me for using such a term to describe us together. Publicly, anyway. I'd have fucked her anywhere, still would if she was here. But she isn't. She's dead.

A corpse.

The loud old fashioned doorbell makes me frown from my musings and look up. Who's here? Why? I snarl at the door and turn from it, ready to head back towards the kitchen. It rings again, followed by a knocking sound against the wood. My head inclines back to it as I pocket my hands and peer at the stained glass. Nothing moves or comes into view. There's just the continued echo of the damned bell holding me still in the corridor.

"Mr. Caldwell?" My heart damn near stops, nearly ripping the guts from my insides as I stumble backwards further up the hall. *Selma?* "Mr. Caldwell? The old man said you were here. Are you?" Christ. My hands grab out at the walls, looking for support or tangibility. It can't be her. She's dead. "Mr. Caldwell, please? It's Miss Cavannagh. I'm here to see the antiques for sale." What the hell is she talking about?

Something moves in the stained glass, a shadow of someone trying to look through it. I freeze, not knowing what to do. And then the bell rings again. Over and over it rings. I step away from the fucking thing, backing my feet up the hall slowly in the hope that the face peering in can't see me. "Oh, for god's sake," I hear mumbled. "Is that you, Mr. Caldwell? Please could you answer the door?" Fuck.

I stand immobile, and glare at the door, hoping that if I stand here long enough the issue will disappear, or fuck off and leave me alone. Is it not bad enough that I have to endure the insanity of ghosts appearing?

"Mr. Caldwell, should I go? I'll have to wait for my car to be pulled out of your bog, I'm afraid. The old man's doing it now." The bog? What is she talking about now? I half move, suddenly concerned for reasons unknown. Or perhaps it's the thought of her voice leaving, the one that sounds just like Selma's. "I'll just wait out here then, shall I?" Yes. I narrow my eyes at the sight of her leaning against the stained glass. "It's not like I've driven over a bloody hour to get here, you inconsiderate arsehole." The last of it is mumbled and full of frustration, something that raises my lips as my foot inches forward without consent.

I wait for a while, neither moving forward nor backward. I just stare at the figure of her body resting against the rippled glass work and wonder what she looks like. Does she look like Selma, too? Why does she have to be British? Who would have sent this enigma to me, and why?

Toby.

The door handle suddenly twists slightly, making me snarl and flick my eyes over the hall, searching for something, anything to help me understand what the fuck is happening before the door opens. I listen intently, hoping for the real ghost version of Selma to say something, warn me, help me. One or the other. Christ, this is irrational. And unfounded. I'm hoping for a ghost rather than the actual human outside the door?

I shake my head, feeling more than unsatisfied with my own irrationality, and take a step towards the door again, bracing my hand on the wall for support. I have to see her, if nothing more than to send her on her way and scare her into never coming back. Sell my antiques? Selma's things? It isn't happening no matter how much my brother thinks I should move on. How fucking dare he do this to me? Nothing is leaving this house. Ever. I'll burn the place to the ground before I let one piece of her leave these walls.

Her jolt and tumble down the steps as the door opens is amusing, enough so that a chuckle comes out of me, but the moment she turns to look up at me, I can't breathe. I hold onto the doorframe, choking on my inability to move or speak as I look at her. Her hands splay on the steps as she begins to pull herself upright, the crease of her suit exposing her legs and drawing me away from her eyes if only for a few seconds.

"Mr. Caldwell?" she asks, climbing up the steps to stand. I can't say anything, regardless of the fact I'm trying. I nod and try once again to pull in breaths. "Oh, good. I thought you were out. I'm Miss Cavannagh. Shall we get on with it?" Still there are no words to be found, but I find myself nodding at that, too, as she stares at me. "Are you alright, Mr. Caldwell? You seem ill. Pale."

Ill. A good word for what is currently circulating my thoughts.

Madness is more fucking appropriate.

I lick my lips and gaze at her eyes again, allowing myself to be drawn into the blue depths I know all too well.

"Lighter hair," I eventually muse, barely restraining the need to reach out and touch it. It falls around her cheeks, tumbling just as Selma's did, but it's a little lighter in colour.

"Excuse me?" she responds as she fingers it and frowns. "Lighter than what?" Nothing comes out of my mouth at that. "Is it a problem? I can assure you it doesn't impact on my ability to value correctly." I watch the way her lips move around the words, listening to the British lilt behind the slight Americanism, and devour the image of lush pink lips. "If we could just get on with it, Mr. Caldwell. I'm sure you're busy and it's a long drive back for me."

Something snaps inside me at her words. Back? She's leaving?

I take my hand from its position on the doorframe and extended it to her, hoping she'll simply put her hand in mine and leave it there, forever.

"Miss?"

"Cavannagh," she replies, taking it and shaking it firmly, and then trying to pull away. I don't let her. I close the distance between us and stare into her eyes instead, waiting for more language to fall out so I can bask in it some more. "Mr. Caldwell, could I have my hand back?" she eventually asks. No, she can't. "Because it's a bit strange to be holding your hand on a first meeting." I've met her a thousand times before. Walked with her. Talked with her. Eaten, holidayed, drank with her. I've fucked her a thousand times, too, rolled on beds and held her naked skin to mine. Ground myself into her pussy, drank from it. I glare at the internal image, letting my eyes caress the slight pinking of her cheeks as she keeps gently tugging at my hand. "I really think we should…."

"What do you think we should?" I mutter.

She shakes, her whole body trembling in my hand. I feel it travel through her fingertips as she stops trying to pull away and just stands there. The sight makes me imagine all the things we should be doing. It's been a long time since I felt the desire to bury myself inside something because of sentimental reasons, but she's so like Selma. Perhaps even a reincarnation of the woman I loved.

"I, well, perhaps the antiques?" Fuck the antiques. Fuck anything but just standing here so I can watch the way she moves, or flinches, or even the way she's beginning to look amused by my behaviour. "Mr. Caldwell, really. This is flattering, but I'm here to do a job," she says, bracing her other hand on mine and snatching my hold away. Job. Yes, I suppose she is. Not that she's taking a damn thing from here. "Shall I?" she says, nodding past me into the house.

My eyes narrow at that, but before I can find the words I want, she picks up her bag and proceeds to duck past me into the hall.

"You have a beautiful home," she calls, swaying down the hall and dragging a finger along the walls. It's not nearly as beautiful as the little thing that's currently striding towards the centre of it, hardening my cock with every footfall. "I'm excited to see the Phillips works," she says, turning to the right and disappearing from view. Is she? I scowl, surprised at that. They were cheap when bought. I can't even remember where they are.

I turn the corner and gaze at the sway of her ass, remembering the way I used to smack Selma's when we fucked. "I was told they're on the gallery landing. Shall we start up there and..." My feet rush to catch up with her, not hearing the last of her words as I realise where she's intending to go.

"No," I snap, grabbing her arm harshly and pulling her away from the spiral staircase. She snatches her arm back instantly and glares as she backs away into the foyer, causing me to sneer at her anger. "No one goes up those stairs."

"Why?" she immediately retorts, looking confused. Why, is none of her business. I pocket my damned hands again for fear of just throwing her on the floor and fucking her. "I can hardly do my job if you won't let me see the work, Mr. Caldwell."

"I don't need you to do a job." Her brows rise as she rubs her arm, making her seem aloof and capricious. Possibly about to bolt for the door.

"Then why am I here?"

I can't think of an answer apart from the fact I'm not letting her go. And the fact that she's so direct is becoming an issue for my ability to think rationally. I just want to look at her, watch her, and listen to her. Fuck her, actually. I want to fuck her. And kiss her, kiss Selma again. I want to feel her on my skin, trace my tongue with hers and remind myself of Selma's love.

I glance around, unsure what the fuck to do.

"You want a drink?" I eventually mumble out, hoping it will go some way to apologizing for manhandling her.

"No, thank you."

I hover at the bottom of the stairs, sneering at the black carpet and chastising myself for my inadequacy. The silence carries on, something I'm normally comfortable in, but not this time. I frown, flicking my eyes across to her and not attempting to make the atmosphere any more relaxed as she stares at me. She's so like her—the way she stands, the slight raise of brow, the haughty disposition. Long legs, tight waist, slender fingers that will grab on, no doubt. Dig in. And her lips echo kisses from long ago. God, she's beautiful. So beautiful. Like a sculpture of the perfect creation.

"It's cold," she eventually says.

Is it? I hadn't noticed.

Blowing out a breath and straightening my back, I pull at my tie and try to find a way to make her stay a while longer at least.

"Miss Cavannagh, we should start in the ballroom at the back," I offer, pointing back past her towards the kitchen.

"You have a ballroom?" she says, startled as she uncrosses her arms in anticipation and brightens her frown into a smile.

"I do," I mutter, walking past her and crossing through the back corridors towards it.

"You're not much of a talker, are you?" she asks, her heels clattering on the wooden floor behind me. "More physical." I stop and turn back to her, holding my hand up instantly to stop her colliding into me.

"I shouldn't have touched you. I apologize. It's just the spiral staircase, it…" It what? Holds criminals at the top, ones covered in blood and wallowing in their own excrement?

I look at my hands, checking the bruising around the knuckles, and then frown at the thought of what I did yesterday to dog number two. What's upstairs is no one's business but my own. Nothing else needs to be said. "No one goes upstairs. It's not safe."

She opens her mouth. I stare at it, waiting for her to dare questioning me.

"That's okay," she says, smiling so widely I nearly stumble back at the brilliance of it. "You're forgiven. Just this once, though, Mr. Caldwell."

I smile back, desperate to hold her hand to my face and hear my name whispered from her lips. She tilts her head, still smiling and beginning to giggle a little at something. "Are you okay? You've got that look you had outside going on again."

I turn and continue to walk again then stop as she gasps behind me. "Is that a Hopper? But it can't be." Before I can stop her, she's wandered into Selma's study, heading straight for the small sketch on the far wall. "Where did you get this?" she asks, pulling glasses out of her top pocket and sliding them over her eyes to see close up. "It's fascinating. I didn't know anyone had these." Fascinating is a fair assessment of my current thinking. Everything is fascinating about this woman.

"What's your name?" I ask, surprising myself by wanting to know, given her likeness to Selma. I should want nothing more than to keep imagining she *is* her. Just hold that name in my mouth and use it, often. Perhaps even gag whoever this is and force her to change her name.

"Madeline," she murmurs back, as I inch my way inside the room and watch her studying the pencil sketch. "Seriously, I didn't even know these were in circulation. How much did you have to pay?"

"A lot," I answer. But then it was our two year anniversary and Selma loved Edward Hopper. I had art dealers scour continents to find it, eventually making an old woman in Chile an offer she most definitely could not refuse to procure the thing.

"I bet. It's charming. I could absolutely sell this for—"

"It's not for sale," I cut in, furious at the thought and heading back out to continue on to the ballroom. "If you could follow me, Madeline."

What the hell am I doing? I don't want to sell anything. Not one fucking thing is leaving this house. Certainly not anything to do with Selma. And yet, I can't get this woman out of my mind or field of vison. I don't want to.

Fuck.

I storm into the ball room, footsteps crashing around the huge expanse creating a rhythm of their own.

"Oh my word," she says behind me. I look back to find her wandering into the middle of the space, looking up at the ceiling and spinning herself around slowly. “Have you actually held a ball here?” Yes, our wedding night. One I have little desire to remember with Madeline Cavannagh in the room. “It’s astounding. If there was just some music, I could practice my waltz. Do you have any?”

“No.” Waltzing is the last thing on my mind. Fucking is closer to the point, and the longer she speaks, moves, twirls, or is even alive, the closer I’m getting to just taking what I want.

Consequences be damned.

“I have,” she says, digging in her bag and producing a phone. “Can you dance, Mr. Caldwell?”

“No.” Fuck, yes. Dance, no. Only with my wife.

My dead wife.

I stare at her as she proceeds to flick through her phone and walk around the space, eyeing up the paintings and vases on display.

“So, which would you like me to sell for you?” she asks, unbuttoning her jacket and revealing her shapely frame as she drops her bag on the floor. My cock rears inside my pants, ready to cause damage, but then some music sounds in the room, followed by her heeled feet moving cautiously.

She suddenly springs into action, her hands in a faux hold as her body begins gliding around. “I’m sure this is inappropriate,” she says, quickening her pace a little and starting to circle. “But what girl gets the chance to dance in a proper ballroom, hey?" I stare in near disbelief as she continues on, her feet moving exactly, albeit whimsically on occasion, until she glides past me with a smile on her face and spins again. "I mean, the day is turning chaotic anyway because of your bog, so why not? Which ones, Mr. Caldwell?" she calls again, her body now spinning at the bottom of the room past the double formal doors, which lead to the spiral.

"The Shitzner, the Riechlebach and the Jones impressions," I reply.

I don't want to sell any of them, but the more I watch her, the more I need to watch her, nearly forgetting the reason we've come in here or my dogs above us.

"Okay," she says, once more gliding past. I step back, giving her more room to circle the space. "Are you sure you don't dance?" Yes. But something's telling me I should. My feet bounce quietly, listening to the beat of the tune. I'm desperate to pull her into my embrace and fuck her until tomorrow comes.

"No."

"Perhaps you could if I knew your name?" she laughs out, as she does another lap of the room. "That would make this more fun, yes? We could pretend."

I watch a bead of sweat drip down her cheek as she comes by again, and halt the need to lick it from her skin, or at the very least create more of it. Fuck. The way her body moves, it's everything Selma was. Lively, elegant, full of vigour and transparency. She oozes Selma's very being, holds all of her in fingertips, and she's not even aware of it. She breathes as Selma did, sharp intakes of breath on the correct note, and long sighs as the melody cruises by, her hair swaying in time with her shoulders.

I've snatched hold of her hand and waist before I know what I'm doing, drawing her close to me and resting her against my cock as we dance forward. She gasps, tightening her grip on my shoulder, and immediately moulds her body into mine. There isn't one second of awkwardness or confusion; we just blend together, crafting a music of our own as we spin.

"Jack," I mutter, half debating kissing her, or fucking her, perhaps even just continuing to dance all night to feel her back in my arms again.

Selma.

I close my eyes and remember our wedding dance as we continue spinning. I remember the feel of her in my arms, the way she said she loved me, and the moment she put my hand on her stomach, announcing our child. I can almost see the crowd around us now, hear their chants of congratulations and raucous calls for more speeches. I can smell her, too—blossoms and faint traces of freesias. Springtime's freshness, all basking in one solitary person.

"Jack," she whispers into my chest.

I tighten my hold to the point of bruising the woman, spinning us again as the chorus rouses me further. I'm never letting her go, never letting this sensation go again. She *is* Selma. At this moment, and for whatever reason, Selma has come home. She's here in this room and dancing with me again.

My fingers begin to indent her skin, testing my resolve to remember the woman who *is* actually here. Even her flesh feels the same beneath my hands, malleable and ripe, ready for devouring, loving in my own way. I rest my nose above her hair, breathing in the scent of a newly formed Selma and relishing the thought of the first drive inside her. Just to feel her again, fuck her, be inside her so the world will right itself, and then we can bring Lenon back, too. All of us together again, living, breathing. "Jack?"

The sound of my name coming from her mouth again makes me smile, the tone resonating deeply and engraining itself. "Jack, please?" I know how she feels. I can feel it, too, this desperation to make love. To make us whole again so we can be free of the last year or so, be a family again.

I kiss the top of her head, circling us around the floor once more and readying myself to put her down on it. Just here. We'll fuck right here and remember our wedding night so I can imagine the feel of white silk in my hands and tear at it. "Mr. Caldwell!" Something slaps out at me, bringing me acutely back to the present. “Jack, for God’s sake!”

I stop and frown, sliding us to a standstill and looking down at what appears to be an angry woman. Selma? No. Madeline.

I shake my head and let go, backing away instantly and wondering what the hell just happened, again.

“What the bloody hell is your problem?” she spits out, swinging herself away from me and heading for her bag. The music abruptly cuts off just as quickly, causing me to scowl. “Do you often hurt women for fun?” I scowl further at that, my feet backing away. “Let me give you some advice. Don’t ever touch a woman unless she asks.”

“You did ask,” I mumble, confused at the lack of Selma as I glance around the room. Where has she gone? Was she ever here? I move towards the windows, frowning some more as I listen for voices. “You asked me to dance with you. We danced.”

“I danced. I’m not sure what you ended up doing,” she snarls out.

I turn back to see her rubbing her arm again and snatching her bag from the floor. “And stay the hell back,” she snaps again, pointing at me and glaring some more. “This was a mistake, Mr. Caldwell. I’ll wait outside until my car’s out of the bloody bog.”

She storms out of the room, leaving nothing but irritating emotions, feelings, and hatred behind as she goes. I stare at my hands, not knowing what they've done and feeling widowed again for the lack of her gripping them. So much so that I fume after her, entirely disposed to get her back in my arms as soon as feasibly possible.

"Sel..." I halt my fucking mouth, shaking my head as I pass the kitchen and hurry on to the hall again. "Madeline, wait."

All the response I get is heels clattering and an open front door, the house damn near rattling with her fury. I storm straight out to her, more than intrigued by what she thinks I've done. If she only knew what I could have done had I chosen to, or perhaps had more time to think of my dead wife, she might just be a little more pleasant with her fucking tone.

"Don't touch me," she says, her hands splayed in front of her as she backs down the steps and sniffs back tears. "I have mace. I'll scream." She's right, she damn well will, but that will be at the moment I actually do something worth screaming for.

I hold my hands up and slowly put them in my trouser pockets, signalling the surrender of whatever evil she thinks I might become.

"I haven't done anything, Ms. Cavannagh. Calm down," I say quietly, walking down the steps towards her and giving her the room to breathe she's asking for. "We just danced, which you requested if you remember. You're a beautiful dancer. I might have become engrossed in you." Or the memory of Selma and the way she felt within my grasp.

She sniffs again, raising her hand to her face and wiping at the tears that are beginning to stream from her eyes. It's at that moment that a smear of makeup is wiped clear, highlighting the blue yellow tones around her bloodshot eye. "Who did that to you?" I ask, infuriated by the vision enough that I move forward again thoughtfully.

She widens her eyes, her hands coming up to her face.

"It's none of your business," she snaps, shielding the bruise and turning to start walking off down the lane towards the garages. I follow and watch the swing of her ass again, intrigue now beginning to piss me off. "Please, Mr. Caldwell. Leave me in peace. I'll just get my car and go home."

I watch her pull her dark curls across her eye, trying to create a fringe to mask the bruising as she carries on, which causes resentment to well inside. Someone has done this to her, beaten her intentionally. Perhaps that was why she reacted so fiercely to me touching her.

I gaze past her, noticing the black Range Rover ramped up on the stands in the workshop, Bob beneath it and liquid pouring out all over him. Seems little Ms. Madeline won't be going anywhere without support.

"You won't be going anywhere," I say, still watching her ass move. She turns and storms up to me, hovering her finger in the air and about to pounce with that attitude of hers. I hold my hands up again and nod at the workshop. "Your car, Madeline. It's broken. I can assure you that's not my doing. Quite the opposite."

"What?" she squawks, spinning back around and hurrying over to where Bob is fucking about with bits of metal. "Oh god, what's happened?"

"Oil coming from your suspension, lassy. You right crunched her up. It'll take a while yet."

"Jesus, it was just a fucking field," she bites out, throwing her bag on the floor and sinking to her ass alongside it. "It's supposed to go off road."

I smile at her language, temper, and ire, and then stare at the bruising around her eye again as she gently runs her finger over the area in thought.

"Does it still hurt?"

"Oh, go away," she whispers, dropping her head into her hands and resting them on her knees, only to pick them up and then knock them against her knees again. It brings back memories of Selma again, the same spit of annoyance coming from her on occasion.

"Madeline, this is my house, my road you're sitting on, and thankfully my ass you'll have to kiss to get yourself out of this mess." Her head shoots up, first flushed with a frown of annoyance as she glares at me, and then suddenly brightening into one of her ill offered smiles. "Which cheek would you like?" She frowns again and wrinkles her nose, obviously disregarding the idea. "Then stay here by all means," I reply, walking to Bob and levering myself down beneath the car to see the suspension. "I could use a distraction like you."

I chuckle at the thought of using her as I check out the damage. Nearly destroyed is a fair analysis of the situation.

"How did she do this in the bog?" I ask Bob quietly, noting the mangling along the suspension rack. The man shrugs his shoulders and throws the last bit of metal to the ground as he begins wiping his hands. "The kitchen needs a good clean. You could work off your board and lodgings until the car gets fixed," I call up, nodding my head at Bob to carry on as I climb back out.

By the time I've gotten out of the pit and back up onto the road, Madeline is nowhere to be seen. I swing my body round searching for her, eyes narrowed at where the fuck she's gone as I scan the parkland. She can't leave.

Chapter 6

Madeline

I don't know who the hell he thinks he is trying to order me around. Kitchen cleaning? I'm not playing that game anymore. The days of Madeline Cavannagh doing anything a man says are long gone, certainly after whatever the hell that performance was in the ballroom.

I felt the moment his hands latched on tighter than they should have, and I felt my own eager reaction to it regardless of the fact I didn't want anything to happen. It was my need as much as his, pure and simple, like a freight train had charged its engine and was going to railroad me into something one way or another. My protest was infuriating and a lie if truth be told, but it did scare me. *He* scared me. His hands reminded me of Lewis'. Cool, calm, collected, and then like a bear grappling for its prey. Holding it still and readying it for the kill it deserved.

And Ballroom? What was I thinking? Dancing my way around like some queen in her little kingdom was stupid, and wholly unsuitable behaviour for a woman trying to act professionally. It's just, it was beautiful in some ways, almost dream worthy. It reminded me of the hopes of adolescent children, my adolescent childhood, where dancing class was all I had to get me away from the chaos at home. Before Lewis, before battered limbs.

My hand flings the phone about, desperately searching for a signal as I amble around the fields. It doesn't find one. It hasn't done since I entered the estate. Wealth and phone signals don't mix around here, it seems. Great. And here I was being all haughty and storming off again, thinking I could just call the breakdown response people and stick a finger up to Mr. Downright Edible. Seems I can't even do that effectively on my own.

Looking up into the sunlit sky, I feel the tears threatening again. They came filled with joy when he took hold of me and started dancing, happiness mingling inside me for the first time in who knows how long. Then they came again when I felt his hands tighten on me, reminding me of bruised skin. And then again as I ran for the front door, scared and frustrated with my fervent response to the thought. And then one last time, filling me with feelings of self-loathing when he saw the bruising around my eye. He was judging me, thinking me weak and incompetent.

Presumably the make-up wore off with the tears, or maybe the sweat we built up dancing loosened it. I don't know, but one thing I do know is he made me feel incapable and alone, inadequate maybe. Confused definitely.

Callie was right; I don't know how to be on my own. I've forgotten how. Whatever Lewis is or was, he was always there to bail me out of trouble, simply a phone call away when I needed him. I miss that about him, about us. I don't miss his aggression or the constant worry of what was coming next, but I do miss the sense of two, a couple, being with someone who is always there.

I stare round the grounds, blinking my tears away and reaching into my bag for some foundation to hide my past. The last thing I wanted was the look of consideration he gave me. I'm a professional, here to do a professional job. No one who has the remnants of a shiner around their eye looks professional, let alone capable. I just need to get home and forget about this one, lucrative as it might have been. It's over now. I'll just have to find another job in the near future.

"Was one bog not enough for you?" his voice calls from somewhere. I instantly look down at the floor, wondering what he's talking about, to find myself perilously close to blackening mud that bubbles at my proximity. I move on the spot, turning and trying to find the way I came in behind me, but there's no path to see. "Stand still," he shouts, still from an unknown position.

"Okay," I call back, halting the stupid trampling of my feets and hovering in place.

A crashing noise followed by some swearing then huffs of annoyance rage through the air at me as I keep looking for a safe route out.

"What the fuck is wrong with you?" he mutters, pushing a branch out of the way so I can finally see him coming at me from the left though the wooded area. "Didn't anyone ever teach you not to wander off?"

"I needed a signal," I reply quietly as I watch him move toward me. "To call the recovery people." I'm rewarded with another huff, hotly pursued by him battling another branch from his path. "For my car?" I'm babbling, probably because I don't know what else to say given whatever it is that has happened between us.

It's unfortunate how handsome he is, even more so since he appears to be coming to my rescue in his pristine suit. Tall, broad, brown eyes I could easily fall into without thought, and a face devoid of any warmth until he smiles, which he isn't currently doing. He's grimacing, probably at the fact that those highly polished shoes are having to tentatively find their way through mud to get to me. I wish I could say it wasn't funny, but it is, and a small snort of amusement breaks from me before I can stop it as his feet slip further into the mud, making squelching noises.

"If you think I'm carrying you out, Madeline Cavannagh, you can think again."

Oh, I hadn't thought about that. I look down at my already pretty muddy shoes and shrug. What difference does it make? I couldn't screw this up any more than I already have done anyway. It's now just about me getting out of this quagmire and finding my way home, which I'm pretty sure isn't in the direction he's coming at me from.

I turn, taking a step out onto a patch of green grass that I think was behind me before I stopped. It holds beneath me so I take another step, too, hoping I've got this right.

"Madeline, stop," he says anxiously, though I don't know why. He's the one sinking, not me. I jump over to the next clean bit I see, heading back out into the field and generally in the direction of the garage, I think. "Will you damn well stand still?" Seemingly not. My feet are almost skipping over the ground to patches that seem sound, suddenly feeling remarkably in control of myself. I can do this without him. I can. I don't need a man to complete me. I'm not incapable at all. "Madeline, watch out for the…"

Oh.

My foot squelches beneath me, my heel disappearing into wet ground and rapidly sinking in over the arch of my foot. It causes me to lose balance, and my arms start flailing about as I try to pull it back out again. All that happens is my other foot starts to sink as I press on it for leverage, making me wobble further into a fall, my bag flying from my hand.

"Jesus fucking Christ," he grumbles at me as my arse topples backwards and hands grab onto it. Nothing's stopping the momentum, though. We're both going down, heavily.

The suction of my left foot popping free increases the fall, sending me flying back into him and crashing against his chest. His arms wrap around me, grabbing at bits he should not be touching, and it feels like slow motion as I watch the afternoon sun changing angle above me and let him brace my stumble.

Eventually, we're just lying in a heap on the wet ground, his hand still wrapped around my waist and the other far too close to my left boob. It's kind of nice, and I find myself chuckling at the image of us down here. Could my life be anymore pathetic? First I dance around his ballroom, searching for dreams that are not meant for me. Then I embarrass myself with bruising and actions of the highest unprofessional order. And now I'm lying in a bog, covered in mud, almost ready to turn over and kiss him for attempting to be a saviour.

"Nothing is funny about this position," he says gruffly, not even trying to remove his hands.

"Oh, I don't know. It's one I've never done before. You?"

And now I'm flirting, brazenly rubbing my hand down his leg and feeling the tension in it beneath his suit trousers. What else have I got to lose? Nothing. And he's attractive, overly so. Callie was probably right. I could do with having sex with someone to get my mind off Lewis, and the man behind me is *all* male. Not only can I tell this by looking at him—I can tell by the feel of his muscles around me at the moment, and the way he isn't the slightest bit ashamed of where his hands are grabbing. I don't know him, and don't really care to. He's fit, attractive, and probably as interested in this moment as I am.

"You should be careful with whatever thought you're playing with, Ms. Cavannagh," he whispers, brushing his mouth around my ear and sliding his hand across my stomach. Why? Why should I? I've been a good girl most of my life. I stayed true to Lewis even though he didn't deserve anything from me at all. And before that I was naive, virginal even. Well, not quite, but you know. And I've got a new life to build now, one just for me. Perhaps I should take control of it somehow rather than letting these men make me feel incompetent all the time.

"Why?" It comes out so quietly that I chew my lip as I say it, maybe hoping to pull the remark back in. There's quiet for a while, and the rubbing of hands, which is getting nicer by the second as I gaze up at the sky, but still he's so quiet I begin to think I was stupid to even say anything.

"Because I'm not open to anything you might want, other than fucking," he eventually says, no remorse in the words.

My brows lift. Well, it's direct. Quite refreshing really. At least that means I won't have to second guess what mood he's in, or whether he'll beat me or not.

"Are you married?"

"No."

"Engaged? Because I won't do—"

"No."

"Right." I'm actually considering this? Here, in a boggy field? What am I doing?

"You should get up."

"Yes, you're probably right." I'm not moving, though.

Nothing moves, actually. Nothing but the clouds drifting by in the sky as I continue to lie on him in the middle of a bog. It's comforting somehow, warming. I can feel his breath on my ear, his chest rising and falling underneath me. It might even be classed as romantic if I think about it long enough, sweet, given his overbearing attitude. There certainly isn't anything sweet about his nature in general that I've seen so far, or where his hand is still lying on my breast.

"You're not getting up?" he says brusquely.

No, I'm not, and I don't seem to be able to speak either. My throat feels parched, like I can't find the will to move at all, let alone tell him I want to. And my privates ache. Why? I don't even know him. Oh god, his hands are pulling my skirt up slowly as his mouth brushes my cheek again, and I'm helping him by hitching my arse around on him.

"You want fucking or not?" I can't do anything but squeeze my eyes tighter together at his words, perhaps scared of admitting it to myself. "I want you to say it."

"I ..." Nope, there's still nothing coming out as his hand inches up my exposed thigh and lingers over my knickers.

"Tell me you want this, Maddy. Are you a Maddy, Mads?"

Whatever is happening stops the minute he says Mads. Rational thought comes racing back, causing me to slap out at his hand, scramble myself out of his hold, and clamber to my feet.

"This was a mistake," I reply in a snotty voice as I search the ground for solid footing again, and attempt to straighten my mud soaked suit.

"Not from where I'm lying," he mutters, putting his hands behind his head and staring up at me.

"You're…" I don't know what I'm trying to say. He's what? Hot as hell? A pig? An animal with a dirty mouth? I've got no right to say that. We're both here, me having let him touch me, him lying there with an erection waiting for me. I lay there on top of him, not moving. No one forced me to do anything. My name came from his lips, the one I can't take anymore, and it changed everything. I heard Lewis in it, heard his fists coming for me, and now I feel like a fool again.

I brush some soaking mud from my jacket and button it back up to protect whatever feeling I'm confused about. Perhaps I'm embarrassed, or annoyed at myself. I don't know, but now I can't even find words to initiate conversation away from whatever this has been.

He doesn't say anything. He just looks at my lips for a while, frowning, and then eventually turns his face away from me as he gets to his feet.

"You're a cocktease. Still," he mutters, walking straight past me.

I pick up my bag, contemplating the words and frowning at his back. If I knew my way out without him I'd damn well do it on my own, but I don't. So I wait as he tests out each piece of ground with his feet, and eventually follow, watching his ruined suit flap around with his movement. I don't even feel like I can snap back at his remark as I jump into the places he's stepped on. It's true in some respects. Well, it will seem it to him I'm sure—dancing with him, lying in boggy fields and lifting my backside round on him as he hitches up my skirt—all good tease material. I'm not, though. Never have been. Never had a chance to be without fear of getting beaten because of it.

He mumbles to himself as he keeps going, grumbling about something I can't hear. I don't suppose I want to either. It's probably more about me, and his cock, something neither of us should be thinking about, regardless of the fact that I am. He looks so stylish, even with the mess we've created. It's the first time I've noticed the cut and quality of the material. Who would have thought he could be so lacking in refinement with his 'you want fucking or not' statement?

It makes me wonder who Jack Caldwell really is underneath that suit and this huge house he owns. Not that I care or will do any research on the matter because this has just been one of those things. One of those odd and unusual things. A bit like my dancing earlier.

The ground becomes firmer as we approach a small stream and head through it to the other side. I shake my head, trying to see only the garage I need to get back to rather than this man, but his hand reaches for mine and hauls me up the bank. It's disconcerting as he holds onto it that bit too long again, just like it was earlier when I first met him. I stare at him, waiting for him to release it but he doesn't. He just holds on, barely managing to loosen his grip as I try to tug it away gently. It makes me start imagining things I shouldn't even be contemplating, certainly not after him telling me I'm a cocktease, but I am. I can feel it in this hand of his, reminding me of ten minutes ago when that same hand was lingering on parts of me it should have been nowhere near.

"You sure you don't want fucking?" His lips twitch upwards slightly, making me stare all the more at how handsome he becomes when he loses that scowl. I tug again until he relents and lets my hand go, my own lips mirroring his as I look down at the floor and then away towards the garage. "Hmm. I'll get your car fixed, and drive you home in the meantime," he says, his hands in his pockets as he turns and ambles the last few steps of grassland up to the road.

"No, it's fine. If I could just use your phone, I'll…"

"I'll damn well drive you home, Madeline." My feet stop as I find road beneath my feet, fear drawing in at his tone and my mouth opening ready to retaliate in some way. He swings his body back to me, anger lacing his every feature and a look that fuels my panic. "Repeat after me. It's fucking simple. Say, 'Thank you, Jack'."

My mouth opens and within seconds his brow indicates his displeasure at anything but hearing the words he wants to hear. I'm not sure what he thinks he's going to do if I don't reply favourably, but given the amount of strength in his grip I'm not sure I want to find out. Visions of Lewis sidle into my mind again, forcing me to look at the floor and nod in reply.

"Thank you, Jack."

He grunts some kind of response and turns away from me to head up the road towards the house, leaving me to trail behind him aimlessly until he leaves me at the door, his finger pointing at the steps and telling me to wait there. So I do, sliding myself down the wall to sit on the grey sandstone steps. It's not like I can get any filthier anyway, is it? And at the moment I just want away from here. I feel lost again. Alone and foolish under his gaze.

I pick out the drying mud on my skirt and jacket, hoping to detach some of it at least while I wait, then give up bothering and stare out into the estate instead. It's quite beautiful with long rolling fields and the occasional plot of woodland peppering the landscape with tall trees and busy hedgerows. And the area around me, imposing and almost unwelcoming as the house I'm leaning on, towers behind me, dwarfing all it can see. I can smell the redwood's musky scent. It's not unlike Jack's actually, woody and deep, giving a sense of age and wisdom. Wisdom—not a word I can use for what just transpired in the field. Nothing was wise about that, but perhaps this is what being free is all about? My choices. My thoughts.

Time potters by and a rumbling sound around the corner draws my attention back to the here and now. I turn to see a dark green Porsche coming around the corner, gorgeous lines showing me every inch of the car I've always wanted. It makes me snicker as I get to my feet and gently walk towards it, desperate to run my fingers across its pristine surface.

It pulls to a stop and Jack gets out, now looking every inch the lord again. He's obviously showered and changed, which causes me to rub at my suit again, hoping for clean. Clearly nothing alters with my appearance. I shouldn't sigh at the vision of him coming at me, a gruff frown on his face like he hates the world all of a sudden, but I do. He's every girl's dream—wealthy, attractive, and holding that authoritative air that simply begs to have you fall at his feet, worshipping the thought let alone the actuality.

I find myself wavering and looking at my attire, unconsciously trying to fit in with his image. I'm trying to regain some element of professionalism again if truth be told, and find some determination to show myself as capable and strong. It's quite hard given what happened in that field, and the sight of him walking purposely towards me, a rise to his brow as I look up at him, has me feeling completely inadequate again.

"Are you ready, Madeline?" he asks, nodding at the car. I peer through the window at the interior. It's as highly polished as Jack, suede seats and chrome elegantly lining its insides. There's no way this suit of mine is going in there.

"I think I'm too dirty."

"That's yet to be determined," he says, a wry smile on his face that instantly makes me forget about the anger I saw fifteen minutes ago. My insides flutter stupidly, making this whole situation even more debilitating to the professional air I'm aiming for. "As far as I'm concerned, at the moment you're only mildly grubby, Madeline."

He chuckles after that, and I find myself gazing at him, bizarrely infatuated with the smile he's delivering. The connotation of his words has nothing to do with the state of my clothes, more like the amount of whorish behaviour I might be prepared to show, I'm sure, but his continued smirk as he glances his eyes over me only increases my inability to look away. "Get in the car, Madeline. Unless you want to stay. Do you want to stay?" No. Yes. Absolutely not. I need to go home. That's what I need to do. I need to go home and talk to Callie about this, and then I need a large stiff drink. Possibly several. "If it makes you feel more in control, you can drive."

I stare at him, letting myself fall into crinkling hazel eyes that are far too consuming for anyone's good, and then walk round and lower myself into the car. Home. Home and forgetting about this little misdemeanour, or perhaps improving on it in some way. Driving a Porsche is a good start.

Chapter 7

Jack

My dick throbs. It throbs with the proximity of her, the smell of her, and the taste of her. It doesn't matter that I haven't kissed her, or that I've held back from doing so. It also doesn't matter that I've gone out of my way to say her name repeatedly, trying to dismiss Selma from my mind. None of it has worked. She *is* Selma. Everything about her. The way she smiles, the way she groans, the way she grips me, and even the way she frowns and berates, not knowing she is doing it.

She's still doing it now as we near Atlanta.

She's frowned most of the journey and stayed quiet, occasionally trying to pull her soiled skirt further down her legs as she drives the car just as Selma did.

"Where do you live?" I ask.

She doesn't answer, just reaches over and taps the address into the GPS then sits back again and looks out of the window, ignoring me. I sneer at her attempt to pretend this isn't happening, annoyed by her denial. She has no reason to be in denial about wanting to fuck. She's following human nature's natural process. It's inevitable.

I stare over at her lips, watching them mould themselves up into a knowing grin, one that reminds me of Selma's coy glances after we'd snuck out somewhere.

"If it makes you feel any better, we could pull over and get the fucking out of the way." She twitches her lips, reminding me of Selma even more.

"I'm not available for only that," she counters, still gazing outside. "And as you say, you're not available for anything other than that, are you, Jack?"

I look back at the road, irritation biting into every part of me at the thought of not being able to touch her again.

"What if I was?" She turns back slowly, a coy glance at my mouth before she turns to look at the destination again. "Something more ongoing."

I glower at my own words, considering what the hell I'm doing. This isn't real. She isn't Selma. She's just a woman who looks like her, walks like her, even talks like her, and apparently drives like her, but I can't rid myself of the desire to lie in her arms and remember a life before this one. “I’d like to see you again.”

“Would you?” she replies, looking shocked.

“Mmm. See how much dirtier than mildly grubby we can get you.”

“Because I’m not grubby enough already,” she says, snickering and brushing at her skirt.

“Not nearly enough, Madeline,” I reply as we drive into suburban back streets. “But I want an honest answer to something first.”

“Hmm?”

“Who did that to your face?” She immediately turns her body back to upright and looks out of the window again, clamping her mouth closed as she does. “I don’t care, but I do want the truth either way. It’s what I’ll want from this arrangement. Truth.”

“Arrangement?”

“Yes. Arrangement.” She nods a little, nothing more, and then clamps her mouth closed, effectively trying to end the conversation. “That’s all I can offer, Madeline.”

“Right.”

Dread fills me as I watch her face disengage, but my statement isn’t about her, it’s about me. It’s the only way I can see this working because desperate as I am to see her again, there has to be a way of separating Selma from Madeline. Dirty and rough is the only way I can think of.

Making love to my dead wife isn't on the fucking cards. It can't be.

I'm so engrossed in looking at her I nearly miss the brake lights in front of me, as the car comes screeching to a halt. I'm about to get out and shout at the idiot when I notice others getting out of their cars, too, all looking upwards.

"What the hell?" I hear her say, as her door opens. She gets out and begins walking away, stripping her feet of her shoes as she does to hurry her pace. I get out, and instantly notice the vast plume of black smoke billowing out into the sky from the next street over. "That's on my street. That could be my house."

I race after her as she takes off along the pavement away from the smoke, her skirt hitched up above her knees. And a short distance later, I catch up with her as she rounds to the left, careering into me and picking up her pace again as she keeps looking upwards.

"Shit, that's… Oh my god!"

I've never seen a woman run so fast. She sprints round to the right, hitching her skirt higher and letting her shoes go behind her. "CALLIE!" she calls, her feet furiously chasing the ground as we near the house alight with flames. I grab at her, stopping her from going onto the front lawn and yanking her back to me. "CALLIE!" she screams again. Black smoke plumes into the air, choking us of oxygen as I try to pull her struggling frame away from the building. She screams again as heat assaults us from every angle, sparks jumping from the flames. I tug her more forcefully, pulling her back into the crowd of people that have come for the show. "CALLIE!" She pushes at me. "Get the hell off me," she spits, fighting in my arms and twisting her body to kick out at me. "My friend's in there. Get off me."

"Madeline, you can't—" She slaps out at me again, her arms flailing and shoving for all she's worth. "Look at the fucking thing," I snap, shaking her body to get her back to reality. It doesn't stop her, and now her eyes are streaming with tears of frustration, too.

"CALLIE! CALLIE!" she calls over and over again.

The faint sound of the fire department rings in the air, sirens getting louder with every passing second as I feel her struggling begin to weaken in my hold. I just hold her tighter until I've finally got my back to a car, waiting for her to calm down or give in. Not because she needs me, but because I suddenly need her. Memories flood me. Sirens and emergency crews. Machines and devices. Monitors bleeping and people in white uniforms coming into my home. The sight of blood, Selma's vacant gaze. Lenon's hand hanging out of that fucking body bag.

"Callie," she wails again, now with little other than despair in her voice as she sinks down my body to the floor. I go with her, wrapping her into my chest as she lays her head into my shoulder and we gaze at the burning woodwork. "What have I done?" she mumbles, choking on a sob as a large chunk of the roof crashes to the ground. "She came to help me and I've killed her."

My hand soothes through her hair, softly caressing her as I frown at her words and watch the smoke oozing and curling. It enrages the building's inferno further, creaking and spitting flames further into the sky with every hiss.

I eventually move us further away, dragging her backwards towards a large truck as the structure groans and begins leaning. "What have I done?" she sobs out, her fingers lying limply at her sides. "She was my friend." I kiss the back of her hair, remembering the feeling of dread and terror. "She was my best friend. My only friend."

She shakes in my arms as the engines arrive and begin their work, until eventually she stops and just becomes still. There are no more tears, no more questions, only the ones she answers when the police officers ask. We don't move when prompted. We stay there, together, watching the building burn and remembering our own memories for our own reasons as night draws in around us.

Time passes and the people around us disperse, seemingly bored now that the show is quieting down. The last of the embers are put out after an hour or so of the fire service battling, and all that's left is a blackened shell of a building, which occasionally topples and crumbles some more.

“I’ll have to go back,” she eventually says quietly, still not moving as she slumps between my legs and watches the uniformed men at work. One of them clears a path to the door, the other dousing remnants of wood still half alight. “If he’s willing to go to these lengths, what hope do I have on my own?” I frown at her words, scanning the area for any evidence of someone doing this purposefully.

“What do you mean?”

“I wouldn’t be surprised if he did this to spite me,” she says, moving with another lamenting sigh and pulling herself up from the floor. “He probably knew Callie was in there, too. He never liked her.” I open my mouth, confused about what this has to do with another man as I stand up and brush some soot from my suit. She wanders away from me, her bare feet slapping at the littered ground around her, mingling with the debris. “I was his wife until two weeks ago, you know?” she says, picking up a piece of plank from the floor and then throwing it back again. She moves along the path the guys are clearing, hugging her arms around herself and looking up at what’s left. “But after the last attack, I left. This,” she says, waving her hand at the scorched remains, “was my attempt at freedom. Pretty useless against men that powerful, huh?”

Rage rears its way through me, rage and hatred for anyone who would do this to her. It brings with it more visions of Selma and Lenon, their mutilated frames filling my mind with anger and loathing to keep my fury live and willing revenge on anything that breathes.

"You should come home with me," I offer, frowning and wandering up behind her to reach for her back. She turns and steps away from me before I can touch her, backing herself up to the house and sneering a little.

"Why? I hardly think that's sensible, Jack. Playtime's over. I think my husband's proved that point, don't you?"

"You're not considering going back to him?"

"What else do I have? My house is nothing but cinder. My free life's over." She turns to look back at the crumbling structure. "Not that it ever really began."

I stare at her for a moment, wondering why she's arrived in my life, and then gaze at what remains of the house. She's right. There's nothing left here for her to salvage. Nothing apart from her hatred. I walk past her, considering my interest in that thought process and nodding at a police officer walking out.

"We're done here," the guy says to us. "If you could come to the station over the next few days we'll fill out the report." I nod again, for some reason certain that it's my position to be involved. It isn't. I don't know this woman and shouldn't care in the least for her, but I do.

"Have you found her?" she asks, looking at the building in a glaze. The guy looks back at her, removing his helmet and shrugging out of his overalls.

"Ma'am, we can't see anything until the building's declared safe." She nods and carries on staring at the house. "The investigators will be here soon. You're free to go. We've got your details."

He nods at us both and smiles solemnly before disappearing to the back of a vehicle, the rest of his team joining him there.

I pocket my hands and gaze at her as she wanders through the carnage, trying to calm myself. I've become furious for reasons unknown. Enough that I can feel the need to beat something coursing my veins. Perhaps it's Selma's vacant gaze that I can still see because of the sirens, or perhaps it's the acrid stink lingering around the place.

"Come home with me, Madeline. Think," I say, turning to walk back to her. "If you still want to go back to whoever the fuck did this then you can go when your car's ready. Give yourself some time first."

She slumps to the floor again, letting her suit get grubbier than it already was and running her fingers in the soot.

"I have nothing, Jack. Nothing but the soiled clothes I sit here in and a bank account stuffed with money I'm apparently not allowed to use on my own," she says quietly, her voice becoming less emotional by the second. "Look what happens when I try. Is that what you want? If I come with you, you'll be in danger, too. He's probably here now." She chuckles, the sound filled with hatred rather than amusement. "Watching us. Getting ready to kill you for helping me." I slowly glance over the area again, willing the bastard to be somewhere useful. "That should scare you, Jack." Nothing scares me anymore. I have nothing to lose. Life is empty now, meaningless. "It scares me. *He* scares me," she continues, her finger still tracing circles in the soot beneath us. "He's got my life all wrapped up in his hands, ready to destroy it over and over again, and all because he can't get his own way. I shouldn't have tried to escape him. I should have known it wouldn't work."

I watch the light decrease in her eyes, watch Selma's brightness disappear, and begin to see Madeline Cavannagh for who she really is. It's disheartening for some reason, and she's becoming darker by the moment, just as I did after their deaths. Her frame changes, her movements slowing to those of unease and anger as she snaps a piece of charred wood. Even her hair begins to somehow lose its lustre. It becomes bland of colour, the chocolate tones within losing their shine.

"Just come home with me, Madeline."

"I fucking hate that name," she suddenly spits, glaring up at me and snarling. "Fucking Madeline. Madeline can't achieve anything, can she?" I raise a brow at her temper then back a step away from her. "Hate it. Madeline Cavannagh, What was I thinking? I don't even have my own fucking life, Jack. Go back to your mansion on your own. Just leave me alone. I don't want you."

The three strides necessary to get to her and lift her from the floor with a firm grip, ready to drag her if needed, are swift and pitiless. She's coming home with me whether she likes it or not. Maybe I want Selma's vibrance back inside her, or maybe I just want to fuck this situation out to its conclusion before I let her go. Either way, she's got nowhere else and I'm not leaving her on this ruined ground alone.

"Get back to the car," I order, pointing back the way we originally came. She glares at me and scuttles away from my tone. I let her move, give her that sense of freedom for now, but keep pointing at the street.

"Jack, I…"

"You don't know what you want, Madeline. And you're not likely to until you can think rationally. For now, you're coming home with me. We'll talk about it tomorrow when I bring you back for the reports." A staring match ensues, one I'll win one way or another regardless of her spirited attitude. She'll be fucking lifted if required and carried back to the car. "Are you ready to explain who you think did this and why?" I grate out. She frowns, her face falling from anger. "Ready for the questions the police will have?" This causes further frowning and her mouth to open, about to protest. "You've got a lot of explaining to do, Madeline. You need to be clear thinking when you do it. For your sake." She falters and glances back at the building. "If your friend was in there, it's now a manslaughter investigation. You ready for that?" She eventually frowns, hugging herself again, and then lowers her head in defeat as she walks to the car compliantly.

~

The drive is quiet again, but this time for different reasons. I spend most of it thinking of my wife and child. Imagining them. Trying to rid myself of the constant scenes of blood and mutilation as we swerve the roads to get back home with no care for the oncoming traffic. She spends most of it morosely looking at the road, barely engaging other to ask if I've seen her phone. I haven't, not since she held it over her head in the bog. We're just silent, nothing making anything easier for either of us until she sighs next to me, breaking me of my nightmares for a few seconds with her barren tone.

"You think things happen for a reason?" she asks, no longer giving a damn about how she looks or what leaves her mouth. I balk at the question, damn sure that nothing in this life happens for a reason regardless of ghostly figures. Shit happens. People die. Buildings burn. Humans are still as reprehensible in nature as they were a year or so ago.

"No," I reply.

That's all I have to offer on the subject as we finally breach the gates onto the main drive. She sighs again in reply, moving herself around as she gazes at the house's lights in the distance.

"Quite the optimist, aren't you?"

Optimism is for fools and religion.

I don't answer, just keep on staring down the dark tarmacked drive so I can rid myself of her. She's too much like Selma, too perfect, even in this scenario. I've felt her aura the entire time we've been together, hovering around us and bringing with it a sense of hope. From meeting her and dancing, to having her body on mine, and finally to this very second as I watch her move and labour as Selma used to. She frowns the same way, sending her pain to me without realising she is doing it. It's comforting, soothing even, filling me with thoughts that are baffling.

It's been nothing but damn well confusing as we travelled here again. I train my dogs; that's all. I train them and make them pay for their sins. None of this is required, certainly not with the fucking hope of Selma attached to anything. She's dead. Gone.

The few dim lights glimmer as we approach through the woods, then the security system kicks in, flooding the forecourt with dull illumination and shadows. I raise my eyes to the third floor, sneering at my dogs and wondering what I can do with them to alleviate this tension inside me. The house is in darkness, no lights left on inside, but I notice something flickering in Selma's dressing room. I stare at it cautiously, but no sooner have I focused on the window than the strange flickering disappears.

I keep looking up, watching for signs of intruders or prowlers as Madeline gets out, but nothing happens. The curtains just hang, static. The room is dark again with no sign of anything to cause concern.

"Did you see that?" I ask, getting out and still staring at the window.

"What?" she replies, looking upwards and barely bothering with enthusiasm as she walks round to me.

"The light on the second floor?"

"No, it all looks dark to me." Hmm. I must have been mistaken, or going mad, which is still possible given the ghosts around.

Rubbing at the bridge of my nose, I walk to the house, trying to remember the last time I slept. Wednesday possibly. Who fucking knows? It's all been a fog of dogs and beatings lately. That and ghosts. Perhaps that's the damn problem.

The moment I open the door she laughs lightly, following me in and keeping her distance as she glances around.

"You don't lock this place?" No, I want the intruders, am desperate for them to come in and try defiling something that belongs to me again. "All this money and you keep it open?"

"They can come if they dare," I grate out.

I head straight for the spiral, flicking on the lamps as I go, and then stand there, gazing up the black steps and waiting for sound. Nothing happens, nothing but the soft padding of her feet as she comes to my side and looks up with me.

"If you just show me a room I'll get out of your way," she says, putting her foot on the stairs. I grab her arm, halting her momentum and pulling her back off the step.

"I don't use the upstairs. I told you it's not fucking safe."

She frowns at me, a look of surprise etched into her features as she wipes some hair back from her face and smears more soot over her cheek.

"How is it unsafe?" she asks, quietly pulling her arm from my hold and then rubbing at it. I growl beneath my ragged breath, irritated that she's asking questions I can't answer. It's none of her fucking business anyway. None.

Why the fuck have I brought her here?

She smiles a little, looking nervous, and takes another step from me, crossing onto the large ornate Chinese rug and glancing around quietly. It's the same rug I enjoyed fucking my wife on by the fire. The same one my son played games on, squealing as I tickled him.

"It just damn well is, Madeline," I snap, dismissing the thought of fucking her there, too, and walking away towards the kitchen before the urge gets any stronger. "Stay away from the stairs."

"Oh, okay," she says gently.

I storm on, animosity in every step, filling the house with my belligerence. Fucking woman. A woman with too many questions, ones I'm not ready for. I've never had to answer them before. In all this time I haven't needed to. Where the fuck I'm going to put her, I don't know. It won't be up those damned stairs, though.

I stare at the kitchen table, frustrated at my thoughts, then look at the drinks cupboard. A fucking drink, that's what I need. A large one.

"Erm, where do I go then? I don't want to get in your way any more than I have to," she says, her voice as light as a damn feather as I hear her feet enter the kitchen.

I don't know. She sure as hell isn't coming into my bed where I can pretend I'm still happily married and life is full of roses. Tangled sheets and morning breakfasts. Words of love whispered in ears. The effortless sense of closeness and harmony that Selma brought with her.

I march to the cupboard and lift out a bottle of whiskey, hoping that rationality will follow. I don't bother with a glass or any sense of refinement. I just lift the damn thing and glug, content in the thought of getting viciously drunk and forgetting for a while.

"Jack?" Christ, I wish she didn't sound like Selma. It's all I can hear. That British lilt hangs around her every word and makes sense impossible. I glug some more, tipping the bottle higher for more down force. Perhaps if I drink enough she'll fuck off and leave me alone. "Jack? Please, I don't know…"

I stop drinking and throw the bottle at the wall, stupefied by my own absurd reaction to her. She jumps at the move, her body vaulting away from me. I watch her from the corner of my eye, hoping she'll be too terrified to talk again and will run off into a corner so I don't have to look at her.

"I'm sorry. Please, just… You offered help and I don't know where to go." She flusters, her frame quavering and nerves pouring from her. I suppose she would be if she's been beaten by a coward. It's something I can use to my advantage, something that'll help alleviate this insanity from going any further until she leaves.

"Past the back of the spiral, fourth room on the right," I grate out, turning my body back to the cupboard and grabbing another bottle. She can stay in one of the old servant's quarters. There's a bed in that one. "Lock the fucking door, Madeline." Unscrewing the next lid, I turn to fully face her and lift the bottle to my lips again. She shakes a little more as she looks me over, cowering slightly, probably scared of my advancing rage as her feet still back away. "That's it. Go hide."

It doesn't take long before she makes the right choice by both of us. She backs out further, her feet silently gracing the floor, and then finally leaves me standing in the kitchen alone.

My hands spread on the old wooden table, the one Selma chose, and I look out through the window into the night. The images and visions spring forth rapidly, reminding me of what is waiting for me in Madeline's arms. Selma's hands. Her sweet singing voice. The sight of her smiling. The smell of her. They crease and blur into each other, finally becoming muddled and distant as I keep swigging more liquor.

"Why are you still here?" I mumble, succumbing to the chair that offers itself for use. I collapse into it, allowing it to hold me steady rather than the swaying that has begun.

"You should be gone by now." Not coming back in reincarnations to taunt me. The whole fucking world could have come here today. Every one of them, and the only one who did has to be a doppelganger of my wife?

I stare out into space, searching for answers that aren't there. "Did you make this happen? Why?" Nothing answers me. No light outside or spectral image. No help of any kind. There's only silence and the occasional whistling wind as the trees outside creak and groan. "I miss you so much, baby." I do. And I'm lost without her. Homeless. Heartless. Void of care or consideration. I exist for only one reason—to punish those responsible.

The dogs upstairs.

My head lolls back as I strip from my jacket and scrunch it to the floor, kicking it away as it lands on the rough stone squares in disgust. Dirty, smeared by smoke and grime as I held her in my arms. Why did I do that?

I rub my brow then look at my hand covered in more filth, streaks of blackened grunge running between my fingers. She isn't Selma. She isn't. She is Madeline Cavannagh. A no one. A woman of no connection other than looking like my dead wife.

My brutalized, bloodied and battered dead wife.

Chapter 8

Madeline

Several hours have passed as I've paced around the house not really knowing what to do with myself. It's beautiful. Old, distinguished, slightly reminiscent of the ghost story the façade outside offers. It's got all the corners and nooks to worry about, the occasional cobweb dangling to highlight its aged appearance.

I've wandered aimlessly, quietly opening doors and peeking inside. Every room is lovely, put together perfectly with matching curtains and designs, but it's devoid of love or care. It's feels like a film of grime has come down on it, killing its warmth. A bit like me now.

Hollow and cold.

A woman did this, or certainly a designer. It's not a man's style. Its English country gent, but with a touch of renaissance about it. The floral patterns on some of the walls clash with the tartan heritage cloth dotted about, and the heavy old oak brings notions of Scottish heritage, thistles engrained into the wood on some pieces. It's attractive, and if it was any other day, I'd be smiling, I'm sure. I'm not, though. I've got nothing to smile about. My world is decimated.

He's made it so.

Again.

I crawled into the bed last night, tossing and turning for a while until eventually I must have drifted off through my tears. Where Jack was for the night, I don't know, and don't know why he told me to lock the door either. I did, though. I preferred that thought to the possibility of anyone I didn't know coming in. Given that he doesn't lock his front door, I suppose that's what he meant. Although, I'm not convinced. I saw something in his eyes last night I've not seen before, something dark. It scared me. Gone was the man who held me back from the fire and protected my stupidity. Gone was his care or comfort. He was replaced by something that looked blank, indifferent.

I stare into the fireplace and remember the smell of my burning home, the one I'd hardly set up yet. I've tried not to think about it. Tried to tell myself it wasn't my fault, that perhaps it *was* an accident, but I know it wasn't. Deep down I know it was Lewis or someone he sent. I wish I had tears left, but I don't seem to be able to find any. I'm just lost and drifting with no sense of direction. Maybe I got rid of my tears yesterday or through the night. I don't know, but it seems no matter how much I try to grieve for my lack of independence or think of how terrible it all is, I just can't find the thoughts I need. I'm numb. It all seems distorted, as if nothing quite makes sense other than the fact that I know Lewis did this.

And he needs to pay.

At some point this morning, while I've been floundering around half dazed in this dressing gown, I've come to the realization that nothing will change if I go back to him. If anything, going back will make it worse. I was right to leave. I did the right thing by me and my future. It's not like I haven't been living in hell for the past few years anyway, terrified of every move I make. I might as well be terrified and on my own. At least I have some power that way, some small element of control to use going forward.

I can use that control. I can use it and focus on vengeance for the one friend I had to help me onwards. He took her from me. She's gone, taken along with the house he destroyed. Killed.

All because of me.

Something's switched inside me now, or maybe it happened overnight. I'm not sure. I spent the drive back here last night feeling emotional, scarcely holding in the need to fall into Jack's lap and cry my heart out. In fact, I probably would have if he hadn't been so cold towards me. But this morning I don't feel like that. I feel emotionally lifeless, and this blur in my mind only heightens that sensation, not really giving me anything to grab onto other than hatred for the man who did this.

My husband.

I might not be able to have him committed for rape anymore, and I might not have the evidence to have him hauled in front of the law courts for his previous behaviour like I originally planned before I chickened out. I might not even have the capacity to prove he did this to my house, to my friend, but I damn well have the ability to make him pay for his actions.

Death, presumably, is easy enough to achieve if you don't care about repercussions.

If I go back to him, he'll beat me again. If I try to hide, he'll find me again. If I try to run, he'll chase me again. There is nowhere to go other than to stand and face him. And I'll do it with a gun in my hand this time. He'll either back down or he'll die. I don't care which. I'll either get caught, or I won't. I don't care about that either. He must pay for what he's done. He will pay. His wealth, his father, his family—none of them will help him out of this one. I don't even want to see him rotting in jail anymore. I want him dead, departed from the planet so I don't have to think about him anymore. I want freedom, even if that comes with a jail sentence. I want sanity.

And I want revenge for Callie.

God, do I want that.

I circle the room I'm in, tracing my fingers over the furniture and collecting the dust that lingers on them. No one's been in here for some time. It feels cold, motionless, still beautiful in its slightly dirty state, but unloved and disused.

Thick reams of powder lift off the surface of a sideboard as I draw the shape of a gun in the dust, swirling my finger to mimic smoke from the end. It's peculiar to think of me doing such a thing, not normally my style at all. I used to be bubbly, a happy-go-lucky sort of girl. Lewis ruined that. Whatever changed in him when we moved here started the process of me becoming what I am today, and last night finished me off. There's nothing left. No niceness, no anxiety, no thought of doing the right thing. There's certainly no hope of me being happy and contented with white picket fences and quiet family streets. He's taken that last shred of faith I had, burned it to the ground as if it was something to be scorned, scorched even.

Perhaps it was. Perhaps I was dreaming to ever think it was viable. I suppose I just hoped he'd leave me alone, realising the mistakes he'd made and giving me a chance at freedom. He clearly won't.

"Why are you in here?"

The sound of Jack's terse voice shocks me, making me spin to look at the door. He's half naked, still in his trousers from last night but with no top on. I stare, barely acknowledging the skin on show. He's flawless. Unadulterated. Toned, long. Skin the colour of honey and ripples goes on endlessly. It's something I should notice, but at the moment it means nothing to me. I feel as empty as this room did minutes ago.

"I'm wandering," I reply, gazing at his lips and waiting for whatever he's got to be gruff about.

There are a few seconds like this. He looks back at me, flicking his eyes between my face and the old dressing gown I found hanging in my room. I wish I wasn't losing myself in hazel eyes that frown insidiously, but I am. I'm willing that man from last night to keep coming at me. The darker the better as far as I'm concerned. Perhaps it'll help engrain my new persona, make me strong enough to do what needs doing. My mind is so bare I feel incapable of anything other than honesty about who I am, what I want. What I'm becoming. Not that I quite know what that is yet, but that man who lingered over liquor can help me with that, the one who scared me as he smashed bottles. Perhaps if I can conquer the way he made me shake in fear then I'll be ready to take my revenge. Be more prepared.

"You naked under there?" he says, nodding at the dressing gown.

"I don't have much choice. No clothes available," I mutter, tilting my head at him and breathing in husky morning masculinity. He grunts and leaves the room, the slight snarl developing on his mouth increasing whatever thoughts I'm having about underhand manhunts.

"I'll get you some."

I lean on the doorway, watching him leave and pulling the robe tighter around me.

"You going to be in an arsehole mood all day?" I call out, hoping that he is.

I don't want nice Jack who dances around ballrooms with me, or sensible Jack who thinks logically about situations. I need whoever that was last night. The one who brooded and dwelt in darkness as he downed alcohol. I need him to help me on this journey.

I turn back into the room and sigh, ready to let myself linger in the mood I'm falling into. What else is there to think about? Nothing. He's right, though. Clothes might be good.

My thoughts make me slump down into a sofa, coughing slightly at the plume of dust that envelops me as I do. Christ, someone could really do with a cleaner. Doesn't he have staff? Surely a place this big should be looked after by people. Maybe he's one of those eccentric types who lives alone in the country, hoarding things. I don't care. I've got plans to make. For a start, I need somewhere to live. I suppose the insurers will need to be contacted, and then I've got police reports to file. The cops said something about that. Going back to town. And Callie's parents. Oh god, I don't even know who they are or where they live. They need to know, though. It's about the only thing I feel anything for, enough so that my eyes well a little, tears threatening as I finger the sofa and pull at a loose thread, trying to picture her smiling face yesterday before I left. M&M's. She was eating M&M's. And laughing at me. Always laughing at me.

They need to know.

"You okay?" he says, as a load of clothes are thrown by my side on the couch. I don't look up at him. What's the point? He doesn't care if I'm alright or not. I don't know why he's being nice in any way. Instead, I lift the stack of clothes—plain blue skinny jeans, about my size by the look of them, and a brown, tight fitting t-shirt. Both women's.

"Do you have guns here?" I ask.

"What?" he replies, his voice low and cautious.

"Guns, for killing people with?" I slowly look up at him, undoing the robe around my waist as I do, not in the slightest bit embarrassed by my nakedness. What's the point in that? He's already seen my tears, seen my fury. There's nothing left for him to see other than love, and there's none of that left now. "It's a simple question." I reach out for the t-shirt, shrugging it over my head and then standing up, leaving the robe behind on the sofa. His frown increases more than usual, if that's possible, and at the same moment his eyes travel over my exposed crotch and skin. I reach down for the jeans, not wanting any more than to get dressed and learn how to shoot a gun. "So, do you have guns?" I ask again, yanking my legs into the jeans and then bouncing to get my bottom into them.

"Yes." He might have said it, but there's hesitation in his voice.

"Good, where are they? I need to learn how to use one to kill with," I say, making my way out into the hall and following it down past the stairs to get to the kitchen. "With all this space around the house I should be able to learn quickly enough."

"Madeline, that's not the answer you're after. You need to forget this and move on."

I swing around mid-stride, daring him to carry on. How the hell would he know what I need, or what will make this go away? How would he have the first clue about how I'm feeling or what I need to do to make this right again. Forget it? Dismiss it like it's nothing to think about, just another little dalliance in life that should be disregarded?

Lewis destroyed my home and killed Callie, and the last shred of me along with her.

"How would you damn well know? Living here in your playboy mansion, having sex with women at will with no thought I should think. Playing with people must be so much fun." There's a menacing narrowing of his eyes, then a sigh, followed by him walking towards me slowly with apathy entrenched in his eyes.

"I suppose that's what you would think," he says eventually, walking past me and stopping by a part of the panelled wall. I watch him for a second or two, noting the way his muscles twist around, and try to calm my wandering thoughts back to killing.

"What else is there to think? It's all there's been to see."

There's no response to that. What could he say? It's true. His hands are rough. His vocabulary rougher regardless of the wealth that surrounds his frame. He's clearly just another man who thinks he can play with whatever falls into his lap, me included. No more. Not now I've seen what I need to do. I thought I was in control before. I wasn't.

I am now.

He points at the panel, misery etching his features as he steps away from the woodwork and huffs out a breath.

"Take your pick." I look at him, unsure what he means. "Push on the panel."

Charlotte E Hart

THE SPIRAL

My hand gently eases at the grained oak, trying to find access to some secret cavern. Nothing happens until I increase my pressure. It snaps back and slides downwards, opening a small closet. I peer into the back of the dingy space, searching for a light. There isn't one I can find, but the glinting of metal shines back regardless. Three shotguns and two handguns, all safely secured to the wall, an array of bullets and cartridges loaded neatly on the shelves next to them.

"Pick one up," he says. "Feel it. It won't solve your problems, I promise you that, but if you think it will, try." He walks away from me, back in the direction he came from, past the spiral and to the left. And then he's gone, leaving me staring at guns without any real ability to use them.

I gaze at them, lumps of metal resting onto each other, and then look back up in the direction he left in. I don't need him. I don't. I wish that thought sat as comfortably as the words, but it doesn't. It's something about the way sadness crept into his eyes as he gazed at me. Or perhaps the way he said 'try', as if the very word made him melancholy.

My hands fidget at my sides, unable to actually pick up the things as I glance back at them. They're alien to me, not something I've ever used or thought about using. Lewis had one—hell, most of America has one, but not me.

I suppose I'm still too British, not quite able to see them as normal and feasible for use. Although, Lewis isn't going to die unless I pick one up, is he? My life won't be free. Nothing is going to change unless I take control and do something about it.

I force my hand forward, knocking the panel first for some semblance of reality, and then link my fingers around the chrome handgun to lift it from its holstered position. It's heavier than I thought, and the grip's bumpy, wider than anything I've ever held there, awkward. And cold, it's bitterly cold, like it's been in a fridge. I hold it up, inspecting it and trying to find a comfortable position for it as I feel my breathing increase. It sits clumsily in my grasp, as if it's got no reason to be there. It has, enough so that I find myself tweaking it around.

Opening and closing my thumb around its base to force it into a more comfortable position, I tremble around it. My finger hovers over the trigger, unsure about safeties or bullets as I lift it to my eye-line and stare down the top of it, hoping for aim. My blood heightens as I begin to believe I should be holding it, that it's in my hand for a purpose. Perhaps it's the feel of it warming in my grip, moulding itself to me and making me feel at ease with its cumbersome shape.

"Hold it with two hands," his voice says behind me. "Cup your left hand around your right." I don't know why I'm smiling, but I am. He suddenly makes me feel like it's all worth something, like this fiddling about with guns is workable somehow.

"I thought you didn't care," I say, jiggling with my grip and trying to find what he's talking about to no avail. His hand slides around my waist, pulling me back into him as he lifts my left hand, closing it around the right and securing it into place.

"I don't, but I won't have you killing yourself either. Keep it close to you. Look down the barrel for precision." He shoves my head forward, lining it up with the barrel correctly. "Your left hand will help keep you level and straight. You're right is for trigger pulling and aim."

"Okay."

"And you need to calm your breathing. You're scared of it. Don't be. It's nothing without someone holding it. Just think of it as a piece of iron, useless unless you power it."

I breathe out slowly and then inhale again, letting his body move me around as we aim at things in the hallway—a vase, an old locket in a picture on the wall, the dotted moulding around the cornicing. Each time he believes my aim's true, he nods, then swings me to a new angle, bracing his foot behind mine to ensure I'm straight. Eventually, he lets me go and backs away. I keep pointing at things, finally getting used to the feel of it and the way I need to hold myself, until I end up pointing at him as he leans on the wall, arms and legs crossed.

He stares, doing nothing else. The look is enthralling in its untroubled attitude. There's no fear or concern etched in, no worry that I'll actually pull the trigger. I need to find that emotion, use it. I need vague and blank, or cocky and self-assured. Having said that, I don't suppose he needs to be worried or bothered. It's not loaded, I'm sure. Either that or there's one of those safety features on it that hinders the mechanism.

I creep closer to him, staring down the barrel and watching his lips lift a little.

"You going to shoot me, Madeline?"

Still he stares, relaxed as ever with the beginnings of a grin. My own mouth twitches into a half smile, overly consumed by his attitude. It's not like Lewis's. It seems justly superior in some way. As if he's earnt his stripes, worn them well and deserves his respect. What for, I don't know, but it makes me see Lewis for what his brashness was: childish. "Or should we get on with the fucking now?"

My frown descends again, annoyed at my lack of power given that I'm aiming a gun at his face.

"I'm holding a gun, Mr. Caldwell. Could you be anymore stupid? I'm the one in charge."

There's utter silence for a minute or so, nothing but air floating around as I half pace and he stands perfectly still staring at me like I'm something unusual. I don't see why. Nothing's changed as far as I can tell. Only the fact that we're back to talking about sex rather than killing. My, how my life's changed since I met this man. Sex and killing.

How clarifying.

I gaze at him, inching my feet over to the left in a charade of escape, all the time readying myself for giving in anyway. There's no way this thing's loaded, and I wouldn't shoot him even if it was. He knows that. And for whatever reason I'm about ready to capitulate to sex. Maybe it's the stalking I'm doing, or the fact that for just a few minutes he's managed to take my mind off my miserable attempt at freedom and make me smile. Either way, Callie's dead. There's nothing I can do but make Lewis pay when I'm done learning to use this thing in my fingers.

"On the stairs," I blurt out, flicking my gun towards the large spiral like I'm in a movie. He continues with his slight smile, probably now because of my moves as I cross my legs towards the first black step, but I see the falter in his eyes. Whatever those stairs are, or however unsafe they might be, they make him nervous. He's bothered by whatever's up them. That, and the fact that I'm holding a gun, makes me feel alive for once, completely in control of what's happening in my life.

I tighten a small smile, interested by the thought that I've set him off balance.

He kicks himself off the dark wooden panelling suddenly, uncrossing his arms and still smiling as he makes his way to me. I back away, rapidly increasing the length of my strides from his to avoid capture.

"You've got a gun. Why are you backing up, Madeline?"

"It's not loaded," I reply, feeling every inch of power and control drain from me as I quickly glance around.

"How do you know?" he says, quickening his stride until he's directly in front of me, lifting my hands and pushing his forehead into the barrel. "You'll never know unless you pull the damned trigger, will you? Pull it."

"I... " I have nothing for this. My hands shake, jiggling the gun around on his forehead, to the point of him pushing against it harder to keep it still.

"You don't know how to fucking kill, do you?" he says. No, I don't suppose I do. The thought of those words makes my body sag as his finger comes up to my face, surprising me and tracing down the right hand side of it. He smiles softly, crinkling his eyes. "You wouldn't know how to. You shouldn't either. You're too flawless for that sort of endeavour. Look at yourself. Beautiful, elegant, graceful." He looks my face over again. "Vicious promises aren't for you. Vengeance either. That's my job." He sighs and licks his lips, looking at mine and pushing the gun into his head some more. "Your future should never have been taken from you like this." I stare at him, bewildered by what's coming from his mouth. "The sun should still rise and set with your smile."

I back away, drawing the gun with me and removing it from his head as I gaze at him, stunned at this romantic version of normal that has no business in this room.

"What?"

"Do you know how faultless you are? It wasn't your fault. It was mine. I'm so sorry."

What the hell's going on? What's he talking about? His fault?

He moves again quickly, lifting the metal back into his head regardless of my attempt to halt the movement, both hands holding it still against him. "I miss us, baby. Pull it. Set me free."

There's nothing but space and silence as we stand there—me, holding a gun to his head, and him looking so utterly peaceful and at ease with that fact that it makes me wonder what he's thinking about as I stare at him.

"Jack, I don't know what you're talking about."

"Say it again," he says, closing his eyes and crawling his hands to my cheeks again, tentatively brushing his thumb back and forth. "Pull the trigger and say my name, baby. I want you safe again."

I gaze at his strong, stone-like jaw, a carefree lilt of happiness caressing his mouth. He seems sentimental, as if he's remembering another time and happily relaxing in it. His dark hair's tousled, roughed about and lazily framing his face, and the morning sun glints off the gun, streaming in through the windows behind me and sending splinters of light over his chest as his ribs heave in slow, deep breaths.

The whole thing sends an eerie feeling through me, all my power suddenly evaporating at his demeanour. I try to move the gun away from him, knowing this has turned into something I don't understand at all, but he snatches it back, pulling his hand from my face to cover mine with his and hold the gun where he wants it to be.

"Jack, I don't know what I'm supposed to do," I mumble, unsure what's going on as I try to lever my hand from his. I'm not shooting him no matter how much he might appear to want it. That's not why I'm here. I need to go, not be here doing this. I need revenge. I need to find Lewis, kill him and stop this happening to me again.

The sigh that comes from his mouth as he eventually opens his eyes is never-ending. It matches his look as he gazes at me. If someone had ever tried to get inside me before now, they failed compared to this stare. It's filled with love, adoration even. Why, I don't know. We hardly know each other, but his shadowy brown eyes just sink into mine, somehow connecting us. I can feel it as we linger in this moment. It's odd, almost unearthly. As if we've known each other a lifetime. And I can sense something, something that's not mine. Distant thoughts circulate in my mind, ones I can't latch onto for fear of losing whatever this is between us.

"Neither do I," he says quietly, finally letting me inch my hands away from the gun and then taking it from me to droop in his hand.

We just stand there again, looking at each other. I don't know what to do or say. Everything's gone strange. Even the air smells different. Freesias, or certainly spring flowers of some sort, permeate the room instead of the dusty wood smell that's normal around here. And I swear to god there's a tear in his eye. They're welling with them, subtly maybe, but the influence he normally holds so well, the one he held only a few minutes ago, is disintegrating around him. Vanishing.

My hand moves to his face, just wanting to comfort him in some way. I'm not even sure why. It's like my arm has its own mind as I run my fingers into his hair, gently brushing it about. He instantly closes his eyes again, letting his body give in to my touch with no thought of stopping me. And for some reason, it all feels alien yet instinctual, the way my hand moves, and the way he moans beneath it, tilting himself into my fingers as he finally lets his body fall to the floor beneath us. It's like a memory, like I've achieved that same reaction before.

I follow him down, still running my skin over his and bringing us closer together, unable to stop myself for reasons unknown. My other hand gently touches his shoulder, for the first time feeling his frame with no clothes on. It's solid, toned to perfection and yet lithe under my touch, warm and pliable as it oozes masculinity and reminds me of a love I once felt.

"I love you," he muses, tentatively reaching his hand forward to my body, unable to see it yet knowing exactly where he's going.

Love?

I frown at the word as his fingers reach the back of my neck, perfectly placing themselves without any vision to get him there. There's no love here, none that I know of anyway. There is something, though. I can feel it, no matter how much I deny it. But I don't love him. I hardly know him. Yet there's a presence, a force maybe, something drawing me to this man that I can't describe. It's fragile. Delicate. It's faint in the back of my mind, like a tunnel that's not quite opened, filling me with connotations of joy as I continue stroking his hair.

His fingers pull me closer, close enough that I can feel his breath on my lips. Kissing. It seems so personal, such a close thing to do. And I can feel myself pulling back from it, hoping to keep the distance we've created to keep me safe and isolated. Sex would be okay, easy, simple. Just like the killing I hope to achieve. Final and non-descript, but nothing about this sensation is simple. I can sense complication and barriers, feel their challenges ahead of us, their hurdles, but I can't stop myself moving forward into him.

It's so very gentle, so hesitant, a bare whisper of touch as our lips meet, dry and feathering. My breath shakes out of me, the muscles on the back of my neck fighting a little but giving no real resistance to the movement other than fear. It's not even fear really. It's more like trepidation, like part of me is desperate to deny connection of any sort. It'll weaken my resolve to do what's necessary to Lewis, perhaps remind me that beauty does exist.

"I love you," he whispers again, the words blown between our lips, and I so want to believe them. I feel the sentiment catch in my throat, my own words wanting to rise out of me and repeat back to him. My head shakes softly, barely containing lucid thought in the middle of whatever this is. I don't know him. I know nothing of Jack, nothing, and yet his mouth's on mine now, slowly moving us into a deeper kiss as his hand grips tighter and his tongue gently traces my bottom lip. It's all so beautiful. It's so perfect that I can feel my own tears coming, writhing their way behind my closed eyelids and threatening me with some madness I don't understand.

"I want to feel you again. Let me," he says, rubbing his hand into my neck and drawing me closer. It's everything a perfect moment should be. It's filled with sentiments of hope and courage, optimism. A future worth living and people worth loving. It's not something I've felt for a while, if ever, certainly not beneath the hands of a man, and I can't help but revel in the sound of his words, hopelessly loving him for them.

Chapter 9

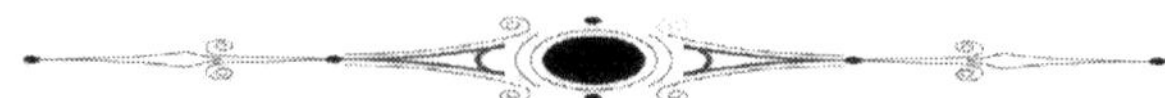

Jack

Selma.

Warm skin and gentle fingers adorn my face once more, her lips gracefully meandering her way around mine. My heart lurches, hastily trying to hold onto its rhythm while she falls into my arms again. This makes no sense, but there's nothing here but love and commitment. Nothing but times past and feelings of worship for the woman I love as we hover in strange shadows around the room. She's here now, resting in my arms and desperately moaning her need for connection.

She moves, pushing herself into my embrace and deepening us. It's enough to rid me of whatever last shred of reason I'm clawing onto as I skim under her t-shirt and tug at the hem.

"Jack." I can't tell if it's real or not, don't care. All I can hear is her echo in my ear.

That's enough.

I turn her onto the floor, feathering her with as many kisses as I can for fear of losing her again, and draw the fabric up her body. She smells so good, flooding me with more memories and thoughts as I lick across her stomach. I bite into it gently, wanting to hear the groan, feel the reality of her between my teeth. She moans instantly, screwing into herself then straightening and presenting herself for more. My hand trails up her legs as I move up her body, pushing her open and inching my hand to the top of her jeans to flick the button.

"Yes," she hisses, her hands still in my hair, tugging me about as she begins to grind into my frame.

My fingers gently run over her as I push the zip down, inching my hand in bit by bit and moving my body up to her face to gaze at her. Fuck, I love watching her come. Always have. No one has ever looked as she does. I love the rapture in her eyes, the way she grits her teeth, and the way her cheeks blush on the final scream.

I sink my hand downwards as her mouth parts, air filtering onto my face from her mouth, and breathe that in, too. It reminds me of her scent, as a shadow looms over the pair of us, casting us further into darkness. The sun might have gone, but the vibrancy of it hasn't. It's here, beneath my hands and waiting for me as I delve my first finger in.

She moans, instantly widening her legs for access and squirming against me. I relish the feeling of her gripping and twisting to help me get deeper, and forge another finger in, widening her further and languishing in the sound of her moans.

"You always were greedy," I murmur, lowering my mouth and swallowing her moans as our lips connect again.

She writhes beautifully while I probe her as I used to, wanting to give her every second of my adulation and waiting for the squeal to come. She always was a squealer, little temper tantrums getting in the way of our playtime. I push on her clit, helping her on her way and rubbing it back and forth as my fingers continue delving in and out. Everything is still so familiar—the sound of her, the smell, the way she moves beneath me as part of me.

"Make me come," she says, suddenly beginning to wrench at the top of her jeans, barely removing her mouth from mine as she does. I help her with that, too, grabbing at the other side of them to ease their path down her legs until finally, she's bare under my weight, her body undulating as she strips her top away.

"So fucking beautiful," I mumble, dropping my head to wrap my tongue around her nipple. She moans aloud, grinding herself down onto my hand and stretching her own out behind her. I smile, remembering the way I tied her hands occasionally, held them down before I knew what

I was doing in that regard. "You want me to play?" I ask, not caring in the slightest either way. I'll do this for hours with no need for kink. She's enough, anyway I can get her. I'll simply spend an eternity lapping over her skin and sinking myself inside it.

"Jack, please. Please…"

It's yet more moaned torment as I turn my hand inside her, watching her writhe against the red Oriental rug as I create more irritation for her. She breathes her pleas like life depends on us making love. She sings them from her soul, just as she always has, nearly scorching the sky with clarity in the middle of this stormy obscurity we find ourselves in.

I increase pressure on her, turning to look at my fingers slipping in and out.

"So fucking sexy," I mutter, bracing my other hand on her stomach to hold her still. She's always been a mover, wrangling her way around the floor so I can't finish her off. And she still is as her legs try to push away from the torment, her stomach muscles propelling her away from my fingers. "Stay fucking still," I snarl out, rounding her body and lowering myself between her legs. Just a taste.

I chuckle, knowing that I long to be down here for hours, too, dipping my tongue as often as I choose and gazing at her fighting against my mouth. Not this time, though. This time, the first time in so long, I'll fucking eat her out desperately. Chew down on her and pull her into my mouth, grabbing her to me as I do.

I pull my fingers from her and wrap my hands under her hips, yanking her along the floor and down onto me. The rug crumples with my force, rippling around us as she yelps out in surprise.

"Oh God, Jack, I can't…" She can, and she will. She will wait until I've had my fill of her taste, and squirm until I'm ready to devour her more.

I rub my nose around her, letting the scent of her intoxicate my senses more. *Selma*. Not one woman has smelt as she does. It drives me mad as I suck the smell in, hardening my dick infinitely as I push my tongue out tentatively. I lap gently at first, desperate to elongate the moment and let her taste linger in my mouth. It's fucking heavenly on my taste buds, beautiful, like wild flowers in spring woods, all mixed with sensual decadence.

The gentle laps turn ravenous as I let my wide tongue find its way around her again, licking and remembering its perfected course as it surges around. She groans and moans, tipping her hips into my mouth, her hands bracing the floor to lift herself into me.

"Jack. Oh god. Please…"

Lowering one of my hands, I try to undo my belt as she bucks about in my hold. I chuckle again, lifting myself off her and up onto my knees to rip at my pants. She's still writhing, her frame barely discernible in the shadow I'm casting over her and the murkiness in the room, but I know this woman. I don't need to see her. I can feel her. Her outline is mapped in my mind. Her curves. The way her body flows effortlessly as she moves. Her long slender arms, her nails and the way they embed themselves in the moment of orgasm. I don't need visuals. All I need is her sound as she keeps moaning beneath me.

"Jack, yes. More."

I close my eyes as her hand wraps around my cock, tugging it towards her, delicate hands nimbly grasping at what she wants. I hover in the moment, remembering her mouth's intensity and the way she swirls her tongue, aching with need for her to do it again and remind me.

"Suck it," I almost growl, desperate to have her warmth around me again as she begins to stroke me back and forth. She doesn't; she torments me as much as I have her, the occasional flick of her tongue here, a kiss on it there. I grunt, grabbing at her hair and hauling her towards me with little care for her comfort. She squeals a little, reminding me of her fragility. It's not something I give a damn about at the moment. I want to fuck my way back into her soul any way I can. Her pussy, her throat. I don't care how. I just need to join, to remind us both what we've been missing.

Her lips part as I push on them, and then warmth envelops me, sliding itself up my shaft and causing me to tighten my ass in response. I could come instantly, barely holding off the need to pump viciously into her throat and erupt, but her moan echoes in the room again, haunting the mysterious nightfall that's descending and giving me a new focus. I grasp hold of the sound as my fingers grip onto her head, guiding her down onto me as I shove in deeper and close my eyes again.

"More, baby," I murmur, sliding myself in further as her hands grip my ass and pull me towards her. She slides her mouth back, running her tongue around me as she goes and then forges back onto me again, swallowing and causing me to growl in pleasure. "Fuck, that's good," I groan out, pushing my cock back and forth in her throat and relishing the tight restriction around it.

Her lips meet my stomach as her teeth grate on me, gentle little nips as her fingers dig into my backside and then she slides away again. Back and forth. Long fluid strokes as one hand leaves my ass and begins to fondle my balls. It makes me desperate to come, enough so that I shove hard and true, angling her head for long rampant thrusts into her throat. She gags once, changing her position so she can handle more of me. One, two, three heavy shoves. And then more, listening to her constant moaning and groaning beneath my hands, feeling the texture of her skin in my fingers and nearly crying at the memory of it.

No. I shake my head and grit my teeth, winding her hair into my fingers. Not like this. I want to fuck her, make love to her, and feel her clamping around my cock when I come inside her. I want to remember that. Give her that moment, give myself that fucking heavenly moment.

I pull her off, just stopping the imminent flow of come from leaving me and push her to the floor again. She yields immediately, not questioning or fighting. She just pushes my trousers off, helping me rid myself of the last barrier between us. She knows, doesn't she? Knows how precious these moments together are. She understands me like no other. She always has. She knows the darkness, the light. She holds me together when I crumble, breaks me open when I close down. She knows me better than I know myself.

Her legs open and draw me down onto her, as her mouth lands on mine with ease and we mould together. "Now," she whispers, her lips and teeth clashing onto mine. "Make love to me, Jack."

I could come the moment I sink into her, our bodies joining with no interruption. We hardly move at first. We just wait, our mouths too desperate to kiss to concern ourselves with making love. This is making love, all of it. The need, the ache, the sense of closeness. I can feel her inside my mind telling me she loves me and holding me in this darkness, reminding me of summer's warmth.

The same warmth I haven't felt without her.

"I love you," I whisper, feeling her hands twine into my hair and her feet hitch up onto my back for comfort. "Closer, pull me closer, baby." She wraps her legs tighter, resting her hands on my face and staring into my eyes.

The first gentle pull out and then forge back in effortlessly sends me into idyllic dreams. She moans aloud, tightening her hands on my cheeks and refusing to take her eyes from me. I wrap my arm under her, lifting her into me and resting my forehead on hers so I can gaze at her, pushing into her again, and again. I know those eyes so well. I've been lost in them so many times before, wished they'd come home so many times. And they're vibrant again now, full of life and vigour. They beg with need, showering their wonder on me and saturating me with love once more.

I slowly drive every inch into her, hoping for a miracle to bring us all home again. She isn't real; none of this is, I know that, but I can feel her regardless. I can sense her in this madness as I grunt, my throat catching with the exertion as I forge in again. Perhaps I'm desperate to prove she is real, to verify this as meaningful somehow. Maybe I just want to prove that she's alive, breathing, and here with me, loving me again as she lingers in the air. I can almost hear Lenon's voice, hear the wedding bells ringing, sense the moment I fell in love with her. She *is* real. I can hear her groans of desire, feel her fingers biting into my neck as she pulls me into her. She is here. *Selma* is here, now, proving she still loves me as I fuck into her and wait for her orgasm to bridge our dreams together.

She rises beneath me, her body suddenly gliding to a stop in the middle of this blackened delusion, her mouth trembling under mine as I keep pushing into her. It's all I need to realise reality. Just her moment of quiet and it's all tangible around me. Real. Every muscle tenses between us, every sinew poised and waiting for the heavens to open, gracing us with freedom. My body primes, come driving itself from the depths to flow into her. And finally she moans, a sound that wrecks my mind and nearly destroys it as all around us blurs into insignificance. There is only these seconds, the two of us, together again and fucking, making love, remembering, reminding. Both of us in the very spot where we made our child.

Together again.

I lie for a while, letting my body relax into her and sensing the last of my come find its way home as she brushes at my hair. Fucking perfect. I can't find the will to move, and couldn't care less what I should be doing or whether this is real or not. As far as I'm concerned, this is the only thing I should be doing. Madness or not. If I have my way I won't be doing anything but this for a very long time. Selma is home. She's here with me, still stoking my hair and holding us together.

"That was nice," she says, letting her legs drop from my back and loll to the floor beside me. I rub my face against her breast, gently nipping at the nipple that happens to fall into my mouth. "You're good at that."

"Hmm." I can't find words yet, don't want to. Words might change the air around us, break whatever fucking spell we're under. And it isn't me who's good, anyway. It never was. It's always her—her and her ability to harness me.

I eventually open my eyes, staring across her body towards the empty fireplace, then breathe in deeply, enjoying the smell of us in the air rather than the usual dust ridden barrenness. I smile, sliding my cock casually and remembering Lenon running through the room, his little hand swinging a sword around while he chased imaginary dragons.

"I've missed this," I murmur, kissing her ribs and then continuing to flick my tongue around her nipple. "Missed you." She laughs lightly, filling me with more dreams and visions. The time she spilt white paint all over the kitchen when we first moved here, the way she always asked me to do her necklaces because she couldn't fasten the clip, and the way she giggled when I tickled her. Christ, I love tickling her. If I could be bothered to move, I might do it now, but I can't. I'm far too engrossed in the quiet and peace around me to attempt moving anywhere.

The darkness of the room starts to brighten out, flecks of light beginning to filter then pour in from the window again. I watch them dapple the floor, flickering through the old stained glass, casting blue and amber tones at me and ridding the space of the murkiness that had fallen. I frown at the colours, knowing what will happen soon and closing my eyes again in hope.

"Jack."

The sound of my name reverberates in my mind. It isn't real this time. I can tell. She's disappearing, leaving me. I tuck my head into the body beneath me, pulling in rapid breaths and trying to keep her here, hoping at least the scent will stay.

"I don't know why you keep saying that. It's not like we really know each other," she says, her hand running through my hair.

Tears prick my eyes as I fight to keep them shut against her skin. *Madeline.* My hand scrunches into her skin, twisting it, hoping beyond all hope that I'll hear Selma again, desperate to before she leaves me alone and in pain again. She shrieks, yanking herself away from my hold and rolling out of the way, my spent cock slipping out of her as she does.

"The hell was that?" she spits, scrambling to her feet and backing away from me.

I don't look at her. I can't. Instead, I sigh and brace myself on the floor, ready to get up and go to my room, to search for some fucking sanity.

"I'm sorry," I whisper, lifting myself wearily and looking anywhere but at her. The gun catches my eye, discarded by the sideboard. I walk to it and pick it up with every intention of putting it back in the gun cabinet so I can leave.

"What the hell is wrong with you? We just made love, didn't we? I'm confused, Jack. What the…" She doesn't finish her sentence, but stops as I notice her feet back away further. "Jack, what are you doing?"

I don't know anymore. Nothing is real here. I can't work out what's going on myself, let alone explain it to her. Brightness then gloom. Fog and mists. Darkness then dappled flickers of light. I just want Selma back, and Lenon, and this house filled with joy like it once was.

I shake my head, trying to get the sight of her out of it or bring the other Selma back into vision, but they blur, the two of them becoming one in my mind. I stare back at the brightly lit mahogany fireplace then flick my eyes up to the stained glass, searching for the dark again and wondering where she's gone, or if she was ever really here. The sun blinds me, glinting off a heart shaped amber piece. I smile at it, blinking and remembering the bridesmaids' dresses and colour of their bouquets.

"Jack, put the gun down." It was such a lovely day. People cheered around us and offered their congratulations, slapping me on the back and telling me I was batting above my weight. They were right, all of them. "Jack?"

I turn, still smiling, but now at how similar she sounds. Even the huskiness of her concerned tone is the same. I don't know why she's concerned, but I look at her fondly, appreciating the apprehension regardless.

"You need to put the gun down, Jack. Come on," she says, her body hesitantly moving towards me. Gun? I search for it, wondering where it's gone, only to find it in my hand pointing towards my chin. I fiddle with it, intending to move it but let the metal linger instead. "Please, give it to me, yeah?" I try to move my hand like she asks, but something stops me as I stare at her naked body. She's so like Selma. "We can go for a walk if you like. Some fresh air?" I smile again. Warm, fresh air. She liked that, too. We walked a lot, especially in spring. She liked the bluebells.

"It's Maddy, Jack. You still with me?" I narrow my eyes. I don't know that either. Nothing makes any sense anymore. Maddy? Who's Maddy? Selma. Where's she gone? I don't know if I'm with either one, or both. Is this Selma, or is Selma Maddy? Why has she come back?

Who is this in front of me?

The gun moves, its texture running along my chin then up to my mouth. It would all be so easy if I just pull the trigger, or if she had done it earlier. I'd be with them then. We'd be together and happy again, like I was ten minutes ago. There wouldn't be this constant confusion, and I wouldn't be alone anymore either. I'd be whole.

"Am I going mad?" I ask, not knowing what to think as my vision swims a little and she moves again. "You're not you, are you?" She looks at me, her lips quivering and reminding me of our first time together.

"No, no, you're not mad, Jack. You're just tired," she says, her feet getting closer as I watch her light skin glide in front of me. Madeline. But she smiles like Selma, and moves like her, talks like her. "I'm not surprised really. You gave up your bed for me, didn't you? Slept on the sofa? Very chivalrous. Just give me that and we'll get dressed. I need to see my car anyway, or you could show me around the woods?" The woods. Yes. I'd like a walk in the woods. I could see the treehouse, imagine Lenon in it. Hear his laugh again. "I saw some on the west side of the house." Yes, they're my favourites, too. Tall redwoods, forever reaching over the house and protecting it from harm.

Not that they ever fucking did.

I grip the gun tighter again, pressing it inwards and feeling the rim cut into my lips as I imagine the fucking dogs upstairs. "And I need another kiss, anyway. Don't you?

You can't do that to me and then not kiss me again." Kiss. I suck air in deeply, tasting her on my mouth over the taint of the metal and smelling the air still filled with love around us.

Her hand is on the gun before I know what's happening, wrangling it from my hold as she spins her body round into me to point it away from us. She backs up, forcefully, shoving my body backwards into the fireplace, causing me to grunt at the impact. Pain ricochets its way along my spine, giving her the chance she needs to snatch the gun from my hand, but somewhere in the commotion the gun shoots loudly into the air. Everything stops as she falls back against me—sound, time, even the house becomes eerily noiseless. Everything's silent, but for her small whimper and the sound of it hanging in the air.

I freeze, unable to see what's happened or to whom as I close my eyes and plead with God not to do this again. She whimpers, her body fully collapsing into my arms without trying to stop herself falling. My heart hammers in my chest, rattling the sound around my mind as I haul myself back to the present.

"Madeline?" She doesn't answer. There's no sound at all as I grab her and lower her to the floor. "Madeline? Talk to me." Still nothing. Panic swells as I slap the gun from her hand and kick it away, furious with its presence. "For fuck's sake, talk to me." She whimpers again, then starts sobbing quietly as I shove at her body. “You okay? Where did it get you?” She mumbles something and tries to roll herself away. I don’t let her. I keep searching her skin for any sign of blood, prodding it and poking her, lifting and turning. I’m nearly fucking hysterical trying to find the injury, desperate to ensure that whatever is here, or *whoever* is here, stays here, with me. “You can’t leave me. Talk to me.”

“I’m alright,” she mutters, curling herself into a ball and starting to push me away. I carry on checking her, hardly hearing her speak or believing what she’s said. I’m too consumed with the thought of her dying. “I’m fine, Jack. Get off me,” she says again, sniffing back tears and gently pushing me again. I half step away from her then carry on inspecting again, still convinced she’s injured. “Jack, I said I’m fine. Just leave me alone so I can get up, will you?”

“But you’re not. The gun fired. It hit you. You... I heard you...” I’m frantic to correct whatever I’ve done. Fraught. My hands still fuss at her, lifting her and moving her over to the chair as she tries to push me off her again.

“I said I’m fine. Stop. It shot over there somewhere. I just bashed against something.”

I look where she’s pointing, needing to see the bullet myself to ensure it hasn’t gone into her. Her finger leads towards the damn spiral.

"You sure you're not hit?" I ask, turning to see her body curled up in the chair. She nods, her full lips still trembling a little as she stares back at me and wipes her eyes.

"It was just the noise, it shocked me." I look her over again and then spin back to the spiral, needing to see the bullet. I don't know why, but I need to. Fucking gun. Stupid.

"Why did you try to kill yourself?"

I snarl at the sound of her, annoyed at her directness in the middle of whatever the fuck this is. My fingers scrub my brow, unsure how the hell to answer.

"I didn't," is all I can say. I don't think I did, anyway. Or maybe I did. I'm not fucking sure at the moment.

"You held a gun to your mouth." Mmm. I finger the carpet on the bottom step, scouring for a bullet and glowering at the thought of the fuckers upstairs. "After we'd made love. Aren't you slightly concerned by that?" I shake my head at the steps, stretching to reach the third, fourth and fifth ones. "I mean, why? Was it that bad?" I twist my face to her. Bad? She was exquisite, always has been. *Maddy.* Christ. I turn back again, choosing the task of finding the bullet rather than trying to explain it to her.

"I'm sorry if it wasn't… I wasn't…"

My foot hits the bottom step as I let her talking ease me on, all the time trying to keep my head level and calm, but the blackness of the carpet hinders my sight, everything blending into it effortlessly just as a damn bullet hole will.

"Where the fuck is it?" I mutter, irritated.

"Why don't you go up the stairs?" I freeze, hardly able to breathe at her question as I hold onto the curved bannister securely. "And don't give me that shit about it being unsafe. We're past that now. What's up there?" I snarl into the air away from her, hiding my true feelings on the matter and glaring at the sweep of the steps in front of me.

"I told you, it's unsafe. That's all."

There's silence behind me as I grip the spindles and lower myself to look at the carpeted steps, running my fingers across them. Still nothing. I look around, searching the rich brown woodwork, then skimming my eyes across the panelling behind it. Why can't I find the fucking thing? I have to find it, see it for myself. It'll tell me everything's okay, that I've not let another woman down.

Chapter 10

Madeline

I don't know what's happening as I stare at his limbs hovering around the stairs. His climb is so slow, nothing like his movements everywhere else. He's normally so strident with everything he does. His walk is fast, persuasive even. In charge. But now he hesitates with every inch he moves forward, checking meticulously for whatever he's looking for. The bullet, I assume. Why, I don't know. It doesn't matter. We're both alive, thanks to me.

I let my teeth chew my nail as I grab a rug off the back of the chair and pull it around my shoulders. What the hell just happened? It's insane. Pointing guns, then making love, then pointing guns again. It's like the whole place is enchanted with dark magic, making me, or maybe even us, do things that are in no way normal. I felt that when we made love here, beneath my feet. And we did make love. It wasn't sex. We were connected by something. It was powerful, something I've never felt before.

I tried to laugh it off when he talked to me as if he knew me better than he does, tried to blank it out and just enjoy what was happening, but it was impossible to deny. Something was mystical about us together, potent and yet so fragile I hardly dared believe it was real. And now I think about it, as I watch his naked form scrabbling about, it started with me dancing in the ball room. Why did I do that? That's nothing like me. It's whimsical, something I would have done as I child. Not something that grown up Madeline would ever do, or Maddy for that matter, certainly not with Lewis still in my mind. And where did the clouds come from?

I tip my head over my shoulder to look at the sunlit sky outside. There's nothing out there but bright blue and a huge yellow globe shining through the glass at me, sending shards of orange and blue across my skin. They're the same colours he had floating on his skin when he held the gun to his chin, brushing it around his face as he did. I wasn't scared by that, which mystifies me. I felt calm despite his strange behaviour, as if I knew he didn't really want to do it. It was only in the last few minutes that I panicked a little, choosing to grab for it when something in his eyes changed.

"Jack. What happened here? Was it…" Something special?

He stops his movements and turns to look at me, his deep hazel eyes narrowing as he frowns at me and sneers. I gaze at him, hoping maybe he understands because I sure as hell don't. I'd like to, though. If only so that I can get it out of my head if I have to, before I put my clothes back on and get on with my life and plan.

There's no response other than some muttering about not letting someone down. Perhaps it's just me then. Perhaps that *was* just sex and I should remember the reality of what's happening here. I'm an over-night guest, one who, for whatever reason, just had sex with this man before I stopped him killing himself.

That's all.

Nothing out of the norm.

I sigh and relegate myself to the facts as I lift from the chair and look for my clothes. It's time to get on with stuff. Callie, my house, and then Lewis. I've got revenge to get on with. I stare at the gun, ready to pick it up and do some real damage with it. It glints at me, reminding me of my new purpose as I try to rid myself of this whimsical feeling.

"I'll get dressed and call a cab," I mumble, scooping my jeans up and shrugging into them. I don't want to shower. I'll leave him inside me for a while, think about mystical encounters that'll help me through what's to come. The thought makes me smile a little as I pick up the gun and wonder about safety catches. "Where's the safety on this thing?" I ask, turning back to him and grabbing at my t-shirt. He's busy searching the stairs still, his body tense as he scours the carpet.

Oh, for god's sake.

I walk to the stairs, skipping the first three and tucking the gun into my back pocket. If finding the bullet's so damn important then I'll help. "I'm fine, Jack, and so are you. It doesn't matter where the thing is."

"No," he shouts, snatching at my ankle as I trot by and turn the curve past him.

"Why? They're just stairs. What's the problem?"

"I... They're unsafe. You can't…"

Unsafe my arse. There's nothing wrong with this spiral of stairs. It's beautiful. Old, solid and dependable, it'll probably last longer than either of us. My bare feet trip up another step, as I tug my t-shirt over my head, looking for the impression of a bullet as I go.

"Madeline, don't…" I spin to look at him, suddenly slightly concerned by his alarmed voice. He looks fraught with anger, his mouth parted and breathing heavily as his naked body reaches for me. I hover, flicking my eyes around for what could be unsafe about the structure. "Come back down. You can't go up there." I stare down at him, watching the way his whole being seems anxious about something, almost like he's having a panic attack. "Please, Madeline," he says, his glower deepening as he comes up a step further.

"They're just stairs, Jack." He looks straight past me and sneers, barely acknowledging my presence in front of him.

"Get off the fucking stairs. Don't make me come for you." Come for me?

His vacant gaze slowly turns back to me, a chill somehow thrown in my direction with its intensity. I freeze to the spot, remembering the man who drank alcohol and frightened me last night, and any sense of power I was rekindling seems to disperse to the stupidity that lies in little old Mads. I quiver in thought, my finger coming to my mouth so I can chew on it as I move a step lower.

"I was just trying to help you find the bullet." Still he stares, making me feel more uncomfortable by the second. I lower another, hoping to make the scowl of annoyance disappear. "Not that I know why you need to see it so much."

"To make sure," he barks out.

"Of what? I'm alive, so are you."

"Are you?" I don't know what that means. I look down at myself, pretty convinced I'm alive and fine. There's no blood stains, no wounds on offer. Nothing hurts.

"Of course I am," I reply, edging closer to him. "Look, no holes, no injury. Madeline Cavannagh. Alive and well."

He eventually nods but doesn't stop looking at me as he takes another slow step, a look of sadness now replacing his anger. It's an almost palpable emotion that washes over him, reminding me of only a short while ago when he was so focused on me. I can almost sense those flashes again on the floor, feel him inside me, his lips on mine. It all felt so linked and true, regardless of the fact that it wasn't, still isn't.

"Jack, listen. I don't know what happened here, but shall we just get on with getting me gone so you can get on with your life, and me with mine?"

"You can't go," he mutters, reaching his hand for me again. "I don't want you to go anywhere." Can't?

I nibble my thumb, watching his hand in front of me. What does he mean can't?

"Why?"

"You just can't."

My eyes sweep around the room, wondering if some new mystical thing is about to evolve. Nothing happens. It's as bright as it was before, rays of gold falling through the glass windows.

"This…" My mouth falters, unsure what I'm trying to say but entirely sure I'm mad for wanting to say anything. "I don't know what this has been, but we're not doing it again. It was strange," I say, my hand waving at the space around us as if trying to search for reasons I don't have. "I don't need strange. I need stable and efficient. Real, tangible. I need to find a new home, Jack. Rebuild my life and find Lewis so I can end this once and for all."

"I love you." My mouth gapes, my hand hovering mid swing around the room.

"Don't be stupid. You don't know me enough to love me." He continues his stare, no waiver in his words to recall them. "I know you said it before, but that was the heat of the moment and …"

"I've always loved you. Come down the stairs."

This is utterly absurd. No one falls in love this quickly. I'm not even sure I want to love again. I haven't got the strength for that yet, or the happiness regardless of this feeling I have buried inside aching to explode all over him. I need Lewis dead for that to come out. I need him gone and his threat removed.

A glare glances over my face at his irrationality, and I consider just running past him and calling that cab, but my feet are glued to the spot beneath me. It's like they're not real, like I can't feel them all of a sudden, let alone move them.

The building creaks and groans as I stare at his face, disbelief wracking every part of me at his sincere expression. He means it, doesn't he? Believes it. It makes me put my hand on the bannister, gripping it to make sure of the reality around me as his hand stays fast in the air, waiting for me to take it and accept his offer of love. Perhaps he's hoping that we'll be together forever, make babies for this big old house to endure and live happily ever after in some sort of dream.

I frown, thinking of dreams that do not happen for me and pushing them away as I remember Lewis' attacks. I screw my face around, still feeling the hint of bruising marring my eye and shuddering at the thought of another man telling me how to live. It's not happening, regardless of this man and the way he makes me feel. Something's not right here. Odd. I can't think straight, and why is it getting dark again?

Oh, enough is enough. I need to get out of here, deal with things. This is not real. I must be in some kind of nightmare I can't get out of. In fact, maybe my car's actually alright, and my house, and I'm really just asleep in my new home waiting to wake up. Callie will be waiting for me downstairs, probably having been out all night with some new man.

"I need to go," I mouth quietly, my feet trundling past him without thought for his hand, trying not to look at him anymore. Perhaps if I keep my head down I can avoid another declaration of love. I don't know who he's saying it to, or why, but those words don't belong to me. I don't deserve them or own them.

My arms fold into each other as I walk along the corridor towards the front of the house. I'll wait outside, or maybe even walk around to my car. If I could just get a phone signal I could call recovery myself and leave when they got here. Although, where I'll go I don't know.

I snatch my bag from the side table on the way into the hall, and then push my feet into my still muddied shoes. I'm instantly haunted with visions of fields and dirt, which in turn make me think about the man walking up behind me. I can hear his bare feet padding along, sense his proximity long before he reaches me.

"I have to go, Jack. Don't try to stop me," I call out, not turning to face him for fear of this rationale leaving me again.

My hand grabs the bronze door handle, swinging it out wide to walk into the sun, only to find darkness staring back at me. I halt, confused as the wind whips past my face and a low fog creeps its way across the ground in front of me.

"What the hell?" I mumble, as I gaze at it rippling the bottom of the stone steps. It's like a sea of rolling waves, foreboding in its swirl around the gravel beneath it. And it's daytime. It's the middle of the day. Where's the sun?

I flick my eyes to the sky, wrapping my arms around myself for warmth as I search for the golden globe that was there five minutes ago. There's nothing up there but clouds and a dim light casting over the top of the woods. Maybe there's an eclipse I didn't know about. "Where's the sun?" I ask, gingerly lowering my feet into the fog.

"Stay inside," he says from behind me somewhere, his voice like silk again now that he's away from the spiral. No, I can't stay inside. I need to get my car and go home. I dig into my bag, hoping that maybe my phone will work this time, but I can't find it anywhere.

"I need to use your landline," I muse, finding myself twirling around in the mist as it licks its way up my legs. He doesn't answer as I wander further into it towards the trees on the far side of the drive, but then I don't suppose he will. He doesn't want me to leave, does he? He wants me to stay in this fantasy and pretend it's real. It's not. Can't be.

I touch the back of a tall redwood, staring up at the spread of branches as I circle its girth. It's glorious as it towers above me and the mist swirls around its base, as are all the others around here. I look back at the house as I come round the far side of it, watching the way the lights dot the boundary and twinkle beneath the fog. It looks just like a ship below water sailing on by, and its beauty makes me smile as I gaze upwards and start walking towards the garages.

Charlotte E Hart

THE SPIRAL

The road seems shorter as I wander over. Perhaps it's just that everything's covered in this mist, I'm not sure, but I'm there before I know it, having trailed my hands through the billowing swirl of white as I went. The old man's there, a small shaft of light illuminating the end garage as he walks around and tinkers with things.

"How's the car doing?" I ask, looking at it still up on ramps above the pit.

"I've ordered the parts. They should be here soon, lassy."

"Oh, okay. And you can fix it then?"

"Surely can."

"Good. That's great." Okay, I'll just have to hang around a bit longer, which is a bit of a shame but there's no point calling recovery if it's nearly done anyway. "Thank you. What's your name by the way? Sorry, I never got it first time."

"It's Bob, lassy. I look after the old place. There's only me now."

"Well, nice to meet you, Bob, even if it is in unusual circumstances."

I rock on my feet, and watch him continue to potter around as I wonder what to do. I can't really go back inside. If I do it'll get all odd again. It's not something I want to deal with. I just want to get in my car and get out of here, perhaps find some sense of normal again. I snort at myself as the mist drifts around my feet again, and I glance back out into the darkened air. Normal? I haven't even got a house to go to anymore, let alone any sense of normality. I suppose I'll have to go to Callie's place first, find her parents' number and then find a hotel room.

"Funny weather," I say, inching myself onto an old chair to stare out into the beauty of the nightly vision. It's haunting really, like one of those old creepy movies, but it's got a real sense of calm about it here. There's no trepidation or hostility, no fear. It's just quiet and serene.

"The old house sits in a dip in the land. We get all sorts here. Think the headland pulls the damp air through us," he eventually replies. Oh. Okay. Must be reasonably normal round here then. Not that I've ever heard of it, but hey. If he says so.

"You got some good prices yet?"

"What?"

"You said you was an antiques dealer?"

"Oh, yes. There's plenty in there to sell if he wants to sell it." Not that he seems to. In fact, I'd almost forgotten that was what I was here to do in the first place. He didn't seem very affable to the idea, though, did he? I'm not sure why I was ever called here, actually.

He doesn't speak again, and I get to a point after a while where I feel a little uncomfortable, so I get off the chair and amble back out into the mist again, ready to wander back to the house.

The journey back takes me longer this time, or perhaps I make it so. I'm not sure, but the fact that I can't stop gazing up at the massive place probably slows my pace. It's magnificent as it rises from the mist covered ground. It dominates the landscape around it, giving the area a sense of strength at its centre. The frontage may look old but there's no decay on the outside. It's as solid as the principal spiral of stairs within it.

That thought makes me question the stairs again as I keep my legs flowing through the grey expanse of low level fog. Why should he be scared of me going up them? Everything seems to be odd around them. He changes. I change. I feel something near them, something guiding me. A memory that isn't mine maybe. It isn't like me to have sex with strangers. It's as bizarre as dancing in the ballroom.

A shriek and sudden brush against my head has me ducking down, flustered at whatever's hit me as I search the area. There's nothing to see at first, only the continued shrieking and cawing as I back away from the noise. And then I notice the flap of a wing flitter through the fog a few feet away. I focus on it as it gently batters the mist around, trying to see what it belongs to and inching my way forward again. A crow appears as the density disperses, its wings still flapping about as it hops and jumps around. I smirk as it tilts its head, eyeing me up with its beady black eyes and snapping its beak almost noiselessly.

"Where did you come from?" I ask, glancing around the area to see if there are any more of them. There isn't, just this lone one who's still prancing and ruffling out his jet black feathers. It's only after a while of watching him move that I notice something around his right leg, a clump of mud maybe, by his foot, but it's not clear enough to see. I inch forward again and bend down to him, willing the moon to come out and illuminate the ground beneath us, but that's not being helpful at all.

The crow dances again, and I realise that perhaps he's not dancing at all—maybe he's trying to dislodge the muddy clump.

"You need help with that?" I ask. What is wrong with me? Now I'm talking to birds in this insanity? I roll my eyes at myself and stand back up, utterly perplexed by what the hell's happening around here. My eyes sweep the area, looking for what I don't know, but as they do I hear the crow cawing madly as his wings bat my jeans. "Okay, okay," I say, still smiling at the sound he's making and crouching back down.

He stares at me, his feet hopping backwards away from me as he twists his head about.

"Okay, let me help," I mumble out, reaching my hand to him and flicking some of the fog between us away.

"I'll get it off. What is it? Let's have a look, shall we?" His neck twists again, looking awkward on his body as he looks me over. I don't think I've ever noticed a bird watching me before. It's eerie really, slightly disturbing in the middle of this fog and darkness. He reminds me of horror stories and ghouls. I snort out a small laugh, glancing around me again to check for concerns. There's none to speak of, other than this odd weather. "Come on, birdy. Let's get you free of whatever that is."

He's huge up close, much bigger than other birds, and as I gently reach to touch him, I realise I've never been this close to one before. I think I went to the Tower of London once when I was little, saw them there and the Beefeaters guarding the place, but I don't remember crows being so big. He dwarfs my hand as he lets me touch his wing, all the time twitching his head around ready to fly off if things don't go his way.

I gaze at him, slowly running my fingers along his frame until I reach his leg, which makes him instantly hop away again.

"Come on, I can't get it off if you don't let me." He inclines his head again, opening and closing his beak as he does. "You've got to trust me, yeah?" He snaps his beak again, offering nothing but distrust as he opens his wings and waves them about. I can't say I'm surprised, but he's the one hovering around. "Surely you didn't fly over here just to wimp out on me? Because we don't do wimping out, do we?" Not anymore. I've done my years of wimping out. The beady eye blinks a bit, his beak suddenly closing and stilling as he wanders closer again. "Okay, let's get it off then. What have you got yourself wrapped up in?"

He lets me pick him up carefully, and then rests quietly as I start picking at the clump around his foot. It's sodden with wet mud and grime as I begin to tug, trying to cause no damage to his tiny bones as I do. "It's really wedged, huh?" I say, continuing to talk to a bloody bird in the middle of the fog. Something is very odd around here. I flick at a bit and my nail gets caught, enough so that I've got to rip at it to get my finger out, but as I do the last glob of mud comes with it. "Oh," I cry as I stare at what materialises. A ring. A filthy one, but a ring nonetheless. It's not a ring like they'd put on pigeons. It's a proper ring. "How did you get that around your foot?" I tap at the metal, not sure what colour it is and trying to work out if it'll slide over his claw. "And how are we going to get it off without hurting you?" He squawks in response, snatching his foot away from my hand and turning his black eye on me again. "Perhaps if we…" He struggles in my grasp, pressure building in his wings as he tries to open them out. "Now, now. Stop being melodramatic. You'll just need to squeeze your foot together a bit. It'll slide right off if you're brave enough. You're brave, right?"

The flapping and struggling stops enough to give me time to squeeze my fingers around his toes, pressing them together and pushing at the ring as I do. Wings flap again as I lose my hold on him slightly to give me room, battering me around the head and flicking about in my line of sight. But I keep hold of the leg, letting him scramble about on me to get away. “It’s coming,” I snap out, trying to avoid his frantic fluttering around. “I’m sorry, but if you’d just stay...” The final tug sends me reeling onto my backside, letting go of his leg and clutching at the thing I’ve managed to pull off.

I land with a jolt on the wet gravel, snorting at myself and searching the ground for him to make sure he’s okay. He’s nowhere to be seen. There’s nothing but the mist still hovering around and a distant caw resonating in the air somewhere. Gone. Great.

“You’re welcome,” I muse, lifting my hand to get a look at the ring. It doesn’t sparkle or glimmer. It’s as soiled as it was when I first saw it, so I rub my fingers over it to clear some of the mud off. There’s an impression on it of some sort, travelling the circumference, but again I can’t see clearly enough here. If the sun would come back it might be helpful.

I pick myself up and walk back around to the front of the house, staring at the sky and still wondering what’s happening around me. Crows and mist. Night time in the middle of the day. Sex sessions with someone I hardly know. It's all completely odd, and all I should be thinking about is getting out of here, but for some reason all I want to do now is go back in the house and wash the dirt off this ring. The thought hurries my steps, making me swish through the fog until I'm back in front of the entrance again. The caw sounds above me somewhere, so I turn back, gazing at the tall trees and searching for him as I climb up the stone steps to the house. The sun instantly starts to break in the sky behind the redwoods, spreading itself luminously out on the horizon and brightening everything around me. I stare open mouthed, bewildered by its sudden arrival again, watching the dense fog surrounding the ground ebb away to nothing as the colours of summer bleed back into the area.

"What the hell?"

"I said stay inside," Jack's voice says calmly from behind me.

"I know. I just…" I wander back down the steps again, not believing what's just occurred as I rub the ring in my fingers to make sure it's all real. "The sun. Look. It's back again. Where did it go?"

"Come inside, Madeline," he says again. I shake my head, trying to put some semblance of normality into what's going on as I turn to look at him. He's there, standing just behind the door, the light now cascading into the porched area and making him glow as he lurks in the dark.

Charlotte E Hart

THE SPIRAL

"What's happening here? It was dark… and then the sun… I found a crow and he–"

"Madeline, come inside." Yes, maybe that's a good idea. Although, as I stand here looking at him, the sight of him confusing me yet more, I can't quite work out whether it is or not.

"I need to wash the ring off," I say for no particular reason as I look at the circle of dirty metal in my hand. "The crow was wearing it and…" I can't find words anymore. Nothing seems real. But this ring in my fingers is real, isn't it? That means the crow was.

Confusion wracks me again as I hover, unable to make a decision. Perhaps I should just go and wait by the car until it's fixed. Nothing odd happens there. It'll be normal and then I can get out of here, ridding myself of this strange place as I go. "I think I'll just go and wait by—"

"Inside, now!"

His tone makes me jump, the ring tumbling from my hands as his shout sounds out. I immediately lurch down to the gravel to find it, for some reason desperate to clutch onto the reality of it in my fingers. It's the one thing I can hold onto in the middle of this strangeness. It's solid, dependable in my grasp, not unlike the house. I scrabble around, lifting and turning gravel to find it until I finally see it glinting back at me and scoop it up, then waste no time turning my back on him to head back to the car. There'll be water in the garage. I can clean it there. I have to leave and find normal again, no matter how appealing he looks standing there waiting for me.

"What's that?" he says, yanking at my arm out of nowhere. I stop, trying to pull my arm from his grasp as I wonder how the hell he got to me so quick. My fingers close around the metal, hiding it behind my back to keep him from taking it from me. It's my one piece of rationality here.

"It's nothing. Just an old ring I found. The crow landed and asked for my help." That sounds outrageous. Even in this scenario.

I stare at him as he frowns at me in reply, not knowing what else to say. It's the truth. It is, outlandish as it might seem. And I don't have to explain anything to him anyway. It's not like he knows what the hell's happening around here either. Some time passes with nothing but silence in the air. I don't know why, but I can't think of one thing to say. Maybe it's because I don't know *what* to say anymore.

"Show me the ring."

"No. I'm just going to go."

His grab at my arm, then wrist, has me spinning into his hold within seconds. He prises at my hand, levering it open with little effort and then shoves me away from him with a gasp as my hand unfurls. We both watch as it tumbles to the ground again, bouncing on the gravel and nearly disappearing before he chases it down frantically.

"Where did you find this?" he snarls out, turning his back on me and quickening his strides back into the house.

"Hey, that's mine. I want it back," I call out, my feet hurrying to catch up with him as I reach out for his arm. He shoves me away again with little thought as he continues onwards up the stone steps and rushes into the house. For the life of me I can't stop myself from following him. I know I shouldn't, but I don't even try to stop myself keeping up with his strides as he heads straight for the middle of the house. He halts as the spiral comes into view, glaring at it a little and then muttering to himself about something.

"Why did you fucking come here?" he snaps at me, rounding on me so suddenly I falter backwards on my heels. "You shouldn't fucking be here." I open my mouth in reply, confused. The antiques. I came for the antiques. He knows that. Antiques he doesn't want to sell. "You're... You should leave. You're not supposed to be here. Go."

He strides on again, leaving me shaking in the middle of the hall, staring at the spiral and not knowing what he's talking about. He doesn't want me to leave and now he does?

Right. I will then. Screw all of this. And screw that ring, too. I'm going. He's right, I shouldn't be here. It's clear he doesn't want anything valuing, which was the intention of me being here. I suppose he's right. I tug the gun from my pocket and place it on the table, knowing I'll never have the bloody balls to pull it anyway. Whatever this is, or has been, is pointless and stupid.

My eyes flick to the Chinese rug, remembering a short while ago when he lay on top of me, made love to me. The sun spots dapple the floor again on the very place we lay, and the smell of metal still hangs heavy in the air from the fired gun. What was all that? If I shouldn't be here, what happened there? And why is this mist and darkness hanging around half the damn time? And why the crow? It's baffling, bothersome. It feels incomplete, like I'm lost in a world I can't regain strength over.

I sniff the air again, letting the tinge of metal remind me of what he was about to do. Would he really have shot himself? Why? I stare back at the spiral, suddenly too interested in its endless curve for rational thought to interfere anymore. Who is he?

And why can't I go up those stairs?

My feet have me turning towards it instantly, determination welling in the pit of my stomach as I follow the stripes of light that filter in from the windows opposite. I'm going up them. I'm going to find out what's happening around me. I've got time before that car's fixed. Perhaps I'll find out what's going on, or perhaps I won't, but I'm damned if I'm going to leave without finding out why I feel like I'm falling in love with a man I don't know. And he told me he loved me, that he'd always loved me. Why did he say those things? And I know he meant them, I felt them, deep inside where truth exists. They were real. They were the tangible I'm trying to get to.

Well, in the strangest sense of the word, anyway.

Chapter 11

Jack

These damn hands become rawer by the second as I plunge the ring beneath the flow of water again. I can't get it clean, can't see the engraved markings. No matter how much I scrub the surface it just won't come clear of grime.

I grimace, grinding the metal between my fingers, hoping for one small flick of soil to dislodge. Nothing does, but I know this ring. I can feel it in my heart. It drops onto the ceramic surface, my feet stumbling away from the sink and nearly giving way as I continue to falter in thought. Her wedding band? Why? And what fucking crow?

My teeth grit, bearing down on my clenched jaw as I glare at the sink, trying to build the momentum to go back to it. I need to get to it again, but the stone slabs seem endless as they layer the space between it and me.

Charlotte E Hart

THE SPIRAL

Tugging at my shirt collar, I slowly scan the room, willing someone to come and help. As always, there's no one there. Empty. This whole fucking place is empty. Unused, unloved, somehow now sick and fucking tired of grieving. It putrefies around me, just as *they* are doing beneath the ground. She'll be nothing but decay and rotted flesh now, her glow extinguished by dogs who came in the night and took what belonged to me.

I half heave, swallowing the bile down, and yet again attempt to move. My foot hovers, locking my leg in place and disabling my ability to move onwards. So I lean on the wall, my head banging against it as I close my eyes and try for logical thinking. It's a fucking floor, that's all. Nothing to concern myself with. I just have to move. One step in front of the other. It's only four or five paces. Simple enough.

My eyes focus again, my muscles steeling for another attempt. Nothing moves. I just freeze again, my whole body refusing to move until I just slide down the surface and give in to this pathetic response. Even in death I can't reach her. Can't help. I couldn't stop the dogs, and now can't even hold the ring that I gave her when I promised her the world.

Gazing at the old light blue cupboards and tracing the woodwork up to the top of the white ceramic sink unit, I imagine her standing at it. *Selma.* I can feel her in this room more than any other. She loved it in here, often spending hour upon hour cooking, creating our perfect family meals. And I can hear her voice now, too, calling me to peel potatoes, or help her get something out of the ancient stove. I smile at the thought then hear her babbling to Lenon, trying to get him to eat the last of his vegetables. He never did, often times throwing it over her rather than letting any of it past his lips.

Jack.

My head shoots up, searching for her presence as my name is shouted loudly into the air, sounding almost scared. I scramble upright, desperate to help her and try to set the past straight.

"Selma?" I call, turning from the kitchen and launching into the hall as I glance around wildly. "Baby, where are you?"

I love you, Jack.

I speed up, running the halls and searching the space for her to no avail.

"Where are you?" I call again, running for the ballroom.

All becomes silent as I slide into the room and stop. I listen intently, waiting for noise, a signal, anything to give me a hint at her whereabouts. There's nothing but the usual. Large ornate chandeliers swing slightly above the wooden expanse of floor, the spread of sprung boards reaching to the far end. I frown, trying to work out if the sound was real or not, and then watch the red baroque curtains at the end of the room billow under a heavy breeze that should not be there.

My brow furrows further, my eyes searching the floor to ceiling windows for one of them to be open. None are that I can see, so I tentatively step forward some more, pocketing my hands and scanning the area again. Nothing occurs of consequence. No ghouls, no apparitions. No blinding lights or darkened corners. It's as it always is. A huge expanse of memories.

Nothing more.

I smile at the first few that come to mind, letting them wash around inside and remind me of her, then glower at the argument that happened in here once. I deserved the scolding she gave me as she talked about our son's needs, telling me that life was not the same now and that I'd have to stop working so late.

She pleaded through her tears of anger, her knees sinking to the floor as she clung onto me, begged me to be home more, be a father more. And then I remember the outcome of that kneeling and begging. It's as crystal clear as the droplets hanging in the lights above. Her breath, her moans. The way her eyes hardened as we argued then softened at the first strike of her ass. A snort breaks from me as I watch the floor beneath me, vividly replaying the fucking that came after the quarrel. She was always testing me, pushing, arguing and bickering, but she was my wife and held every right to put me in my place.

I smile again and spin slowly, embracing the need for her to show herself as I wait for something to happen. Whatever the hell this is, I want more of it.

"Selma, if this is real somehow, it needs to stop, or you need to talk to me and explain," I say, wondering what the fuck is happening in this house. I might be mad, probably going fucking insane in all honesty given the dogs upstairs, but I won't be played with. Not even by her and her return. "Much as I love you, you're being a devious fucking bitch now."

I swear I hear her laugh. It's enough to broaden my lips as I wander into the middle of the ballroom and open my arms wide. "Are you here? Show me."

Nothing moves. Even the curtains stop wafting into the room, but I see the light decrease for the first time, actually notice its fall around me. It comes down the windows in stages, cascading gently and falling to the ground along the framework until it eventually makes it to the ground.

I chuckle slightly, staring out into the black night and imagining her switching the lights off as the shadow creeps along the highly shined parquet towards me. "You never did like the lights on, did you?"

Charlotte E Hart

THE SPIRAL

The last of the brightness disperses instantly, vanishing from the huge breadth of the room and leaving me with little more than the slight influx of light from a full moon. I chuckle some more at the thought of her defiance, or guidance. Neither of us knew what we were doing. We weren't so much young, just naive, immature maybe. But days had turned to weeks, weeks to months, months to a year or so. Something changed with us after Lenon came along, changing our needs along with it. She talked of needing space, but not wanting to be away from me. It was something neither of us understood, nor found comprehension in until we finally found our balance together.

"Will you answer if I ask? Is that how this works still?" That's how it all worked before. She'd call me a good man—a good and decent man. The master of her fears and tears for giving her room to breathe again. The only one to hold her together in the middle of her storm. "Why are you back?"

Wind whistles through the room, flashing by my face and causing me to step away from its freezing chill. I turn to the mirrors lining the inner side, hoping to see her reflection in them, or even just a ghostly mirage to make this seem plausible. She isn't there. Only my own image looks back, alone in the room and dwarfed by its vastness. I gaze at myself, wondering what she saw in me, and watch my frown deepen. A scowl she called it. A permanent scowl. One that only she could remove with her idea of humor.

"How's this going to work, Selma? You going to haunt me for the rest of my life, or are you trying to tell me something?"

Something moves in the reflection. I can't really tell what it is. Maybe the light changes, or perhaps the curtains flicker again. I don't know, but something happens as I stare into the mirror. So I stand still and wait for whatever she chooses to bring. There will be no more running from her little games or taunts. I'll ask and she'll damn well answer, just as became our way together. I'll have her on her fucking knees again if I have to, force the answers from her, irrespective of the fact that she's dead.

Jack.

I don't answer the sound in the air, or perhaps in my head. I won't, not until she shows herself again or at least gives me some answers to my questions. I stand still, tilting my head at the image of myself and considering how mad I am. Insanity is a new experience for me, regardless of my dogs who drive me there. I've wallowed until now, happy to stay within these walls and let the world outside rot as I punish the damned, but now, this new madness is becoming amusing, something to be toyed with. Harnessed. Enjoyed even.

Another chuckle bursts out at this new insidious nature of hers, sneaking back from heaven's gate to show me something. It's just like her, just like her beauty. She was light and dark. She was effortless and hard work. She was tears and laughter and summer days. Deviancy and niceties. The nimble caress of gentle rain on skin, and the sneering possession of hell's fury.

Light begins to brighten up the glazed expanse of one window pane behind me. It spreads outwards from a pinpoint as I stare at it through the mirror. Cream tones began to change and dilate, casting a shape of kinds as I watch on in wonder. Still, I don't move, nor change my stance or scowl. I'll wait until she shows me what she came here for.

The lines creep closer to each other, pink tones encroaching on the creams, blending into each other and forming what seems to be a face. I stare at it, not recognising the new male reflection, which blurs and bounces between reality and folly.

"More," I mutter, not understanding the reasoning for the image as I continue gazing and imprinting the face further to memory. Dark eyes, dark hair, hollowed cheekbones and jaw line. It isn't a face I'll forget in a hurry, nor one that resembles the current image she's showing me anymore. It's the fast one, his fucking features already embedded.

"He's paying for it, Selma." The face blurs again, dispersing to almost nothing and beginning to fade back to black again. "They'll pay until they die." A low growl sounds in the room, making me confused at her thoughts. "No. Wait. The others?" I want to see the other faces, the two other dogs, so I can remember what they looked like when they destroyed my life.

The colours turn again, more imagery coming as the second dog's face takes form. He's the runt, the snivelling little one who whines about his bruises. I snarl at it, remembering the way he pleaded for his life as I locked the cage behind him the first time round. And then the last of them shows, the lighter hair changing the features slowly to show dog three. He bleeds weekly, somehow drawing me back to him more rather than the other two. Not that I give a fuck about any of their pain. They fucking deserve it. All of them. "I'm so sorry, baby. I wasn't here."

The creams come again, once more merging and changing, offering a softer vision than the hardened tones of the previous face. Until the final image makes the scowl dispense from my face. She's there, smiling at me softly with a slight curve of her lip. Her blue eyes gently blink as she shakes her head a little and hovers in my sight.

"Selma." I pull in a long sigh and let her eyes haunt me with no fear. She's the most welcome sight I've seen in some time, and I feel myself getting lost in her eyes without any other thought. "Still so beautiful." Her dark curls bounce as she shakes her head slowly, lips parting as if she's trying to say something. I watch them intently, waiting for a reason this is all happening, but nothing comes from them. She just hovers and blinks slowly, filling me with feelings of light again. I catch the swathes of curtains beginning to billow slightly from the corner of my eye, a deeper darkness descending at the same time. It makes me stare harder, willing her to stay close so I can forget reality and linger here with her, but her hair begins to change before I can speak. It shortens and straightens a little, lush folds coming to replace the curls. And, at the same time, everything lightens. Her skin tone pinks more, the olive tones changing to ivory. "Madeline?"

Jack

"I don't understand what you're trying to tell me," I whisper, turning myself around to see the vision more clearly. The moment I do, the image begins to dissolve again, the room losing its blackened state by the second as the sun peeks into the far corner of the ballroom.

I stride forward, for some reason needing to touch the spot she emanates from before she vanishes entirely, or perhaps sense her closer. "No, Selma. Don't go again. I need you to..." I don't know what I need, can't find the words anymore in the middle of whatever this is. "I need you back," I mumble, my hand finally reaching the spot on the window where she was.

The frosted glass almost stings my hand as I press against it, willing the slow creep of fucking sunlight away again. "Selma, please answer me." Nothing happens again as I watch the luminous light crawl along the floor, sucking itself back to the position I stand in. Until eventually, the last dark fleck of Selma disappears from my black shoe and the sun glints off the shine of it again.

I lean my forehead on the window, still palming the glass and closing my eyes, searching for her face again, but all I can see is blurred edges and hazy reflections. Nothing is clear, nothing as clear as the last vision she's left me with. Madeline.

"Jack?"

Mmm.

I suck in a breath and hold onto her sound hovering in my mind. At least I can still hear her. That's enough for now. She'll be back again soon enough. I know that now. She's got things to tell me. That thought alone satisfies me. Just the very thought of knowing she'll return and help proves more worthwhile than I could ever have imagined.

"Jack?"

I turn as something pokes me in the back, glaring at the sensation and barely seeing Madeline in my line of sight until the haze dissipates completely. She frowns at me then folds her arms around herself as she backs a step away.

"What is going on here?"

"What?"

"It's all odd. The fog, the dark that's just disappeared again. I saw it when I came into the room just now. It's not normal. None of this is. I want answers." I smile at her, enjoying the way her face quirks as Selma's did. She furrows her brow and glances nervously around the room. "It started in here when I danced, which was nothing like me by the way." I look her over, remembering that first dance and how she felt in my arms. "And I've just been up the stairs. There's nothing wrong with them. Nothing there but empty rooms and locked doors on the third floor. What on earth is happening?"

"Are you you, Madeline Cavannagh?"

"What?"

"You. Do you feel like you?"

"I think you need a drink," she replies, "Of course I'm me."

"You sure?"

"What the hell are you talking about?"

"You're not, are you?"

I reach for her hair, making her jump away from my hands. She glowers a little, attempting to remain in control of something neither of us are in control of.

"I think it's best if we stop all that," she mumbles, backing away from me.

"Why?"

"Because you... Well... And I… It's not normal. Something's not right here."

"Hmm. Perhaps you're right," I reply, walking past her and heading for the kitchen. I need to feel her wedding band in my hand again and for some reason I'm now relaxed enough to go and retrieve it.

"Where are you going?" she calls, her heels clicking across the floor behind me and reminding me of times past. I stop, swinging myself back to her and picking her arms up into dance hold before she has a chance to avoid them.

"Are you really sure you're you?" I say, swaying her and then forging us into a slow waltz. "I don't think you are. I think you're someone entirely different from who you think you are." She frowns again, probably trying to work out what the fuck I'm talking about. I'd explain further if I knew, but I don't yet. I only know what Selma has shown me, and Madeline Cavannagh is part of that mystery. "Do you remember the feel of me against you?"

"Hardly difficult, we're dancing," she replies, huffing and trying her best to keep distance between us. I pull her closer with a sharp tug, breathing in her scent and not allowing one inch of space to interrupt my musings.

"Not that, Madeline. The fucking. Do you remember the fucking? Here on the floor beneath our feet? The way you bit your lip on the first strike, making it bleed." She rears away again, her body struggling against me to break the connection I'm forcing. "I think you need reminding who you are, Madeline," I whisper, swinging us around the corner and lengthening my stride. "Shall I show you?" She shudders in my hands, her frame straining for release as she tenses and tries to stop her feet moving with mine. "There's no point fighting it anymore, don't you see? It's all connected. Can't you feel it? You belong here, don't you?"

"No. I want to leave. I–"

"Do you really?" I cut in, keeping us dancing, regardless of her attempts at freedom. "I'll protect you this time. I will."

I just keep us twirling and gliding, tightening my hold on her and hearing my own tempo in my head. The sound of our wedding dance is so clear as we travel the floor. It rings around the room as our feet move seamlessly, commemorating the feelings I have for her and driving us closer still. If anything, those sensations grow stronger than they've ever been, dismissing images of brutalised bodies and blood. I feel them rising inside my heart, reminding me of love and happiness, of evening walks and babies crying in the middle of the night.

I smile as Lenon's cries of need filter into the song, imagining his little hands reaching for me in the darkest depths of night. For once, they aren't covered with blood, or just lying limply at his sides. They're loud and vibrant, grabbing for me and clinging on like children do.

"You must remember, Madeline. Close your eyes and let me guide you. We'll find it all together." She yanks at my hands, trying to free herself from my fingers as her steps falter. I hardly feel her try, choosing to carry on and submerge myself and her into something whether she likes it or not. It's why she's here, so we can remould ourselves, link.

Selma's showing me the way.

"You're mad," she stutters, still struggling and eventually managing to loosen her hand from mine. I grab at it again, halting my spin and winding myself behind her body so she has little chance of escape. Maybe I am. In fact, I'm becoming surer of it by the hour, but this *is* happening between us. Selma appeared the night before this woman arrived, telling me to go home and wait. And then Madeline arrived for me, bringing with her all the feelings I've been left without.

I stare at her in the mirror facing us, watching the way her mouth parts under my gaze and her exertion, and then pick up her right hand as I hold her close. She feels the same in this position as Selma did, her ass sliding itself neatly alongside my cock as I bend slightly to tuck my face into her neck. My fingers hold her hand aloft, nudging her face with my own so she keeps her eyes connected with mine in the mirror.

"What's missing from this hand, Madeline?"

"Nothing," she mumbles, her voice shaky as her eyes fidget about. I smirk at her, drawing my lips along her jaw and barely containing the need to unzip my pants.

"Think, Madeline. Remember." She shakes her head, presumably confused and trying to avoid the topic. There's little point in that now. We're bound to each other, some part of me knowing it even if she doesn't yet. "You know who you are. You must know. You came to me."

"Jack, I…"

"How familiar does my name sound on your lips?"

"I don't know you, Jack. I don't know what this is about and I just…"

"And yet we fucked on that rug you always loved." She gasps at that, stilling her erratic moves. "We made love, didn't we? Tell me you didn't feel that. Tell me you don't feel it now."

She shakes her head again, closing her eyes and trying to wriggle free once more.

"It's not real. None of this is," she whispers, sighing out as I clamp my hold more forcibly and grind into her. "I don't know what it is, but I have to go. My house. Lewis…"

Anger flares inside instantaneously, raging its way through my insides at the mention of another man's name. I push her to the mirror, squashing her against it, intent on driving only one name from her lips. Mine.

"You will fucking remember, Madeline," I snarl, rubbing myself into her back and dragging my hands up her thighs. "Which version of me makes you remember: the one who's begging to fuck your ass right now, or the one who made love to you on the floor?" She shakes, her head instantly rising to watch me again as she stills, frightened.

"No, please."

There aren't no's anymore. I won't hear them again. Not from her lips, or mine. Whatever is happening around us, *is* happening. I'll force it forward if I have to. I'll fuck her ragged, bleed her dry of indecision until all she can do is breathe my name and remember our time together. She *is* Selma. Somehow the two are the same person. Whether she believes it yet or not isn't relevant. She will believe it. I'll make her believe it.

"Tell me which one or I'll choose for you," I say, yanking on her jeans and groaning as my cock grinds into her leg.

"Jack, this isn't right. It's not real," she replies, twisting in my hold to try to turn towards me. I growl at her and push her hand to the mirror, irritated with her weakness and lack of cooperation.

"You'll fucking stand there and look at me until you do remember," I snap out, lifting her other hand and placing it on top of the other.

Those are the last words of discussion I have. There are only orders now, ones she'll know well when she remembers how to answer them. I'll fuck the sentiment into her instead, force her to remember the first time I took her ass, then maybe force her to remember the first time she felt my belt, begging for more of it time and time again after that.

She wriggles and writhes, bucking against my hold and trying to dislodge herself. It riles me up further, enough so that I clamp onto her wrists and drag them behind her back for leverage, pushing her whole body into the mirror.

"Jack, please, I don't want this," she murmurs, her voice wavering with every syllable as she gasps at my strength around her wrists.

I don't care what she wants. She doesn't know, not like I do. She'll only know when this is done. She'll feel it then; she'll feel the pain, the surrender, the aches we forge between ourselves. And then, eventually, when I've almost exhausted the life from her and myself, she'll feel the thing I already know. She'll feel *us* again. She'll feel the love that no other compares to. She'll believe it. Neither of us will need ghosts or visions of mist and darkness, and neither will question or doubt the ache inside. We'll just know, and then no one will tear us apart again.

She whimpers as my fingers bite in harder, her legs buckling a little under the pressure I'm using on her. Good. She can go to the floor where she's most workable. She'll enjoy it down there, labour there beautifully. She'll groan and mewl like she used to, beg me for help like she once did. She can have all my help to remember. I'll keep going until she understands what her coming here means and how relevant she is.

I force my hold harder, turning her as I do so she ends on her knees at my feet.

"That's where you stay," I murmur, pushing her head onto the floor to make her realise this is very fucking real. Nothing is changing here. The only thing that will change is her attitude. "You don't move unless I say. You don't speak unless I ask." She gasps and quivers, still fighting my hold slightly and pushing her luck as my fingers wind into her hair. "Keep fighting and see what you get."

I hear the first sniff and push her head harder onto the wooden floor, remembering her need for the tears to come first. She always cried in the first few minutes. It causes me to close my eyes as I crouch beside her, listening for the honest sounds to finally leave her body. The heaving sobs start then, her body trembling as her chest rises and falls under my hand. I will the noise inside, letting the sound revive my honour for the woman I adore. She cries so prettily in her distress, unleashing the honesty she once kept buried from me, and setting us both free of lies as she crumbles.

"More," I bark, gripping her hair tighter and scratching my nails into her head. It was never the first ones that mattered; it was the ones that came after them. They cleansed her enough to start the process, enough for her to begin begging for help. "All of it." She chokes on the next set of tears as they come.

Her head heaves from the floor, and she braces her hands out, searching for air as she sobs out another round and shivers. I let her carry on, soaking in the sounds and smiling as they come thicker and faster. Selma's coming. She'll be here soon. I can feel her in the way this body grinds itself into my fingers, feel the tension in her neck disbanding, the anger finally giving in to my power over the situation. "You done with your whining yet?"

She shakes her head, her body convulsing on the next snivel that consumes her throat. I lick my lips, readying myself for action as I stand and let go of her hair. She's about done. Almost there, just as she always was. Time will mend this rift—time right here where it all began. It was dark that time, pitch black, the middle of the night and the dead of winter.

Charlotte E Hart

THE SPIRAL

I sneer at the reflected image of myself as I unbutton my shirt slowly, garnering the loathing needed for this next adventure and knowing the room will darken of its own accord. I don't need Selma's help for that, or her guidance. Not anymore. Ghosts aren't the thing this body beneath me should be scared of. Her reality is the thing she should concern herself with for the time being. Her reality that is about to change.

Chapter 12

Madeline

I don't know what's happening to me. I can't breathe through these tears as they come from the depths of me. It's like I'm ripping out years of them. Like they were just sitting beneath the surface, bubbling away and waiting for a reason to finally come out.

Coiling my legs into myself, I just let the sensation have its way with me as I shiver here on the floor. I'm too afraid to open my eyes for fear of more hallucinations, but so desperately in need of looking at him again I don't know what to do. None of it makes any sense to me. It would take nothing for me to get up and leave. I could even have chosen to walk away when I came back to the ballroom in search of him, but I didn't. He looked so sad as he leant against the window, nearly crying out at something, and now he's making me feel that way, too. So sad. So very miserable and alone.

My legs tuck in tighter, inducing some kind of foetal position to consume me as the tears keep falling from my eyes. I can't even say why they're coming; they just are. There are no visions in my head as I wind my arms tighter around my waist, no sounds of Lewis's voice scaring me either. There are only two things inside my head: darkness and him.

"Finished?" he says, his tone angry and snappy as the word echoes around the vast room.

I shake my head again. I'm not finished at all. It's like they're not even my tears anymore. I'm weeping with no way of stopping them, and no real desire to try. Whoever, or whatever is inside me just keeps coming, battering my heart with hurt and pain. And the only thing I can hear is his name being repeated. *Jack, Jack, Jack.* I don't know what it means, and I can't stop it.

"Yes, you are," he says, grabbing the back of my jeans and heaving on the denim until I slide across the wood in his grasp. I don't try to fight. I just keep my eyes closed, for some reason allowing his power to take me wherever he chooses as more tears come. They almost feel like blood dripping along my skin now. They're thick and hot, swelling my eyeballs beneath closed lids and binding them together.

"Take your clothes off." My head shakes again, barely hearing his words over my sobs as his hands leave me, but understanding them nonetheless.

"I don't… don't want to," I stutter between more choked breaths.

The recourse for saying no seems to enforce more anger because I'm tugged and pulled instantly, my body straightened with little care for my wellbeing as my clothes are torn off. There's nothing seductive in his manner, nothing romantic, not like our earlier encounter. He strips me with no care or thought, and all I seem to be able to do is allow it, not caring for the naked eventuality of his hand's work as my frame slumps to the floor. It just causes me to curl tighter again, hoping to stop the tears somehow, or at least find some comfort from them.

Jack

Again his name whispers itself in my mind. It's so full of love, spoken with an endless sense of eternity to it. It's not my voice; it's softer than mine, but it makes my lips twitch between my sniffs and snivels as I open my eyes. It makes them want to rise into a smile and denounce the tears I'm crying. I don't understand.

"Knees," he says, calmly now, all anger dissipated from his voice and a kinder tone filtering in. My flat smile develops of its own accord as I stare at the floor, remembering the man who made love to me by the stairs as

I feel myself pushing upwards. *Knees*. I know what that means. I don't know how I know, but I do. It's confusing, but so simple when I try not to think.

Jack.

His shirt drops by my head as I brace my hand out and draw my knees together. It brings with it his aftershave and that power he radiates. I stare at it, wondering what's happening to me as my fingers drag me towards it and gently grasp the hem. I heard that name this time. Heard it loud in the air. I look around the floor and bring the shirt to my nose, inhaling him into me. Deep, cleansing breaths wash across me instantly, ridding me of the last tear that wants to come and finishing the sobs.

"Trousers." It's another order I know the answer to without thought. My hands discard the shirt smoothly, wrapping it over itself and folding it peacefully onto the floor.

He doesn't move to me from his position some three or four feet away. He waits, his black shoes shining at me as I look at his body for the first time in all of this. He's so tall from down here. His stance exudes confidence, arrogance even. I don't want to question anything anymore, though. I don't want to leave, or run. I don't want to question his authority, or his control. I, or whatever other voice is inside my head, wants to be here. I want to see this, be part of it. I've never done anything like it, but for some strange reason it all feels natural, like an evolution I've already been a part of before this moment.

My hands skim his legs, letting the fabric of his trousers remind me of something I'm not sure about. It resonates, though. The dark brown, thick cloth feels familiar in my fingers as I let them linger on his shin. There's such a sense of love burning through me. It travels my bones like wildfire, crowding me with so much emotion I'd fall back but for his hold on my chin. His lips stay static as I gaze at him and feel shivers begin to wash across me. His lips don't move as he stares back down at me, but his eyes smile a little, one brow slightly cocking as they do.

The silence continues as I brace my knees, becoming more comfortable here by the second as the irrational love consumes all thought.

"Take them off before I remind you what happens when you disobey."

I don't know what that means, but the quiet authority and threat in his voice has me racing to get to his belt rather than lingering in the love I was feeling. My fingers shudder and quiver as I try to loosen the thing, grappling with it so as not to cause harm to his skin. He grunts quietly above me as I stare at nothing but the brown leather, strangely intrigued by the supple feel of it in my hands as I thread it from the buckle.

It doesn't take long to lever the material from him, shoes too, and then he just stands there, naked and gloriously solid in the middle of this vast empty space, waiting for something. I flick my eyes between him and the floor nervously, trying to hear the voice in my head that tells me what to do. But that's empty too all of a sudden. There's no love anymore, no warmth, no sense of direction and no offering of that support I was getting used to. It's just vacant of thought, other than trepidation again as he watches me kneeling before him and scowls.

"You know what to do," he eventually says.

I don't. I don't know what to do. I search for the thought again, hoping there's an answer somewhere. There isn't. It's just a void—a void that's beginning to remember what scared feels like. It's creeping up my ribs and bruising my skin, worrying me into seeing someone who's not here. I know this is Jack, but it's starting to feel like Lewis is here, frightening me again.

Jack.

Did I say that? My fingers touch my lips, struggling to remember speaking as I glance around the room looking for someone else. Nothing moves, and I swing my eyes back to him to see the beginnings of a smirk tracing his lips. "Think, Selma. Quickly." Who?

I stutter out breaths, unsure. I remember that name, though. It swims around inside me like a haunted memory of another time or another place. It may be a dream, but it's real. I've heard it a thousand times and yet I can't quite picture it ever being used. There's no memory of locations or dates, no memory of touch associated with it. No visions. And nothing to help me remember it other than him using the name.

"I don't remember—"

I cry out as his hand grips my hair harshly, dragging me down to the floor and stamping loudly by my ear as he does.

"No!" I scream out, desperately trying to avoid his unexpected fury as he growls in my ear and pushes my weight away. My legs scrabble away from him, real fear reducing my whimpers to ones of horror as I head for the doorway.

He laughs behind me. It rumbles through the room, reverberating off the floor beneath my hands and knees as I keep scurrying.

"Where do you think you're going, baby?" I keep going, hoping the door arrives faster than I know it will. "We're far from finished in here."

I pick myself up, feet scuffing the wood as I reach my arms for the doorway and lengthen my strides to get away. He's grabbed my stomach and is hauling me backwards before I've managed four strides, his wide arm wrapping me back into his hold regardless of my struggle.

He laughs out, amused at me as he walks back the way I came. It doesn't matter how much I struggle or how much I twist in his arms, he just continues chuckling and then drops me to the floor again in the same position I started in. "We'll start again. You know what to do."

I don't.

I look at the floor, terrified by his amusement as I tremble beneath him. I'm so scared—scared of what I'm feeling, scared of what he wants. And I'm so cold and lonely here, no matter the voice that was talking in my head.

"Look at me," he snarls. I can't. I'm too afraid.

He wrenches my chin upwards and raises his other hand into the air. I'm so sure he's going to hit me that I cower away from him, tucking my face into my neck and lowering myself further towards the floor until my nose is by it. He chuckles, gently putting his finger beneath my chin again and inching me back towards him.

"I've never hit you before, have I?"

I flick my eyes back and forth, searching for something to let me know if he has or not. How would I know? He's never hit me, no, but it isn't just me inside my head anymore. There's someone else there now, too.

Jack, help us.

"Help me."

I shake my head at my own voice whispering the words into the air. I don't know what they mean, or why

I've said them. They're not my words. I didn't want to say them. They just came out, spilling into the air as if I have no control in this room. "This isn't real," I whisper. "Something's not right here."

"Everything's perfect. You're perfect. Talk to me. We'll find our way together." His fingers glide up my thigh again, teasing their way to the place that needs them most. "You need to tell me why you're here."

I stare into the dull light from the huge windows, splinters of white filtering in and then starting to dissipate back to a dull grey in the room. It draws me to it, focusing me onto something that I can't quite grasp. "Don't you leave me," he says, a slight crack in his voice that makes me turn my cheek into his face as he tightens his hand on my waist. "I'm not letting you go this time. You're coming home where you belong."

My own hand travels to his face, stroking the side of it as I gaze into something familiar and try to seek sense. There isn't any to find.

I can't think anymore. It's all too confusing. I'm here on the floor, naked, with a man wrapped around me and no sense involved in any of it. My legs try to push me up from my knees, but his body clamps tighter around me as the light decreases again.

"Do I need to fuck you into remembering?"

Oh god, that language. It's suddenly so clear again. His tone, the way he moulds a cadence around his dirty talk. It's so memorable. So resonating. But I've never been here before. I don't…

My head shakes again, wishing I remembered clearly. "I..."

His hand clamps around my mouth tightly, shoving me into the mirror again and widening my legs as he manoeuvres himself behind me.

"You're not leaving me."

It all happens so quickly, as if I'm not even a participant for a few minutes. He's just there inside me, his cock buried with no movement from either of us. And it fits so perfectly, as if it was made to sit inside just me. The heat of my breath tickles back at me from his hand covering my mouth, and a residual memory of being trapped or tied in some way ebbs into my brain. It should frighten me, but it doesn't. It floods me with serene thoughts as his grip tightens to painful.

"Are you ready for more?" he says, his tone gravelly as he breathes heavily against my neck and pushes my shoulders into the mirror further. "How much do you need to remember us?"

My skin still prickles. I can feel it heating my flesh as his body chafes against it and shoves me into a wider position. "Rougher? Shall I choke it out of you?"

I wish I could say my eyes widen in fear, or that my body reacts as a normal one would to the threat of pain, but neither of those things happen. Instead, my insides clamp his cock, surprising me and making me drool against his fingers.

"There you are again," he says, a chuckle barely skimming his words. He slides himself out a little, causing a whimper to leave my lips as I stare at his reflection. He doesn't remove his eyes from mine as he teases the edges of me, giving me nothing to clamp onto again. "You always were best at releasing when treated like this." He rears back away from me, his eyes looking at my back as he watches his own cock glancing in and out with no pressure. "Perhaps you'll remember when we talk. I'll draw your bath, just like I always do." What?

I hover against the mirror, my hands still fixed to it like some sort of glue is holding me in place, and I listen to the dull echo of his feet leaving me, still yearning for him inside me again. But he's gone without another word to explain any further. And I ache here, deprived of him. My mind's confused. My limbs feel cold suddenly, almost lost without his heat wrapped around me. And my brain is muddled, unfocused. The only thing I can feel with any clarity is the sense of loss that seems attached to my soul at his departure.

Chapter 13

Madeline

Eventually, I slump back down onto my backside, still staring at the door and wondering where he's gone and why. A bath, like he always does? I skim the floor with my hand then tentatively pull my fingers across the back of my thigh, still feeling his skin on mine somehow. And I can't stop my own hands from wandering my body, testing areas to make sure I'm real. My skin is prickly, as if it's restless for something. Twitching almost.

"Jack."

The name is so loud and clear that I swing my head around to search for whoever called it out, my naked body stumbling back to rest against the mirror as I do. There's someone else here. Her. It's the same voice that was in my head.

My eyes rapidly search the space, tracing the outline of the great ballroom for anything that moves, but nothing's there. Nothing. It's just dark and still. I look again, curling my legs up into myself and then pushing myself up the mirror to get to my feet.

"Is someone here?" I ask quietly, almost stupefied at my own idiocy as I tentatively step out into the room. There's no response. No light blinding me. No voice or memory in my mind like there was before. "Who are you?" Nothing again.

I look up to the chandeliers lining the path of the middle section, watching for their crystals to move or perhaps for a wind to burst through the room. Nothing happens there either. Oh, this is pathetic. Do I think there's a ghost here or something as ridiculous as that? I pull in a long breath, brushing down the front of my naked skin in an attempt to rid myself of whatever lunacy is happening in this house. I need to leave. Whatever, or whoever, was in my mind has no place being there. And the sooner I'm out of here, the better. Draw me a bath so we can talk? Jesus. We just had sex again. There is nothing here but an attractive man and a slightly weird sensation that seems to happen around him. I need to get back to my real life. Normal.

I shake my head at the room and walk backwards to the doorway, still watching for any movement at all as I flick my eyes around. Again, though, nothing happens as I retreat to the set of large doors, only a cold draught filtering across my calves and feet. But the draught begins to intensify the closer I get to the exit, nearly freezing my feet and whipping up the side of the room as I hurry away from it.

I'm frozen to the spot instantly as the deep red curtains billow, lifting into the space and creating a burst of ghostly shapes from beneath them. My heart races as I stare in terror at what's happening, trying desperately to move my feet. But I can't shift again, like I'm stuck in a damn vortex that won't let me go.

Maddy?

Who the hell is that?

I swing my head from side to side, looking for the woman who speaks so clearly to me to find nothing but empty space and a few lights illuminating the outer edges of the room.

I need you, Maddy.

Breath pants out of me as I watch in mystification, the billow of the curtains trailing off and sending a covering of frost across the floor towards me instead. If I could run, I would. If I could scream, I would, but I can't do either. I'm just frozen and staring in disbelief as a wealth of warmth rushes over me regardless of the ice travelling over the sprung floor. It hovers for a moment, creating a slight crackling on the wood three metres in front of me. Again, I try to back away, tugging at my own weight to lift the pads of my feet as I wrap my arms around myself, but they refuse the movement. I'm just stuck to the spot with nowhere to go.

Slowly, the frost peters away, changing direction and heading for the mirrors, which causes a sigh of relief to spill from me. I watch as it creeps over the floor slowly, all the time producing a pattern of icicles to spread the effort forward until eventually, it reaches its destination, leaving anticipation hanging in the air as to what's next. My mouth opens. I'm not sure what for. I feel like I want to ask a question, though. What's happening? Who she is? How is she able to talk to me? What does she want?

I find myself shaking my head again, dismissing the irrationality and trying to lift my feet again instead. Ghosts? This is just some odd frost. More than likely because of a sudden weather change outside. I just need to get to the door, that's all. Then I can leave. Regain some composure.

The thoughts make me heave on my foot again, hoping it releases this time as I hear Jack's voice somewhere though the door. Whatever is in this room isn't real. It can't be, no matter what I've just been through. It's this house, that's all.

"Thank god," I murmur, as my foot eventually lifts and I gingerly move the other one, assuming that's free, too. It comes loose just as easily, allowing my first step of my own free will since the curtains started swelling from an unknown source.

I turn, ready to leave this madness and make a run for the exit. Exquisite he might be, and infuriatingly intriguing, but none of this is what I need in my life. I need stability not lunacy. My quick walk has me almost at the double doors before a gust of wind slams them closed in my face, almost knocking me off my feet with the intensity of its speed. I grab at the handles, wrenching at it in the hope that it budges, but there's nothing.

I back away again, rapidly, wrapping my arms around myself once more and searching for another exit or way out. There's only the other set of doors at the far end. My feet halt as the freezing temperature increases around them, making me check the floor for ice getting too close.

"Madeline?" Jack's voice calls loudly through the doors. "Open the doors."

"Jack, I can't," I shout back, skirting the outside of the room to keep me away from the frost and heading towards the oak doors at the other end. My head swings back and forth as I move, constantly checking for new visions and threats. "They're stuck. What's going on?" I turn on the spot, staring up to the other end of the room and gauging how fast I can get there. It's a fair distance, and the light seems to be bouncing again, dark then light. "I'm going for the other doors."

The original door rattles as I start what seems an endless journey to the other end, as if he's trying to open them from the outside.

"Open the fucking doors," he shouts, apparently furious all of a sudden.

"I can't. I told you. They're stuck," I reply as I continue my quick step up the side of the room. He doesn't stop rattling them. In fact, the sound of him kicking the doors starts heightening my fear as I speed for the other exit.

I can hear my own breaths as I edge the windows, trying to avoid contact with the frost that seems to be emanating from them. It terrifies me, sending anxieties about more ghostly apparitions, so I close my eyes slightly, focusing them entirely on my end goal, which is that door and escape.

"Open the fucking doors, you bitch," he shouts again, his kicking getting louder and louder as I keep edging my way to the end of the space. I half stop, frowning at his tone and wondering what the hell reason he has to call me a bitch. "This is not… nice."

Nice? Nice? He's right it's not nice. If I wasn't quite so concerned about the odd happenings in here I might well go back and tell him all about not nice.

A soft humming starts as I near the ornate doors, and then I hear a lock clicking. It takes me a few blinks to realise that I did actually see the key in the door turn of its own accord. This can't be real. I did not just see that, did I?

"Jack, what the hell is happening in this house?" I scream back to him, planting myself against the wall and bracing for whatever might occur next. The wind whistles into the space instantly, the thick red curtains lifting from the ground again beneath its squall. The whole wall side of them lifts, creating a sailing wall of chiffon and velvet to crash around the area. "This is not real. It's not." I keep chanting it to myself, flicking my eyes around the floor and praying to God that the patterns of ice don't start stretching any further in my direction. "Someone's locked the other door. I saw the key turn in front of my eyes. Who else is here?"

The battering of the door at the other end of the room stops, leaving me with no other noise than the soft humming that continues and the flapping curtain's heavy material as it bobs about.

I'm here, Maddy.

I jump immediately, throwing myself into the corner of the room for some degree of comfort against her voice.

You know who I am.

I don't. I don't know who she is. I don't even know if her voice is real or not.

It's enough for me to slide down the surface of the wall, lowering myself into a crouch and covering my ears in the hope that maybe it'll all go away. Or that maybe if I shut my eyes tightly enough it'll stop, that this voice will leave me alone.

You felt me. I want him back.

I don't know what that means, and it makes me shake my head, physically shake it with my hands to try to rid myself of her inside my head.

Open your eyes, Maddy.

No. No. I won't open my eyes. I'm not opening them until all this stops and goes away. I'll just sit here, ignoring whatever is happening. Perhaps if I do that long enough she'll stop bloody well talking to me, whoever she is. It's not real. Not real.

He's mine.

"I didn't hear that. I didn't. You're not real." The temperature drops again, making me curl my naked body into itself further as I inch closer to the wall, but the noise of the curtains stops instantly.

Tentatively, I open my eyes a little, squinting into the room to see if anything's changed. The frost is still there on the floor, but the curtains have calmed their stormy tirade, and the white light seems to have dispersed to only small flecks of it around the mirrored wall. I watch it bounce about, nervously scanning the mirror for a sight of a ghost.

There's nothing there, nothing again other than the frosty patterns beginning to dissipate back towards the huge mirrors.

"Stupid," I mumble to myself, looking at the doors that Jack was kicking at. "Are you still there?" I shout up to him, hoping he is. "Try the door again." No sound comes back in my direction. He's ether not there, or he's not answering me. "Jack?" Still nothing.

I sigh out a breath, wondering what to do as I shiver against the wall. This is all plainly absurd. It's a freak weather thing, obviously. It's nothing more than a storm. I try to ignore the fact that the key managed to turn itself in the lock without my help, also discounting the fact the doors seemed to purposely slam in my face. It's just an oddity, that's all. And it's over now anyway. Finished.

Chapter 14

Madeline

I crawl my way back up the wall and head for the closest door, hoping that by some miracle, the lock didn't actually turn and it was just my imagination running wild. Ghosts. It's insane.

A hissing noise erupts in the room the moment I go to touch the handle, making me swing round and back up to the wall again. White light explodes around the space, almost blinding me with its assault on my senses. I raise my arm, trying to protect my face as it gets brighter and then draws back to the mirror, giving me a chance to see again.

"What the hell is going on?" I shout out, shivering in fear.

Scrawled writing begins on the fogged surface of the mirror. Letters and numbers, dates, times, but it all disappears again so quickly I struggle to see its meaning.

I need you, Maddy.

More words appear, jumbled and messy, almost as if it's another language until the surface clears and then I see one I recognise. There, bold as brass and dispersing by the second the name Lewis is scrawled. I gasp, my feet faltering backwards in disbelief. And then, as soon as it disappears, the beginnings of another word. I start forward again, still hugging my frame but intrigued by whatever is about to appear. Why would Lewis be written there?

Slowly more letters appear. First an S, then an E, then an L, until finally the name Selma hovers and then disappears, too. Selma. And then an H, O, M, and E. Home?

I stare, dumfounded by the last trace of an E as it all completely disperses, bringing with it a warmer feeling that washes around the room. I rub my shoulders, wondering what the hell I've just been a part of while desperately trying to dismiss it. There was writing there. Real writing. I didn't imagine it. Storms don't create writing. Wind and frost don't make letters appear in the mirror. I just stand here, still staring at the mirror and trying to understand the meaning of any of this.

The door suddenly bursts open, the slam of it against the wall making me leap away from the noise.

"Why didn't you answer?" a frantic looking Jack says as he storms in, axe in his hand and sweat marring his brow.

"I did, and then you stopped shouting." I respond bluntly, frowning at his perplexed expression. He left me to deal with all of this—left me alone in the middle of this damned ballroom with nothing but the skin on my bones to protect me.

"I've been shouting through that door for twenty minutes," he says, walking closer, which only causes me to back away from him and his offering of all too late help. "Fucking Scottish oak wouldn't budge."

Has he? I didn't hear him. All I could hear was her voice, and then the wind.

I narrow my eyes at him, watching the way his hand grips the axe, and then swing them back up to his eyes for clarity in the middle of this strange drama. He appears to believe himself. He looks almost apologetic for not getting in quicker.

"Who's Selma?"

His frame immediately tenses, his eyes looking anywhere but at me for a second or two before they're replaced with his normal self-assurance, arrogance even.

"Why?"

"I didn't ask you for a question. I asked who she is, which you clearly know."

He takes two steps away from me, two long strides backwards, before turning on his heel and beginning to walk straight out of the room again. My feet are so quick to have me in front of him he hasn't got a chance.

"No. Whatever just happened in here happened for a reason, I want to know what it is. Who's Selma? You called me by her name. And I can hear her."

"It's not something I'm discussing with you, Madeline," he says, sidestepping me and heading out of the room.

Fine. I'll just go up to that third level of the stairs and find out then, shall I? Locked doors are absolutely not keeping me out, because that's all I found when I got up there earlier. I go through that in a ballroom, something he most definitely has an idea about, and then he's not prepared to discuss it with me?

I've turned, hurried past him, snatching the axe from his hand as I go, and picked up speed before he has a chance to even gauge what I'm up to.

"What's the problem with the stairs, Jack?" I call, skidding around the corners to get to the long hallway. I hear his pounding feet behind me as he chases me down, but he's not going to get to me in time. I want to know. Now. And if it takes a bit of taunting to get what I want then that's what we'll do. "What happened, huh?"

"Madeline, no," his voice calls, a sense of desperation now coursing through that arrogant tone. Screw that. I'm going up those stairs and he can follow me or not. I'll smash the doors in to find out what's hiding in this house. Something's not right here. It's freaky, as is he now I think about it regardless of his clear beauty.

My knees propel me into the circular space then onto the bottom step, lurching me onto the next two before he's even caught up. The vision of him sliding around the corner as I turn back to see how close he is, is one of utter rage. I half stop, twisting my body back towards him to ask the question again, my left leg still moving up the stairs.

"Who's Selma? And why shouldn't I go up these stairs?"

"Come down," he snaps, his hands barely containing the need to grab out at me.

"No, I want some answers. She wrote Lewis' name. Why? This place is bloody insane. Or maybe you are." Violence springs across his features, the kind of death stare he had when he held a gun to his own head.

"Get off the fucking stairs."

"Make me." He snarls at me, his features contorting into a look of disgust and hatred, his legs pushing him closer to me. "All there was were locked doors on the third floor. There's definitely nothing wrong with the structure. Stop with all the damned lies now."

"Get out of my fucking house. Leave." No. I have nowhere to go now anyway.

"Really? That's the best you've got? Screw you, I want to know."

I turn again, my legs driving me upwards to the top, and I'm counting as I go. Round and round the long, wide steps, turning slowly and letting my feet move along the pristine carpet. He's not following me, but I can hear him pacing below as the numbers fall from my lips.

"Come down, Madeline, now," he calls, fury etched into his words.

The sound echoes up the stairway, chasing around the space as if it's haunting the area. It makes me smile, reminding me of the woman in the ballroom and her melancholy tone. She was warmer in her manner, regardless of the temperature she created.

"Selma?" I ask into the air quietly, wondering if it might be her name. It's not implausible after all. I did just have a chat with a ghost in the mirror.

I'm not even nervous about her answering. Maybe I'm going mad, too. Or maybe I just want some answers as to what the hell is happening here. I should be going to kill Lewis, but for the time being nothing seems as important as this. It's like my mind has to know. Has to. She wrote Lewis' name. I saw it there clear as day, and then she wrote Selma. Is it her?

Charlotte E Hart

THE SPIRAL

I stand on the step that leads off to the second floor, glancing along the corridor, unsure where to check first or whether to keep going upwards. There was nothing on this floor earlier, just some empty rooms full of luxury furnishings and nothing else.

My hand scuffs the wall, knocking on a protrusion of elaborate plaster work as I let it slide around the oak bannister. I hardly feel the impact as I listen and watch for a response.

"Selma? You there?" I call out again. There's nothing coming back, so I keep climbing and counting the never ending spiral, more interested in those locked doors further up. "I'm going up, Jack. You should start talking before I find out for myself," I call down, peering through the middle of the spiral to see the floor below. He's not there, not that I can see anyway, and his feet seem to have become silent, too. Maybe he's climbing behind me and I can't hear him on the carpet. I turn to look backwards, searching the space, but all I can see is the elaborate bannister as it cascades back downwards. "You coming to get me, Jack?"

There's a low rumble of something somewhere beneath me. I couldn't say what it is, or where it came from. "Selma? Hey? If that was you in there I need to know what you want."

Great. I really am talking to ghosts now. I believe in them, or this one, it seems. I shake my head at myself, letting the axe swing loosely in my hand and chuckling a little as I look upwards. Nothing's happening. It's just silent apart from my breathing and the continued landing of my bare feet on the carpet. Mmm.

I look upwards again, scanning the huge circular galleried landing that's coming into view as the stairs begin petering out in front of me. There's balustrading acting as a wall over the open gallery area, creating a balcony for the entire circle as it stretches the four sides of the third floor. It's stunning, a true masterpiece of craftsmanship and opulence, matching the downstairs to perfection, regardless of the grime and dust covering everything here, but the continued turn of the stairs is disorientating, making me question positioning and clarity in the house.

I finally land at the top, now a little unsure of my purpose as I look at the axe in my hand. Breaking into rooms is not my forte, not something I've ever entertained before this madness.

"Selma?" I whisper, perhaps because the climb has somehow made me recognise the stupidity of all this. Ghosts? Maybe I didn't see that stuff downstairs. Maybe it was just my imagination and now I'm simply being foolish.

I turn, looking back down at the vast spherically shaped wood on the ground floor around the spiral, hoping for something sane to present itself in this strange house. There's nothing there but the table waiting for me. No warming set of arms to hold onto, not that that's what I could call him really. It's just me standing here, alone. "Jack? Are you still there?"

Nothing.

Well, I'm here now. And I've got this axe.

My lip purse at the thought of doing damage as I turn away from the area, twisting my body towards the first door I tired earlier. So much damage over the last few years. My body, my face, my home and possessions. My friend. I lift my fingers to my face, tracing the outline of my eye and wishing the residual bruising away. My new house, my new life, destroyed before it began by the man I ran from. And now this—this house full of strange pain and hurt. Why is everything always broken? Why can't life be plain and ordinary like I wanted it to be? A safe new life, that's all I wanted. One filled with contentment and ease. And yet now I'm standing here with an axe in my hands, ready to break through doors to find answers to questions from ghosts. Ones like:

Who is that man downstairs?

And why do I even care?

My back hits the balustrade, making me realise I've been wandering aimlessly in thought. What am I doing? I look at the axe, its dark wooden handle looking awkward in my grip as the end of it glints light back into my face. I'm just little Mads. Cute Mads. Mads who potters about, making a home out of dreams and hopes. This axe looks as ungainly in my hand as the gun did earlier.

Maddy.

My head rises from the axe, unsure who said my name, or if anyone actually did. I sweep the space, looking for the body attached to the voice, but there's no one there. No white images or mirages. No billowing curtains. No frost creeping along the floors. There's only more silence and the long stretch of stagnant beauty all around me.

Do it.

That wasn't spoken out loud; it was all in my head, like a little voice nagging at me to finish something, to take control of something and make it my own. I look at one of the doors lining the landing from where I'm stood, breathing in some courage to do damage. I've never damaged anything. I've spent my life putting things back together, rebuilding them—my relationship, my face, my life. That's what I do. I don't destroy things or tear them to pieces. I mend things, keep them knitted together even if it is pretence.

Do it.

I feel the pressure building inside me. It's not sadness or regret. It's not anger or infuriation either. It's indignance. Sheer exasperation at how pathetic my life has been, how disastrous the last years of my life have become. Cute Mads has no place in my life anymore. She's hopeless, a waste of time and effort. What did she achieve by putting things back together? Nothing. Nothing but more hurt and pain. She grovelled in the dirt he provided and waded through life's misery while he took the glory for the home she tried to keep making. She was right to die. Right to be put in the ground so that Madeline, the one holding this axe ready to own every part of her life, could go and regain her strength.

Screw it.

I storm at a door in a rage before I've thought more about it, waving the axe above my head madly and hammering it down at the handle with as much power as I can muster. It ricochets off the metal, bouncing back at me and knocking me backwards. So I swing it again, the last few years-worth of hate and hurt and torment firmly levied in my next attack. The blade lands heavy into the frame, a dull thud sounding in the air this time rather than the metal tang of the handle. I heave on the thing, sawing it back and forth to remove it.

"What's in here, Jack? Where the hell are you?" I scream out, years of anger suddenly pouring into my voice as I search for answers. Answers for what, I don't know. Me probably, me and my pathetic response to Lewis' hands coming at me. “Selma? Tell me what the hell you want from me.”

The axe finally pulls free and I swing it high again, aiming better and letting it fall again with yet more power. Who the hell did he think he was treating me like that? What right did he have? How dare he abuse me with no reason? I was the perfect wife. Always. I looked after him, cared for him. Put up with his family, his temper tantrums, his moods. What the hell have I been doing all this time?

The axe lands again, jolting pain through my arm as it hacks at the wood again, splinters falling as I tug at it to get it free for my next strike. It becomes a frenzied attack at some point, my whole body raining blow after blow at the wood with no thought attached, only hatred and pain as I bash carelessly at the old solid surface. I can feel my limbs aching with the effort as I double more exertion into it, hoping to get in. I’m almost not here. Mads certainly isn’t. This is pure venom, levelled at anything that will take it. I don’t give a damn about Jack or who Selma is, or this fucking door. I don’t care about anything but smashing this thing in two. Wrecking it. Breaking something and owning that damage. It’s not like he doesn’t deserve it. He does. He hurt me. Caused pain. Turned my skin into nothing but a rainbow of purples and blues, all at his own whims. He destroyed me. He took something I gave him and made me beg for it to stay in one piece as he ripped it apart daily.

"FUCK YOU!" I scream out, the bellow coming out of the depths of my hatred for him and what he did to us as I land another blow at the wood. Tears erupt, causing my vision to blur as I tug at the handle again and try to catch my breath. "Fuck you and your hands." More tears stream as I remember the nights, the pain, and the effort of smiling through the next day, still too much in fear to actually say something or challenge him.

"Madeline, stop." Jack's voice barely cuts through my frantic attack, making me swing my glaring eyes towards the stairs again, axe hovering in the air above my head ready for another blow at the door. He's stood there, one hand resting on the banister, as he watches me from the step just before the top. "Please."

"Please what?" I snap out, ready to let this axe swing the instant he doesn't answer me properly.

"Stop. You shouldn't see what's in there."

"What do you mean? Why not?" He sighs and looks at the next step in front of him instead of at me as I grip the axe tighter, still rage filled and intent on causing more mutilation to anything that moves.

"What's in there isn't for you," he says, eventually looking back up at me and tentatively raising his leg to the next level, hovering it there. "You should stop attacking the door."

"I want to see what's in this damn room, Jack."

I'm not entirely sure what happens in the next few moments, but watching him, sensing the amount of composure he has somehow calms my hatred of anything that moves. I feel the tension leave my fingertips first. Then I feel the relaxation slowly migrate through the rest of me, filling me with a cooler air than the heated one I've created for myself. It's like just his demeanour is reassuring now he's stopped his raging and swearing, a bit like it was in the ballroom when he stood proud and tall above me and made me do things I didn't understand.

"Is this what you need from me?" he says, but I don't think it's to me. He's looking anywhere but at me, his eyes slowly searching the landing area as if he's looking for someone or something. "Is it? Talk to me?"

"I don't know…"

"You don't know what?" he asks firmly, finally getting his feet onto the top of the landing and glancing at his hand still attached to the bannister. "Come here." Does he mean me?

"Me or…" He raises a brow, slowly tipping his stare back in my direction from its ambiguous gaze around the place.

"Who else do you think I'm talking to?"

"A ghost."

I can't believe I said that out loud, but there are ghosts here, aren't there? At least one anyway. There must be—either that or I'm going mad and this place is a lunatic asylum. The thoughts make me glance back at the door, seeing the splinters of wood scattered around the bottom of it, and wonder if that's the best description of this building.

He's smirking by the time I look back at him, his hand reaching for me as he turns to look at the door behind me. "Same thing, Madeline. You're the same thing."

Chapter 15

Jack

She stares at me as if I've gone mad, challenging these feelings inside. I might well have done, because I can feel Selma's breath on my neck as I watch Madeline gawp at me. Her hand still hovers with the axe, as if she's ready to attack me with it, but it seems so clumsy in her fingers, just as it always did with Selma.

"What?" she says, lips quivering around the words. "What does that mean? What do you want?"

My lips smile at her, finally seeing the blend of the two of them and mapping out how we make this happen.

"Selma?" I ask, turning my eyes down the hall again to see if she appears. She doesn't. There's nothing but dusty old furniture and the darkness of this third floor looming back at us.

"What's in this damned room, Jack?"

"The past."

It's all I've got to give her. The past that I've kept in my every day, forcing it to continue in my memory so I can wreak my vengeance on their skin and bones. "I used to do that for her," I continue, nodding at the axe. Still she looks confused, her body backing towards the door as I take a step closer to her. "You've made as much of as a mess as she would have done."

"What?"

"Chopping wood."

She looks at me again, then at her hand, then back at me.

"It's a door, Jack. What's behind it?" she snaps.

I sigh and walk away from her along the corridor, running my fingers through the dust that covers the tables along the way.

"Why do you want her to see that?" I ask into the air, unsure what my wife is up to and unclear about whether it's the right thing to show her or not.

The air immediately turns as frigid as it was when I burst into the ballroom, making me glance back at Madeline's naked frame. She shivers there behind me, still hovering around that one door that she seems to know holds all the problems beyond it. The thought of one of the dogs catching a glance of her pristine skin makes me glower at myself and open the door nearest to me, searching for a blanket.

I stop on entering, stunned by the room I've walked into without thought. All her things are in here, making her seem so much more alive than she is. It's the place I put them into at first, hoping to hide from them somehow rather than face the truth. My breath halts, the last fog lingering in the dimly lit gloom as I stare into the space and will my feet backwards. They don't move. Nothing moves. No sound. No offer of her ghost to make this comfortable. It's just her dresses. Her shoes. Her jewellery. All of it neatly and carefully laid out on the bed and furniture, as covered in dust and grime as she is.

"Jack?"

I no longer care who said that. I can smell her here, and the aroma makes me smile wider as I move forward towards the bed and grab at something tangible to hold. Silk touches my fingers first, the lingerie laid out as if she were getting ready for a night out, or in. I chuckle at the thought of it, remembering her taste under my lips as I pick up the red garment and bring it to my face.

"Jack?"

It smells of roses, the blush of perfume still heavy even after all this time.

"Jack, the door… Oh."

I pull the silk away from my nose and slowly turn my head to look at her. She gazes around, her mouth open as she takes in the luxury on show and stands immobile in the doorway. She couldn't look more perfect if she tried, other than the colour of that pristine skin. "Is this…"

She trails off, unable to finish her sentence as she walks over to the far corner and I try to come to terms with her in this room. It feels as awkward as it was watching her batter the door, causing me to trail my eyes down to her hand to see the axe still hanging there. Maybe she could put that to a better use, clear the angst out of her system on real life rather than hammer wooden splinters to dredge out the pain.

I watch on as she gingerly reaches out at a fur coat, her fingers barely touching the soft fringing that used to house Selma's neck on cold winter nights.

"Is this her?"

I don't answer. I'm too consumed by her to answer, and suddenly too miserable to offer her help understanding what's happening here. Not that I know entirely, but this woman standing here, touching my wife's clothes and letting her scent mingle with times past, must be a reincarnation of sorts. A ghost sent to haunt me, or renew me perhaps.

She smiles at something, a slight lift of her lip causing me to follow her gaze as she looks down at the floor.

"Nice shoes," she says, reaching to pick the silver heels up.

They are. They were my favourites on her, especially when she wore nothing else with them.

"Put them on," I mumble, unable to stop my dick hardening at the thought. She frowns and glances across at me as I discard the silk in my fingers and pick up a long satin, matching negligee instead.

"But this is her, isn't it? Selma?"

"Just put them on, Madeline."

She shakes her head a little, backing away from them and inching along the wall towards the door again.

"I need to know, Jack," she whispers, looking around again. "I need to understand."

"Why? It is as it is, regardless of why."

She looks startled at my lack of information, her fingers gripping the back of a chair.

"This is... All this is not right. It's…"

I hold the garment up, watching as she flusters around the words and tries to make sense of the situation.

"Ask for her," I say as I take a step forward, pushing the satin at her. She glares at it in my hand, reminding me further of how my wife would get angry in her confusion. “Let her tell you to fuck me again if you need to.”

What was an unfocused glare becomes a look of shock as she backs away again, sliding towards the chest of drawers in the far corner. Time becomes as irrelevant as life as I centre on the shake of her limbs, licking my lips at the thought of what she could look like wearing these clothes.

“You believe this, don’t you?” she stutters.

I nod. I do believe all of this. There isn’t anything to disbelieve. She’s here, in this house, having come from nowhere offering the image of my wife. There’s no other explanation for what is happening around us, and the throb of my heart as it lurches closer to her burns inside to take and forget giving her a chance to remember. It’s alive in here again, waiting for all the segments to slot back together and prove the love I once knew.

I glance at the drawers, wondering whether I should open them and show her the pictures, let her see who she is as she stood there in her wedding dress.

“Can you tell me something, Jack? Anything?”

“Put this on, with the shoes, and I might.” The fabric slides through my fingers as she looks at it, her frown creasing again at the thought. “I’ll show you.”

“The room?”

“No. You don’t need to see that.”

A burst of light flashes in the room, blinding me enough that I stumble back a little and then reach for Madeline. She squeals as I grab onto her, her body folding into mine as I shield her and glance around the space for Selma. Frigid air comes just as quickly, telling me everything I need to know about my wife's wrath.

"I will not show her until I'm ready," I growl as I turn Madeline towards the wall, shoving the satin at her. "Put this on." I reach for the shoes, too, pushing them into her hands and turning my back to wait for my wife's eruption. "You'll damn well wait, Selma."

Hissing sounds out in the room, the door creaking along with it as it shutters back and forth, making me pocket my hands and calm myself. She can fuck around as much as she likes. This will happen at my pace, not hers. "You're being a bitch again, baby."

"This is crazy," Madeline whispers, one of her hands braced on my back, clutching me. I turn my neck to look at her, raising a brow and smirking a little. "I am not mad, Jack. I'm not." Maybe she's not. "I think you might be, though." I smile wider. It's a madness I'm beginning to enjoy. She will, too, if she gets with the damn programme and puts the fucking clothes on.

"Dress, before I lose patience with both of you." Her mouth opens to retaliate, but the sudden rush of wind that bristles through the room has her eyes widening in fear before she can. "Do as you're told and we'll see about showing you something." She stares as I walk away, leaving her exposed in the corner as I head for the curtains. "Now, before my temper gets the better of this whole fucking situation."

My fingers tip the curtains back to look out into the grounds, watching for the darkness to descend and warn me to stay inside. I chuckle as it creeps across the gravel, the low fog following it.

"I'm showing her, Selma," I mutter, uninterested in her hatred of the thought. "That's what she needs first." The door slams behind me, a loud crack coming with the move. It makes me chuckle again, almost waiting for stamping footsteps to echo in the hall outside.

"Show me what?" Madeline asks.

"The past. That's what you want, isn't it?"

I turn to look back at her, and am as stunned as I first was when I walked into this room. My face flattens under the sight, desperately trying to remember the need to do anything other than make love. Satin floats across her curves, highlighting everything that Selma was, is. Even her hair seems darker in this light, shadows casting a chocolate tone across it. And her eyes glimmer in the small shaft of light from the open curtain, emphasising pupils that contract and widen.

"I've known your eyes for so long I can't see anything else but them."

"What?"

"Your skin, your curves. Look at you. Still so beautiful." I reach for the coat near me, desperate to see the auburn fur mingle further into her hair and prove all this is real.

"See, that. What does that mean? Do I look like her? Is that it? Who is she?" she says, lips quivering as I take a step closer and offer the coat to her. "Why do I need that?" I frown at her questions and walk away again, shaking my head and opening the door my dead wife slammed. Dead. She's dead. A ghost. And Lenon is, too. Dead. Both dead. "Jack, where?"

I scowl at the hall as I walk out into it, glaring at the hacked up door as it comes into sight. Dead. All dead. And their innocent mutilated bodies come into my mind as I keep going. Bloody, open wounds seeping out onto carpet. Eyes lifeless and rigid rather than holding the vibrancy Madeline's now show me. Bile sticks in my throat at the thoughts, making me grab onto the wall for support as I edge along the hall and bypass the room of dogs.

"What's in that room, Jack? You haven't answered me," she says, her feet scuttling behind me as she catches up. "Jack, please. I need to understand this. I need clarity of some sort. Why do I feel this thing inside me?" I shake my head again, lifting my heavy feet and taking the stairs downwards the moment they come into view. "Jack, Christ, come on. Look at me. Why am I wearing this? Tell me, please."

"NOT UNTIL I'M FUCKING READY," I bellow, infuriated with the questions when I have no answers to give.

She gasps behind me, something crashing to the ground at the same moment. I don't care. I don't care about anything but getting away from this damn spiral and the dogs in that room. Nothing makes sense. It's all confused, and I can't see anything clearly anymore. The only thing I can see is their mutilated bodies.

Where's my Selma gone?

"Selma?" She doesn't answer as I turn onto the ground floor, eyes searching the corridor for a glimpse of her. I need her here now. I need her voice and some direction, not these unending questions that have no meaning unless she's here. "Please, Selma."

"Jack?"

"Selma? Where are you?"

"Jack?"

Was that Madeline or Selma?

I turn back to look for Madeline and find nothing but the spiral looking down at me, so I spin again and head for the door. Perhaps she's outside in that darkness and fog she likes so much.

The sun blinds me as I head out into it, confusing me as I search the tree line for something to clarify all this. Madeline's right. We both need clarification. I need it. I need Selma here to mingle with Madeline again. The two of them as one. I need that.

"Selma. Come here, now." Nothing happens other than a light breeze blowing the top of the old redwoods. "Fuck you," I snarl out, as I walk out down the steps and onto the gravel. "You started this, you bitch. Get here and finish it." Silence.

I snarl at the lack of an answer, wanting nothing more than her hissing, or the low hum of fog as it creeps the ground to get to me. My fingers roll her ring in my pocket as I think. It was so easy to pick it up after I'd been inside Madeline, like she's a part of its platinum somehow. Maybe I should put it on *her* finger, wake the bitch back up like that. "Stop playing with me, baby. You know how dirty I can get when you piss me off."

"Jack? Is this her?" I swing my head back to the door and find Madeline hovering there, a piece of paper in her hand as she gazes at me. My eyes narrow at the sight, immediately recognizing the old newspaper clipping. "This is her, isn't it?" Fury rises inside me as I remember looking at that crumpled piece of paper. Weeks went past while I did nothing but decay in this house, holding onto that scrap of an obituary. "She looks like me."

"Where did you get that?" I snap, my feet turning back to her. Her eyes widen as I storm over and snatch it from her hand.

"It was in the table. I knocked into it and it fell out. I'm sorry, but if you would just answer my questions maybe we could…"

I can't answer. I'm not ready to answer.

I'm walking away before she has chance to say another word, crunching the ground beneath me to get me to the woods. I'll go and see the treehouse. She talked about that earlier. A walk in the woods, she said. I can sit there for a while, see if this bitch dares to turn up again and give me some answers to use.

"Jack? Jack?"

I hurry on faster. Away. I need to get away from all this, as does she. She's right. None of this is real. It's a fucking ghost story, one I'm accepting out of desperation. She needs to go and leave me with my dogs. Let me be alone with them so I can keep funnelling these beleaguered thoughts onto something concrete. Serve vengeance.

"Go home, Madeline," I call back, as I get to the field and start trudging through to the dirt paths. If she wasn't here I'd get those damn dogs out, beat them. I'd walk for hours just to alleviate the ache in my chest. "Why are you doing this?" I mutter, pushing a branch out of the way and ducking towards the brook. "Why. Why not leave me to rot?" The mud begins to clog my boots, rendering the ground beneath me the wrong damn direction. I don't even know where I'm heading anymore. I'm just going away from Madeline, leaving her so she can make the right choice. Fuck, I should give her Selma's fucking Porsche. She drove it well enough. Then she could go rebuild her new life, not have me holding her here in my madness.

"Jack."

I stumble as her voice sounds, twisting myself back to find her in the sunlight and damn near tripping over a log. She's not there. It's devoid of Selma. No halos or bright blinding lights. No fog. Not even the darkness I'd prefer rather than the nothingness she leaves me with. It's just a dull, mundane spring day. Empty.

"Jack?"

My eyes snap in the direction of the sound, watching as Madeline lifts the heels from her feet and heads towards me.

"I told you to go home, Madeline." She wrangles her way through the undergrowth, finally finding decent footing to bring her within two feet of me. "Take the Porsche and go." Her eyes widen, but quickly soften again.

"I can't," she whispers, glancing around fretfully and tugging at the fur wrapped around her. "I've got no home to go to. You know that."

I stare at her, unable to answer her questions and seemingly unable to make her leave either. I don't even want her to leave, especially not while she's wearing Selma's clothes. The vision makes me smile again as I glance over her frame, finally landing my eyes on her mud covered feet.

"Grubby," I murmur.

"Mildly," she replies.

My fingers fiddle with the ring in my pocket again, wondering what the hell to do for the best. She should go. I'm right in that thought. But this ring in my pocket, the air that continues around us, and Selma's whispered words make it so difficult to enforce.

"Can you walk like that?" I ask, drawing my eyes back up to hers. She nods, using no other words to tell me if I'm doing the right thing or not. Just a nod. An acceptance. "Then we'll walk until I can find the answers you want. Maybe if you talk to me it'll help me find them for you."

Chapter 16

Madeline

We seem to walk for ages, silently travelling alongside each other with what seems like no destination. Not that I mind too much. It's beautiful here. Everywhere is full of sun and spring weather coming from the skies above. Part of me might be waiting for that darkness to descend again, willing it even, but it's nice to take in the view without whatever normally happens around that house clouding my views on sanity. Strangely, though, those odd happenings seem to clarify thoughts inside me. They seem to come with a sense of certainty, something my life has been lacking for a long time. There's an underlying feeling of warmth within that frigid air, one that speaks to me of love and protection, regardless of the fear associated with them happening in the first place. And I've seen her now anyway. There's nothing to fear.

Even if she is a ghost.

She's so like me. There's barely any difference other than my lighter skin colour and hair. My initial response was absolute horror, an odd foreboding coming over me as I gazed at the small photo in an old paper, but then a peace followed that I've never felt before. It flooded me with memories that aren't mine, filling me with the same sense of tranquillity that came when we made love. Everything made sense for a few minutes. I knew the house, the clothes I'm still wearing. His smile. His anger, the same anger that delivered the shout that had me knocking the side table over, the drawers opening instantly and delivering my first real clue about what is happening here. Everything felt like I knew it all already. Like I'd been here before. Lived here. And perhaps that's why when this man beside me made love to me, all the time making love to this other woman, it felt so right.

I shake my head as we wander on, barely acknowledging the ludicrous thoughts as healthy, but knowing every footfall that carries on like it's imprinted in time before me. We're both discussing ghosts without really discussing them. It's as ridiculous as it is necessary, throwing all form of coherent thought on the matter into disarray, but either way, ludicrous or not, the feel of that paper in my hand made me experience something comforting eventually, not horrifying.

Perhaps I should be alarmed by all this. I suppose most people would be, but with little else to go back to, and nothing but a crumpled house and death to deal with, I'm not in any mood to rush away from something that feels contented, even if it is marginally so and ill understood at present.

I sigh and look up again, drifting my eyes across the sky in search of that darkness that will come again soon. I know it will. She'll come now and show me something more, something to make these moments she delivers clearer in my mind.

"How long?" Jack says, as he leads us over to a small glade out of the bluebell filled landscape.

"How long what?" I reply, swinging my eyes to his. "Until the fog comes?" He looks solemn instantly, the harmony of his face disappearing to the frown I'm so used to now.

"No, how long had he been beating you?"

I'm instantly deflated from our quiet and peaceful meander, relegating myself back to the hours, weeks, months and years of abuse. It seems such a harsh word for what happened. Beating. Abuse. But they're the honest words for what I dealt with from Lewis, no matter how long I tried to deny the terms.

"Too long," I mumble, pointing over to a small fallen tree trunk in the corner. He shakes his head at me and pulls on my arm, sending us in a new direction across another path. "I could do with resting," I continue, wondering how far this walk is going to go on before I get some answers.

"Not yet. There's something I think you should see." I nod at that and follow him, trying to avoid the lumps and bumps beneath my bare feet as we push though some trees out into another clearing, and then through that into another one. "Why did it take you so long to leave him?"

I sigh and glance at his chest, trying to find a sensible answer to that. There isn't one, only that love makes people do strange things in hope.

"I don't know. I guess when I was in it I hoped it would stop. Love does that." He snarls, that scowl of his descending. "I've left him now, though. It doesn't matter anymore what happened before. I just have to find a way of killing him."

"You're no killer, Madeline." My own brow furrows. He might be right. Whether I've actually got the nerve to kill Lewis is as questionable as whatever is occurring around us.

He mutters something after that, which I don't hear, and reaches back to guide me through another small path of twigs and thorns, lifting me over the last of it. "Not bitch enough."

"What does that mean?" He doesn't respond, just pushes out into a clearing and then stops about five or ten feet into it. "Oh, wow. Cute."

There, stood in the middle of the small area, is a treehouse wrapped around what looks like an ancient oak. The wooden structure looks fairy like, bits of it haphazardly attached on, creating a magical feeling. I smile at it and wander over, for some reason wanting to run my hands over it and touch its aged appearance. A small wooden slide hits my fingers first, the run of smooth wood sliding under my fingers as I run my hand up to the main section. It feels like a thousand children have played on it, testing its structure with their buoyancy and bounding around for hours on end.

"It's lovely," I whisper, mesmerised by the look of it.

It really is. It screams of fun and children, muddy boots and sticks. Hours will have been spent here by children over the years, all of them finding their own escape in its limbs and trunks.

"It was my son's." My head whips around, shocked by the words, and I find him gazing at me, touching the structure. "Her son, too." He frowns and walks over to me, his own hands slowly running the length of the slide to reach for mine. "She was my wife." I'd like to say I didn't know that, but somewhere deep down inside I do. Just like I know this space I'm standing in now. "You can feel her, can't you?"

"You told me you weren't married, Jack. You lied," I say, smiling a little and remembering the fall in the bog.

"Hardly a lie. She's dead. I'm widowed," he replies, pressure baring down on my hand as he tries to link our fingers. "Not married."

I don't know how the information makes me feel as I slip my hand from under his and walk off towards the other side of the clearing. Dead seems such a rash word for what his wife is. She's here, all around us somehow. She's far from dead in my opinion, no matter how strange the fundamentals of that argument might be.

I sit on an old log, letting myself rest, and stare at him as he wanders around the treehouse, presumably chasing memories in his mind. He's beautiful. Truly. The sort of man women swoon for. And I'm sure if I was any other woman, in any other situation, I'd find a reason to walk to him and comfort away that sadness that's settling onto his face, but for some reason I suddenly feel as morose as he looks, exhausted even.

"He's dead, too, isn't he?" I ask, not really needing the answer. "Your son." I know he is. I don't know how I do but this miserable sensation inside me tells me it's true. Sad as that might be.

He doesn't answer me at all. Maybe he knows he doesn't need to. Maybe he's always known. It certainly explains a lot now. From the first time we met he's seemed odd when he looks at me, and when he touched me the first time, when he held my hand in his, well, now I know why he didn't want to let go. He thinks I am her. That I am Selma, the mother of his child. I'm not.

"You think she knows what she's doing?" I call out, watching him come from the back of the structure and creep through the undergrowth growing up the frame.

"I think she's trying to come home, through you."

"I'm not her, Jack. You know that."

"Aren't you?" he replies, as he arrives in front of me, a wry smile creeping up his jaw.

"No. I'm Madeline, Jack. I've never been her, nor will I ever be her. One life of a lie is plenty enough for me." He chuckles slightly at that then turns away, back towards the treehouse.

"And yet you're still here, Madeline. Why is that?"

"Because I can't leave." He looks over his shoulder at me, showing me that frown again.

"You can," he says, pointing over towards the left of us. "The road is just there. All you have to do is walk through those trees and you'll eventually reach the road you came in on."

I smile at him, knowing full well that if I really wanted to that's exactly what I could do. I could walk further, eventually find a signal I'm sure, and then call recovery to come get my car. It's a simple solution. One that doesn't involve any of these bizarre happenings, and one that would have me back to the world of rebuilding my dream before I know it. Simple. He knows it as well as I do, but I haven't gone yet, have I? He's right.

Why am I still here?

I smooth over the long satin negligee, smirking at the notion of it in this scenario. It's as ridiculous as the thought of ghosts, but I'm not denying it anymore. Something is alive here, something that's not quite right. Us, the ring I found, the visions of Selma and the frigid air that follows her everywhere. And I know things inside me. I do. I understand something I can't quite place my finger on yet. I feel like I've lived here before, loved here and run these fields without a care in the world.

We both know that without any discussion on the matter.

"What's in that room, Jack?"

"Death," he says, no hesitation in the delivery.

"Why can't I see it?"

"Selma can. Madeline can't. It's none of her business." I scowl at him, displeased with the answer but unable to find a sensible comeback to force him to tell me anything. "Come here. Let's see if we can make her come to us. Get her inside you again. "

My feet lift without any real protest, some errant call inside me making me unsure if it's me or Selma responding to his order. Either way, the walk to him feels as calming as it usually does, the strange pull coercing a closeness we shouldn't have.

"Can you climb in that?" I look down at the negligee, not knowing if *it* will stop me climbing or that fact that I haven't climbed a thing in years.

"Where?" He nods up the rickety steps into the treehouse, his tongue rolling over his lips as he does.

Shivers ride my skin the moment his hand braces my back, forging me towards them without bothering to wait for my answer, and I gasp as my foot hits what feels like ice on the first step. I shoot away from it, fear lacing the next step forward. "Keep going, baby," he says, pushing against me until he's behind me and forging me upwards again. Baby? I turn to look at him, unused to the term as it comes softly from his lips. He just nods again, pushing on my coat to get momentum out of my feet.

"Jack, I don't think this is sensi—"

"You're right. It's not, but I want to fuck again, and I want to do it up there."

My feet immediately stop, my head whipping round to look at him with shock written all over my face. I don't know why. Perhaps it's the crudeness of the statement in the middle of this glade. He smirks, apparently not a care in the world as he nods onwards again. "I like fucking you." For the life of me I can't stop my responding smile as I watch his eyes harden a touch, nor can I stop my own eyes looking over his frame again. "Always have done, baby."

I turn again and keep climbing, confused about the last of his words but unable to stop my need to climb with him. It's like something inside me is taking over again, showing me a path I'm unable to veer from. And each footfall becomes colder, my toes scrunching beneath me to try to alleviate the sensation.

"Cold," I stutter out, as I reach the top and gaze around, pulling my coat closer in to shield myself.

"Take it off," he says, holding out his hand. "That's how we get her here. The cold."

Part of me recoils at the idea, and yet another part welcomes the thought. I wish I understood that more clearly as I part the fur and let it dangle down my sides again, the collar falling to my shoulders.

"You always were so fucking beautiful."

A tear wells in my eyes as I watch him slowly peel the side of the coat away from me, some part of me wanting the feelings he has to take hold and claim this moment. He believes all this so much, doesn't he? Needs it even. I can tell by the reverence in his gaze, the near worship of his movements as he backs off to look me over.

"Jack, I…"

"Sshhh." He discards the coat and moves back in front of me. "No more questions now. We'll do what we did best. Here. With Lenon."

Freezing air blasts into the space around us, causing my teeth to chatter instantly as I search the area for fog. There isn't any, but that darkness is coming even if I can't see it. I know that because I know her now. I can feel her inside me with every next gaze he makes. She's channelling in me. My blood boils regardless of this air around us, almost hurting as I watch him watch me.

"You ready for me?" he asks, taking one step towards me.

"I..."

Nothing comes out of my mouth as he moves in and slips his arms around my waist, tugging me into his chest.

"We'll fuck here. On top of our son. Remember him."

His lips come at me quicker than I expect, forcing me backwards towards a tree trunk. They're harsh and unyielding as his tongue drives in, moulding us together with little effort from me. It's all I can do to hang on to him rather than be swept off my feet and thrown to the floor. And I can feel that coming for me. I don't know why but I know this isn't the Jack who made love to me on the floor. This is the harsher version of him. The one who'll fuck with little care for my comfort or stability in the middle of this madness.

Hold onto him, Maddy.

My head rips away, desperate for air from his assault and her voice. Hands are everywhere on me, grabbing and sliding, pinching in to hoist my leg up onto him and around his back. He pushes again, shoving me harder onto the trunk behind me and making me yelp at the pain.

"You'll fuck like we did before," he growls, a harsh bite into my chest causing me to squirm in his hold and attempt clambering away. "Remember us like you should."

Fear etches into me from somewhere, reminding me of Lewis and his power over me. I shake my head, trying to dislodge the memories and focus on Jack's voice, but it's all too similar. His hands, the biting sensation, the hard touch of male all over me, consuming me.

"Jack, I can't do this," I stutter out, trying again to push away from him.

His hold becomes fiercer than ever, his face coming up to mine to stop me from talking at all before I get a chance to think. Lips mould again, instantly warming me regardless of his handling staying as rough as it's become. Something about his mouth reminds me that it's him, though. It changes everything, all thoughts of Lewis evaporating the second our tongues collide again. I grip on again, aroused immediately because of the connection, and barely able to think of anything but him. And then memories come from somewhere. They lash around in my mind, telling me of things I've never known. A white dress. Dancing. The ring on my finger and the sound of applause.

A wedding.

"Oh god," I breathe out through our lips. "Selma."

Just hold on.

It's freefall from there, all the feelings and emotions she's got somehow propelling their way through me with no stopping them. It's not me here anymore. I'm barely holding onto any reality at all as I let her consume me without fight. And it's so cold now. So very cold I can barely catch my breath as he pushes and hoists me further up. Every touch is like ice across me, somehow whispered through me until I'm numb to anything other than his fingers biting in and holding on.

He shoves again, making me howl at the pain as my back grates and grinds against the trunk. It should hurt, I know it should, but instead it feels euphoric, some part of me screaming for more of it even though I should be running from his hold. The negligee gets pulled from my skin, thrown somewhere. I'm not even sure if I did it or he did, or maybe it was her.

Oh god, Selma. She's screaming at me, moaning and calling his name, pushing it through my lips without my consent. It's panted and groaned, as if she's here rather than me and there's nothing I can do, or want to do, to stop this insanity taking hold.

"Baby," he says, grunting as he finally tugs my hips upwards and seats himself inside. My eyes fly open, lips trying to say something I can't find in my mind. "I've missed you so much," he says, grinding into me and cutting through any inch of separation that was left. "You're home, baby."

I do nothing but stare into hazel eyes as he pushes deeper inside me, waiting for something to tell me this is normal, that it's okay for him to be fucking a ghost through me. I can't find anything to say, nothing of my own anyway. It's all her and him. Her moaning. Her clawing at him. Her whispering his name, pulling him closer with my hands.

"Tell me, baby," he mutters, long slow thrusts building their rhythm as he wraps an arm around me and lifts me from the trunk. I don't know what to say, or even if I should, and the moment he drops me to the floor, covering me with himself and still driving in, I know I don't have to. They're not my words to say. They're hers.

"I love you," murmurs from me, barely able to separate my own thought from hers. "I love you, Jack."

Winds whip the air, a crackle of thunder following them as he keeps pushing in, his lips moulded to mine the entire time. It's timeless, precious. Them together. Me breathing for her, feeling every inch of him for her. It's all so serene, a connection coming from them that I feel privileged to be in the middle of. And then that fog comes. I can't see it. I don't need to. I can feel it smothering my icy skin, feel it warming the space around us and bracing me against him with no route for escape anymore. It's calming, levelling me into him at the same moment as she begins to cry. I can feel that, too. It send ripples through my skin, making the orgasm coming chase itself quicker for her. And now I'm crying. I can feel the tears tracing my face and telling me stories about them. Love, honour, respect. It's all so intense, so penetrating. Every emotion they feel is flooding me and wetting his face as his stubble grates my cheek and he keeps up the rhythm.

"Jack, I love you."

I wish I knew who said that. It's not her anymore; it's me I think. All I can feel is he and I, some part of her disappearing as my orgasm crashes and I grip on tighter. He shunts me downwards, forcing my back onto the deck, and rises up to watch me groan out the orgasm. I pant at him, letting the ebb of other worlds fill me with the love they talk of until he lifts one of my legs and tips it over his shoulder.

"One was never enough for you," he says, a dirty smile leaving me breathless at the sight of it, let alone the thought. "Tell me you want more." His belt rubs against me, small nudges of it heightening every freefall towards crashing orgasms. "Let me hear you, baby. Remind me."

I groan again, or I think I do. I've given up caring who's here anymore, more consumed in the feel of him on me than anything else. And I want to see him all, I do. My hands are reaching forward to tug his shirt off before I consider whether it's appropriate. I don't care about anything but this, here and now. He helps me instantly, clawing at his own clothes until he's as naked as I am, neither of us caring for the fog that surrounds us, the freezing temperature, or the darkness that's once again come from nowhere. This is us, the three of us, for better or worse doing whatever the hell this is.

"Jack, please. More."

He levers down, his lips brushing mine peacefully at the same moment as he deepens the drives again, filling me so completely all breath leaves me. Love drifts again—a love that I can't comprehend, yet understand so intensely that my mind nearly explodes at the richness of it. So many memories. So much joy and happiness, all of it coming through her and into me with no fear of me seeing such intimacy.

"Our son." I gasp at the words leaving my lips, another tear pricking the corner of my eye as he covers my body with his and groans. I can smell him—Lenon. I can even see his boyish eyes as this man carries on driving in, filling me with thoughts of carrying our child and loving him, loving them both. And before I know what's happening, I'm sobbing, my hands scratching at his back to pull him in deeper, find something that's lost between us even though I've never known him. But I have known him. I know that now. I've known him for so long I don't think I knew anything before him, nothing that makes sense anymore, anyway. "Oh god, I love you."

He grunts on the final forge inwards, his mouth smothering the last of the words until there's nothing left but the two of us balanced in this fog, barely conscious to any known reality and continuing to linger in this experience with no desire to leave it.

That's all there is now—her, him, and some small part of me clinging onto them in the hope that I might survive whatever this has become.

Chapter 17

Jack

She moves quicker than I'd like, instantly bringing the daylight with her as she heaves at me and rolls away. Fucking daylight. I want my dark back. Selma's there, and Madeline isn't denying me or her anymore. She's here now. Alive again.

"You should get back down here," I mutter as I grab for her leg. She should. She should forget about any reality she knows and come live this fucked up one with me instead, enjoy it.

She sidesteps out of my hand, reaching for the fur coat and shrugging it around herself.

"Maybe, but that's not getting me or Selma inside that room, is it? And I know now. I do, Jack. I know it all. I can feel her."

Before I've processed what's she'd said, she's running, her feet nimbly negotiating the treehouse as if she's been on it a thousand times.

"Selma," I call, rolling myself onto my knees to grab at my jeans and shirt.

Fuck. Conniving little bitch. This is Selma's doing, not Madeline's. She's inside her now, moulding the two of them together, both of them using each other to get their own damn way. She laughs somewhere ahead of me, causing me to shrug into my jeans quickly and discard the shirt in favour of catching up with her.

My bare feet sprint, not caring for the ground that undulates beneath them as I crash though the undergrowth to get to them before either of them see my dogs. I'm not ready for it, and neither is Madeline. And although Selma's clearly already seen inside it, what the fuck she needs Madeline to see for I don't know.

"Madeline," I shout, finally seeing her coat trailing behind her as she scampers through the woods, feet covered with mud as she leaps a brook.

She doesn't reply, just keeps going until she manages to find the main driveway and veers along it, her feet picking up speed again.

"You can't stop this, Jack," she screams back, more laughter following her words.

I career on, pushing every muscle I've got to get to the house before she does, and swerve off to the left to cut through the small wood that lies to the east of the house. Thickets and brambles hang heavy inside it, hindering my path, but the shortcut proves useful as I watch her come into view again. She's to the right, her own feet still powering her along towards the main steps.

She looks across at me, knowing she's not going to make it first. She scowls and suddenly swerves right away from the front of the house, confusing me. "More than one way in, Jack," she calls. Bitch. I watch her negotiate the terrain, her feet nimbly crossing the stepping stones towards the cellar's entrance. The same entrance that will lead her straight to the spiral. It's as if she knows the damn house better than I do all of a sudden. "You'll have left this open, too, won't you?"

Selma.

"Don't, Madeline," I shout, barely containing my animosity for a wife who's managing to outmanoeuvre me.

I turn sharply, trying to get to the main door before her, but I'm not going to make it along the hall in time. I know that. She's beaten me because of Selma's knowledge of the building, not hers. She knows nothing of this place, but my wife? She knew it better than me. All those damn days rebuilding the decrepit monster, turning it into our home, showed her parts of this place no one even knew existed.

A noise rumbles in the distance, causing me to swing my head behind me and look back up the drive. A car's coming. I can see the dust over towards the headland. I whip back to look for Madeline, noticing as she grinds to a halt by the cellar door and swings around, too. She seems confused as she peers at the dust, and then her face drains of colour regardless of the sprinting she's been doing. Her hands fly to her mouth, feet stumbling over themselves to back her towards the stonework. She looks scared, the laughter of moments ago disappearing with every breath she pulls in.

"Jack," she says, her eyes widening as the car keeps coming and kicks up gravel in its wake. "You've got to go. Run."

"Why?"

"That's Lewis' car."

My eyes narrow at the vehicle, annoyed with its presence for multiple reasons and about ready to kill the man who dared mar the beauty of my wife's face. It causes enough anger to rise that I'm walking in her direction and blocking her from him before I've thought any more of it.

She shakes her head at me, eyes wider than before as she shivers against the stonework and then glances back at the vehicle.

"Don't be stupid, Jack. He's come for me, not you. You have to go. Leave." She walks from the wall, pushing at my chest and pointing towards the main steps. "Go, Jack. Hide." I stare at her, unsure what the fuck she thinks a snivelling little abuser can do in front of a real man, then smile at the prospect of showing him what real men actually do to protect the women they love. "Oh God, Jack. I'm not going back. I'm not. Not again. I need the gun. Where's the gun?" She turns and bolts into the cellar, the door opening after a shove so hard it crashes against the side of the building. "Go, Jack."

I turn slowly to watch the car continuing towards me, little care for her analogy of him. He's a fucking abuser is what he is. A weakling. I've been training my dogs for too long to care about something as insignificant as a wife beater and his threats. Perhaps he should join them in their cell, learn what real pain feels like from the hands of someone who gives a damn about delivering it correctly. I'll wait here for him. Show him how real men behave.

The wind makes the dust drift as the black SUV closes in on me. It reminds me of Selma's fog, amusing me as I wait for whatever this fucker thinks he's got for me. It felt so good to hold her again, hear her voice coming at me as she moaned her love for me.

"JACK."

I swing back to the door, my feet instantly picking up speed at her alarmed voice, and head into the cold confines of the cellar. She shouts again somewhere ahead, making me run up the stairs quicker to get to the door by the spiral. It's open when I arrive, no sight of her.

"Madeline?" I call out, trying to gauge her position. She doesn't answer, but I can feel the chill already coming from the black carpet of the spiral. "You here, baby?" I whisper, watching and waiting for the frost to ebb down to me. No answer from either of them again, but I hear the crackle of ice that comes with her, sense it pull me towards the both of them. "What are you up to, wife? You want me to hurt him like I do those dogs?"

The windows fly open behind me, the bluster of wind swelling the curtains into the room as I watch on then turn for the stairs again. "A little dramatic, baby, don't you think?" I snark, chuckling to myself at her theatrics and beginning to climb. "You just need to damn well talk to me. Ask."

Jack.

"Madeline, where are you?"

The old doorbell chimes back along the corridor, half halting me as I consider just going and grabbing the fucker and pulling him up this spiral so he can rot with the others, but I suppose there could be more than just him. Madeline might be right with her thoughts of the guns.

I swing back and head for the hall table, ready to swipe the revolver, but it's already missing. She must already have it, which amuses me more than I'd like to admit. She's ready to kill. She sure as hell wasn't when I first met her, but then she has Selma now. Selma's courage. Selma's animosity and hatred, and fear and pain do strange things to people. Just as they did to me. She can join me in her quest for madness. Join us.

We'll rid the planet of vile thugs and their needs.

"You still here, baby?" I ask, my feet climbing the black carpeted steps again to get to my dogs. I snort, wondering if I should set them loose, let them hunt something and kill prey. They haven't eaten properly for weeks, not that they damn well deserve anything to fill their repugnant stomachs, but maybe this could amuse us all.

I chuckle again and watch the frost creep over the floor as I keep turning the spiral, ready to let it consume any thoughts of reality I had left. This is what we've become now, a torrid disarray of half in, half out. It's Madeline we both want. Madeline we need. And no one's taking her away from us.

Before I reach the top, I hear the main door being kicked at, its one catch holding fast against whatever intruder is trying to get in. Stupid fucker. He only needs to turn the damn handle and it'll open, just like it always does.

We're all ready for him in here. All of us are ready for anything that dares take my sanctuary from me again.

The door to my dogs is open by the time I've arrived, Madeline hovering in the entrance and staring into the room. I watch for a minute, wondering how she opened it, and then decide not to care anymore. There's no point in hiding it now. If she doesn't know already, then Selma would have soon shown her what my life has become about. She probably feels it already regardless of my attempt to shield her. Like she said, she knows now.

My hand eventually reaches for her shoulder, the fur of the coat reminding me of the fucking that ensued on top of Lenon's treehouse—beautiful, rampant fucking, all of it happening in our son's favourite place. She doesn't even react to me as she carries on staring, a strange sense of shock written all over her beauty until I push on her to make her step into the dimly lit space.

She might as well smell it as well as see it.

"Jack?"

"Dogs."

"But…" She looks at me with eyes full of confusion, her hand covering her mouth and nose as we walk in.

"They're here because of you. You'll understand soon enough."

Footsteps echo in the hall below us, making me look back at the door and then close it quietly. Perhaps if we wait in here he'll come find us and let me show him what happens to intruders.

"Will he be armed?"

She glances at me, and then walks forward a few small paces until she reaches the metal bars.

"I don't know," she mumbles, too intent on the sight in front of her to care.

Dog three cowers in the darkened corner like he always does, whimpering and whining, waiting for dog one to show him what to do. I sneer at him, thinking about what use he's ever been to me other than for amusement and revenge. Two waits patiently, his nearly torn off clothes dropping from his piss stained frame as he sits like a good dog, knowing his damn place. But one, he's as intent as he always is as he creeps closer to her. I watch him sniffing the putrefying air, hoping for a taste of something other than me. Some element of pride mixes with the loathing I feel for them, perhaps chased with the memories of what they've meant to me all this time. They've given me credence up until Madeline came here. Given me purpose.

He lunges unexpectedly, an enthusiastic grimace idling his features, causing Madeline to scamper away, his face coming to the bars and hands grabbing at them.

"Jesus," she pants out, quietly backing into me and pulling her coat tighter around her.

"Hardly," I mutter, looking at his filthy face at the bars as I reach for the zapper.

His tongue licks the side of the caging they're behind, nose sniffing again to pull in Madeline's perfume. It pisses me off that he's even trying to smell her. He smelt Selma enough when he raped her, and sniffed the blood pooling on Lenon's chest when he shot him. Fury wells inside at the mere thought, but I quiet the havoc I want to let loose, knowing this isn't the time with other intruders in the house.

"What is this, Jack? This is… I don't know what to…"

"Memories and death," I mutter, listening to the continued echo of footfalls below us, a few voices coming with them. "The past. My present, until you."

She looks at me, just stares, barely noticing anything other than me in this room of rot and hatred. And she's so beautiful like this. She's all I ever wanted. Her and Lenon. All of us together, filling this place with more children and harbouring our love. "They took you away from me, baby, Lenon too. You must remember that."

She backs away a step, tugging her coat tighter in and glancing at the closed door.

"This isn't right. They're people. Why are they in there?"

"They're fucking dogs," I spit out, annoyed with her comparison to humans. "Dogs that ripped you to pieces and left you to rot."

My finger presses the buzzer repeatedly, causing all three of them to wail and rush around the cage, bellowing out their pain and annoying me further as they crash into the bars. So I press again, and again, all the time watching the look of horror on her face and wishing she could remember the pain they caused her.

"Stop, Jack. Please stop," she says, her hands rising to the side of her head as she watches on and drops to the floor in the corner.

No. I won't fucking stop. I'll never fucking stop. And her hiding down there, refusing to see this as necessary only furthers my infuriation. I grab at her arm, hauling her up to drag her back into the middle of the room. She'll damn well watch, hear the noise, see the fucking pain they're in and will it on them with me.

"Your body was raped, split open and beaten by them," I snarls out, one hand holding her still against the bars. "Lenon shot in the chest while he slept, blood pouring from his body." She gasps at that, her own frame trying to wiggle backwards. "These dogs did that to you, to him.

They fucking took you both from me and no one's doing that again."

She rips herself away from me, eyes wild as she thrashes at my body until she's free of my hold and snatches the keys from the side wall. It makes me sneer at her, uncaring for the whimpering that comes from the dogs, and back myself towards the cage door. "And now they'll work for us, Selma. They will. They'll hunt and kill for you. Make sure you never leave here again. I've trained them. Open the door."

My finger goes up to my mouth, hushing everything. The dogs quieten their rapid pacing behind me to the silent padding they've been trained to, dog one leading the pack in his gesture of compliance as he watches her. "Come, talk to them. Let them hear what they've learnt to protect."

"Talk to them?" she whispers with frantic glances at my hand as I hold it out to her.

I nod, waiting for her to see the sense in all this and learn to trust me. They'll protect her now, chase some rabbits for her if she wants that from them. She takes my hand slowly, rallying herself into the woman she should be behaving like. It's almost a sight to behold as she lets Selma inside again, relegating this frightened version of herself to the wings and becoming my wife instead.

"They know you," I say, reaching behind me to pick up the old picture of her on the terrace. Such a lovely day, her hair shining in the sunlight, eyes sparkling like they always did. I hand it over to her, smiling at the intrigue in her eyes as she looks at it. "They've done nothing but look at this picture for as long as I've had them here, baby."

She sighs and looks up at me, a half smile on her lips as she hands it back to me and walks towards the bars.

"Do they have names?"

"No."

"Jack, they must have names."

"None that fucking matter."

Dog one moves in closer as she gets to him, loose jowls hanging in a display of submission as he creeps along with slow footfalls until she reaches a hand to the bars and smiles at him.

"You're okay," she says, the perfect amount of beauty ringing through her tone to quieten any amount of fear they might be feeling. "You're going to be fine now."

Chapter 18

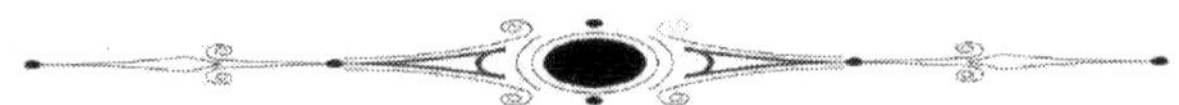

Madeline

I don't know what's happening. These are people I've found in here—three of them, all shivering and scared of anything that moves. Certainly Jack. And the smell is disgusting, as if they've been in here for weeks, months even. Urine, faeces. The tell-tale reek of vomit. It's enough that my eyes are watering and I'm having to hold my breath just to be able to pull in a quick gulp of oxygen when I can.

They're so quiet, all of them, barely anything but skin and bones between them. Blood is scattered across their bodies, along with filth and grime that seems imprinted on them. It's sickening to witness, but Jack says they're responsible for Selma's death in some way. That the three of them murdered her along with their son. If that's true, they probably deserve everything they've got, but it's still not right.

The taller one hovers on the floor by my feet, only the bars separating us as the keys I picked up twitch in my hands. He's told me to open the doors, but I don't know if I should or not by the look of this one's eyes. They're rabid, uncertain. I noticed them when he flew at me, sending me reeling into the corner in fear.

"It's okay," I whisper down at him, crouching and considering offering my hand in the hope he'll be gentle. "I'm going to get you out of here now."

Jack scoffs behind me, making me turn to glare at his mocking laughter.

"You always were too kind, baby." His words hit home more than I'd like to admit. Too kind. Always giving someone a second chance, always giving Lewis a second chance.

Lewis.

I stand up, turning to look at the door for the first time since I found this room. He's here, down those stairs somewhere, isn't he? I walk towards the door and put my ear to it, listening for his whereabouts.

"Ballroom," Jack mutters, sitting on the table and staring at the picture I handed back to him.

I gaze at him, bemused by his apparent boredom. I don't understand why he isn't scared. He should be. This is

Lewis we're talking about. If he's found me, he'll be livid with Jack for being here, ready to kill him for harbouring me, let alone touching me. He saw what Lewis did to my home.

"Don't you care?"

"About what?"

"Lewis."

"No, you have your dogs. A gun in your pocket. Make them all work for you, baby."

Baby? When did that start to feel so comfortable?

He said it down at the treehouse, and earlier than that, called me it as we made love. It feels so familiar, so ground in. Like it's been used a thousand times and acknowledged with the smile that wants to break across my lips. Still I stare, unsure what I should do. Perhaps I should just go down and talk to Lewis, try to smooth things over and then go back with him. It's not like I can stay here forever. I never could have, no matter how appealing the thought. I've only ever been here to find myself, work out how to get even or just carry on trying to live my life again.

I dig into my pocket, feeling for the gun, and let the cold metal mould into my grip. It's as uncomfortable as it's always been. I'm not built for this. I'm not whatever this place is turning me into. I just want my peaceful life again. I want the laughter I wished for, the love I was beginning to feel again for life, even if it was with a man I don't really know.

I stare at him, wondering where Selma's gone from my mind. She'd be doing what he says, wouldn't she? She'd know how to feel about these men in front of me, perhaps feel the vengeance he so vehemently does. But I'm not her, and this isn't right, unless it is.

I'm so confused.

"Jack, this is stupid. I'm just going to go talk to him, work it out." He raises a brow at me, nothing more, then slides himself from the table and walks closer to me.

"You think that will make your life freer?"

A noise comes from below us somewhere, footsteps along the hall maybe. They're coming for the spiral, aren't they? Lewis is. He's coming to get me, make me go back with him.

Save yourself, Maddy. Home.

I half jump at her voice in my head, shaking it to try to find what I want in this situation, as I look at the floor waiting for frost. Maddy, she's always called me that, pulling me back to who I was before Lewis. I shake my head again, knowing I'll never be Maddy again. Too many bruises made her leave. Too many nights in pain.

"My life will be simpler, Jack. I'll talk to him, make him see that…"

The room goes darker, stopping my mouth from voicing my thoughts, shadows looming where the light filtered in slightly until it's almost pitch black. I glance at the men when one of them moans and whines at something, his feet pacing the cage, worried about what's scared them.

"You know better than that, baby. It will only be simpler when he's dead." Jack brushes a finger over my cheek suddenly, warming me into thinking he's actually touching me, but he's not. He's touching her, loving her. "We can be together again then. Just you and me. In this home you made for us." The way the words come make me feel anything but me. They remind me of the haunting memories that come when she's near us, the cold creeping my bones and telling me this is all okay. "You remember it all, don't you?" I do. He's right. And the more he talks, the more I forget the stench in the room, somehow lifting myself above it as if it's just a mere piece of a puzzle that needs solving so we can both move on. "You remember our wedding night? The way I caressed your stomach?" Oh god, I do. I can feel it now as he presses a hand against me in the same spot, his other hand wrapping around my back. "It's all down to you now, baby. It's all in your hands." I can't stop gazing at his mouth, the words somehow deepening *my* feelings for him rather than Selma's. And she's here with us again now. I can feel her whispering across my skin, showing me a way that's not mine. "Just let the dogs out, baby. Let them work for us and then we'll both be free. Kill him."

"Kill." The word mumbles from me, my hand still gripped around the gun in my pocket as I stare into the stormy eyes I first saw when I tumbled down the front steps. It seems so long ago now, like he's another person, too. He's so much softer like this. Calmer. But it's whenever she's here. That's what changes him. For both of us. She makes this work, makes us fit together, and I'm not her.

He nods at the cage again, a look of comfort making me question the lucidity of all of this. He's proud of these people and the state they're in. Proud of himself for the fact that they're here at all. Dogs, he called them. Nothing but dogs.

"They're my present to you, for you," he says, backing away a few steps. "Use them."

The keys in my hand suddenly turn to ice in my grip, the freezing temperature making me jump and lose hold of them. They clatter to the floor, skating sideways, and I scurry to grab at them before it's too late. The tall one's hand has grabbed at them before I can get there, latching onto them and drawing them back into the cage with him.

He looks as surprised as I am as he falls back onto his haunches and fingers the steel in his hands, eyes narrowed, as if maybe this is the first chance at escape he's ever had. I don't know what to do, causing me to look at

Jack for help. He doesn't give any at all. He just stands there and waits for me to do something, a wry look on his face as if something is funny.

"What now?" I ask, turning back to face the tall one and resting my hands on the cage bars. The other two come forward, pacing a little behind the front one and making some noise that haunts the air with more visions of Selma. "Jack? What now?"

I feel entranced by the look of the three of them as the two scamper about behind the tall one, mesmerised by the sight of them acting like a pack of dogs. They don't even seem to move like humans anymore. They're lower, almost bent over as if ready to run on all fours. And the small one fidgets constantly, as if scratching himself and shaking all the time.

Crashing feet on the spiral break me of my trance, making me swing to look at the door again and wonder what to do. He'll be here soon, his hands grabbing at me to make me go back to a life I don't want. Jack said these men would help me, that I should use them. I don't see how, or why. They're just prisoners here, ones I'm sure will run for their freedom the moment they open this door.

"I don't want to go back with him," I muse, closing my eyes and resting my head on the bars. "I don't. I want to live again." The scampering about stops in front of me, their bare feet suddenly silent on the stale carpet beneath them. "I want a chance, you know?" Tears come from nowhere as I say those words—tears I've cried all too often as I remember my life as a teenager, the hope associated with that. "I just want him to leave me alone so I can live." The gun hangs heavy in my pocket as I roll my forehead on the bars, trying to dismiss the idea of killing him. It's not me to be like that, no matter how I want to end my life with him. I don't even know if I can. I'm so full of Selma's love I can't think of anything but life with Jack. "I need help, Selma. I'm not a killer. I don't know what to do."

The gate in my hands unexpectedly pushes open, making me jump back and scurry to the corner of the room. Shit. I brace against the wall, my arms covering myself as I tug the coat tighter in and stare at the tall one. He frowns at me, the twitch in his brow the most human thing I've seen from him so far as he stands tall. The other two hover in the gate, seemingly unable to walk through it as they sniff the air around them nervously.

"Jack?" He doesn't answer, just sits there still, his legs firm in front of him as he crosses his arms and watches on. "Jack? What do I do?"

The sudden burst of speed that comes from the tall one has me trying to climb the wall behind me, desperate to escape his potential hold on me. I go to scream, my mouth opening, and then remember Lewis and clamp my mouth closed as the man stops in front of me, barely an inch between us. He sniffs, nostrils flaring as he inhales close to my neck, then sniffs again as he moves his face around mine. My eyes squeeze shut, willing whatever is happening to stop so I can run, but nothing happens after that. Nothing at all in the minute or so I wait.

This could be the end of me, and perhaps it should be. Lewis could come in here and kill me for my misdemeanour. Or I could do it myself. Perhaps then Jack and Selma could be together, lose themselves in each other. She could take me over, change form with me somehow so this confusion could dissipate. That's what seems to happen when we're close. Maybe that's what this is all meant to be, where it's supposed to end up.

I smile at thought and reach into my coat pocket to close my grip around the gun again, relaxing. My eyes might still be pressed closed, but suddenly I'm far less confused about everything. Any form of death might be the right way forward. Mine. Lewis'. Either way, I wouldn't have to deal with him anymore, at least.

I'd be free then.

Free, Maddy. Home.

"Selma? Is this it?" I whisper, trying to avoid the smell of the tall one under my nose as I imagine them together, us together. It's as warming to me in this frigid room as it always is. As heart softening.

The heat blooms inside my chest, readying me for whatever's coming as I start opening my eyes and squeeze the metal in my grasp. Whatever it is, I want to see Jack as it happens. I want to watch him smile at me and welcome Selma home, see the love in his gaze. Everything has been about this moment, about them joining. And I can feel it so deeply entrenched inside me, as if I never had any other option but to succumb to it. Lewis dead or me dead. That's the way this works for them both. It's why I'm here, so I can let them be together again in some way.

Footsteps echo in the halls outside, making my gaze swing to the door rather than the man in front of me. I don't think I'm even that scared anymore as I wait for the door to burst open and draw the gun from my pocket. I'll either die here for Jack and Selma, or I'll shoot him myself when he enters the room. I doubt I've got the capacity to do the latter, even with Selma circulating my skin. I'm weak like that, fearful. Always have been. Maddy is as feeble in this scenario as she's always been, no matter how hard I've tried not to be. But I'm damned if I'm going back with him again, not after this realm that's shown me true love.

I'd rather die.

Fear begins to ride me again, anxiety rippling through my body as I wait and wonder what will happen when he sees me and Jack. Tears come from that thought alone, some latent thought of love for Lewis encroaching on me. It fills me with times gone by of my own, of the memories in Paris and the way he used to make me smile. Where did that man go? Why? I wish I had the answers as I raise the gun towards the door, barely able to point it for my shaking hands. It would give all of this some reason. It would give my life some reason before it ends or I become a murderer.

Free, Maddy.

"Oh god, help me." The plea wobbles out of me, and I'm unsure who I'm asking for help. I can't do this. I know I can't. The gun that felt so secure when Jack showed me how to use it feels so frightening in my hold now. I'm scared, trembling, the metal juddering about as I try to hold it straight at the door and pretend I'm in control of this. I'm not. I'm terrified of him. Always have been. And he's here now. I can hear him on the outside, hear his voice coming for me. "Please help."

The door crashes in before I get another chance at breath, Lewis' face immediately penetrating me as he storms a foot into the room. He stops and spins his angry glare to me, making me back to the wall again, then flicks it at the tall man still stood in front of me and around the room.

"The hell is this?" he snarls, scowling at the scene, as he fills the doorframe and bores those eyes into me again. I shake still, every ounce of fear I've ever had making me quake at the thought of what he'll do to me. I flick a half glance to Jack and find him stood this time, his scowl as hard as Lewis' as he returns the glare.

The gun in my hand vibrates still, now pointed at the back of the tall man's head. He's moved slightly, getting in my way, and all I can see is his back. It's layered with filth and grime, bits of blood dried into what's left of the shirt that once covered him.

"Come here, Mads. You're coming home," Lewis spits out, offering his hand to me.

Mads. Little Mads. Cute, easy going, forgiving Mads.

Still I shake and point the gun, unsure who I'm pointing it at anymore. I'm not going home with him, though. There is no home with Lewis. There is only pain and humiliation. Hatred and disgrace. The thought rouses my hand, the quiver in it diminishing slightly as I continue to point it towards the doorway.

"You burnt down my home," I mutter, watching him scowl again at my noncompliance. The room stays silent as I watch him, an eerie hush taking over as the other two men quietly scuttle towards the tall man. They hover by him, one of them crouched low as if ready to launch, just as a dog would. The vision puzzles me, but somehow reassures me regardless of its incongruity. It about blocks my view of Lewis completely, allowing me to feel safe behind these men even if they do look like zombies with their absent gazes and mutilated frames. "You killed Callie."

"Stop being a child, Mads. Come, now. Callie's fine. She's gone home. I talked to her. She couldn't get hold of you on your cell phone, told me you'd come to a meeting here." Did she? He must have threatened her to get that information. "I don't know what the fuck you mean about your stupid little house." I frown, trying to work out why he's lying, what he really wants. "And put the damn gun down. You need help. Look at you." I briefly glance down at myself, taking in my appearance. Naked apart from a fur coat, the front of it open as I stand here with a gun, showing off the hand prints of another man who's been inside me. "What the hell are you doing here?" And my feet are covered with mud from running with Jack, laughing, loving. It makes me smile and embrace this cold air, enjoying Selma's hold on my madness. I'm freer like this than I've ever been.

"I tried to get away, but you wouldn't let me, Lewis, would you?" I mumble to myself, the gun rising slightly as I peek through the shoulders of the three. Why wouldn't just let me go? Why? He scoffs at that, a sneer developing on that handsome face to reinforce my hatred of his being. That's what I remember from him—that half sneer, permanently etched in to demean me, belittle me.

"You should leave before it's too late, Lewis. Let me get on with my life free of you."

He takes a step forward, disdain heavy in his movement, his hand reaching for me. I glare in response, my back inching closer to Jack for more protection. It causes another frown from him, enough to stop his movement.

"I don't want to leave with you, Lewis. We're over. Finished. You're not hurting me again." He snarls and begins moving again, ready to push through the three men blocking him, and my hand raises of its own accord, ready to defend myself. "Stay back. I have all the help I need right here, Lewis. I'm warning you. I'll kill you before I let you take me away from this place."

I can feel the trigger on my finger, feel something making me want to pull at it. It's Selma. She's here inside me again, rallying me into killing without thought. I quiver, trying to fight the impulse, but he moves again and panics me into action. I jump back, trying to get out of his way, but knock into the wall in the scurry. The impact causes the gun to shoot into the room without true intention to harm, noise exploding in the confines.

Before I know what's happened, the tall man has leapt for him, sounds snarling through the room in his wake. Lewis turns and bolts, and the other two launch after him, too, all three of them in pursuit as howling suddenly erupts in the house. I run after them, no thought other than what's going to happen when they catch him. I didn't mean to shoot. I didn't. I just wanted to scare him off, make him leave me alone so I could be free.

The second I'm out the door, I see the small man turning the top of the spiral, his feet scampering around the corner, and I triple my pace in the hope that I'll get to them before they do permanent damage. The gun bashes against the wood work as I travel downwards, my own feet stuttering each step for fear of losing balance. Another howl sounds below, already a distance in front, like a pack of hounds chasing their kill. It's sickening to hear, making me bound onwards and keep turning, desperate to end this before it begins.

Too late. That's what I said. Before it's too late. Oh god. They heard that in me, didn't they? Jack said to use them. That they'd protect me. And that's what they're doing now. Protecting me. Killing the thing that threatens me.

"Jack!" I call back, still rounding corners and trying to take two steps at a time. "Jack, help."

I spin my head back, looking for him, but he's nowhere to be seen and I haven't got time. These men are going to kill Lewis, aren't they? They're maniacal. Probably mad, certainly that way inclined because of whatever Jack's been doing. I just need to catch up with them, tell them to stop. They can frighten Lewis off, make him too scared to come for me again, but he doesn't need to be dead. If Callie's alive then he just needs to go and leave me alone.

"Run, Lewis," I shout out, feet clambering around the curves.

I career around the bottom of the spiral, heading straight for the open main door at the end of the hall in the hope I can catch up with them, but by the time I reach the outside, it's black as the night, the fog of Selma already rolling in across the gravel drive and proving ghostly nightmares.

"Selma, I don't want this," I pant out, searching the blackness for them and listening for more volleys of howls. None come other than the faint sound of birds chattering somewhere and the eerie silence she always brings. I lift the gun again, ready to defend myself if needed but unsure what that means anymore. The dogs? Lewis? I'm not certain who should be chasing who anymore, or why any of this is happening. "He doesn't have to die, Selma. We can let him go. We'll be safe then."

You're nearly home, Maddy.

The fog becomes denser as I rush onto the drive, hindering any sight at all. I listen to the last of her echo as I plough through the thick, heavy haze, trying to remember my way into the woods that we were in earlier. I don't know what she means. This isn't my home. This is their home, their life and their love. I'm so confused and panicked that I turn towards the treehouse. Perhaps they've chased him in there. If not, there's always the headland or the bog. It's not somewhere anyone wants to go in this murk, but I guess when you're running for your life, fear of death pushing you onwards, and you don't know when you're running to, anywhere is good enough to escape to.

Sure footing underneath or not.

Chapter 19

Jack

They're running out there.

I can hear them.

I rub the ring in my pocket and then pull it out, ready to put it on the finger of my wife again. She's so close to me now. I can smell her here each time the fog looms over us, taste her in every kiss that Madeline delivers. It's a love that will not be halted by arrogant abusers and their whims. He will die out here, never to be found again. They will kill as they've been asked to do, protecting her at all costs, including their own life should that be necessary. They'll hunt him down for daring to touch her. That's what I trained them to do. It's their chance at repentance, their offer of contrition to her.

All those months of me training them. Teaching them. All those times I beat them as they looked into her picture, warning them of storms that followed when they disobeyed me, and this is what it was for. I thought it just my vengeance at the time. Thought it was for self punishment perhaps. But it has been far from that, far from my own wallowing and self-repugnance. It has been so Madeline Cavannagh could get her freedom, so Selma could help them both come home.

My fingers drop the ring on the hall table as I head out into the darkness and murk my wife so easily delivers, knowing that by the time we return I'll be able to lodge it back where it belongs. She'll wear it again then, have it wrapped around her skin with nothing more to get in our way.

I smile as I wander deeper into the swirl of obscurity dancing around my legs, watching as it claws at me and ripples through my soul. It's her again, stirring the ground around us all, showing herself in the only way she can since they sliced the heart out of her and left her for dead.

Not for much longer, though.

"It's nearly over, baby," I mutter, walking towards the howls that keep coming in the distance. They have the same tone as they do when the chase is nearing conclusion, the same morbid desperation to kill revving them up to rip flesh from limb and eat their prize. It's another thing that makes me smile into the night, gazing at the tall trees that shroud this old house with their cover. "You happy now?"

She doesn't answer, but warmth sweeps around my legs, enthusing me with the thought that she's nearly here with me. I don't know what will happen to Madeline. Perhaps she'll stay in some form, part locked in this spectral mirage we've all made happen. Or maybe she'll disappear, never to return and hinder my view of Selma again. I don't fucking care in reality. My wife is nearly home. She's almost with me. And our son will come with time, his endless chatter making me feel like a father again.

The thought has me looking back at the car, wondering what I should do with it. It should be removed so that no one can find out he was here. Perhaps old Bob can organise that when this is done, find a way of drowning it in the bog. It's deep on the other side of the brook, deep enough to disappear into. Everything disappears in there.

For once I haven't brought the zapper with me. There's nothing to punish them for anymore. No reason for me to continue with my retaliation now that she's coming back. It doesn't matter anymore. They can go after this, or die out here in the wild. Perhaps they'll just guard this place from now on, not knowing how to return to reality now I've stolen that option from them. They can hunt these grounds, cry their pained howls into the night as we sleep safe in the knowledge that nothing will ever happen to break us apart again. They're barely human now anyway. That's been crushed out of them. All they have left are the base instincts to hunt and survive, the latter of which I've only just provided.

The thought makes me chuckle to myself as I keep walking, crossing though the first brook to wander towards the headland. That's where they are. I can hear their continued cries from here, the smaller one shrieking to keep up. Fucking useless dog. He always was the lacking one. It wouldn't surprise me if he didn't even touch my wife while the other two took their fun. His dick certainly isn't big enough to fuck anything successfully.

"JACK?"

Madeline's loud voice rebounds at me from somewhere, a slight frenzy about it. I peer through the gloom, hastening my pace from its relaxed amble. She shouldn't be in any danger out here now, but knowing her she'll have fallen feet first into the bog all of her own accord. That image makes me chortle quietly, the memory of her tumbling onto me that first time coming back to remind me where this all started.

"Jack, help me."

Help her? I smile and then frown in thought. There's nothing left for me to help her with. My dogs are doing that now. The only thing I need to ensure is that this man doesn't take her from the ground beneath our feet, that she stays on it so she can be fused into my wife somehow.

I quicken my pace regardless, brushing the scrub away as I turn through the thicket of brambles to get to her voice. Apart from that it's so quiet out here, no sound other than the occasional call of dogs in pursuit, their disposition so familiar to me regardless of what they're in pursuit of. Some would say it's miserable and melancholy out here, this permanent nightfall obliterating what should be spring days, but to me it's nothing but light and effervescence irrespective of the darkness that surrounds us all.

It's the return of those I love. A re-birth.

Spring will come tomorrow.

A small field lies between us, the spread of it heightening the distance it'll take to get my wife back to me. It might happen by the time I've trudged these last few metres. She might take over completely when the sound of the chase concludes. I wonder about the sound that will come or the vision that might occur as I open a small gate and close it quietly. Will light explode, some spectral reincarnation making her appear within Madeline's form? Or will the fog just dissipate, receding into Madeline's body to form that darker hair I long for.

I snort, amused with my interpretation of ghostly ramblings. Perhaps none of that will happen. Perhaps she'll just look at me differently and I'll see nothing but Selma as I gaze at azure eyes and remember our life together.

The tall hedgerow breaks open onto the headland as my feet choose my route through the last of the bog, and then I turn to the sound of dog one yelping enthusiastically. It's nearly time. He's almost there like the good damned dog he is. I smile again and follow the noise, hurrying to ensure I'm there this time. I want this vision, want to hold it inside so I can consider my job done for a wife and child I didn't protect. I need it. This whole fucking thing is as much a penitence for me as it is for them now. I want to see her acknowledge what I've done for them, tell me I was right to do it. It's all I have to give them, all these bloody hands could do to rectify my mistake.

"We need him dead, don't' we?" I whisper quietly, searching the area and hoping for a glimpse of her. "Clever Selma. Is that how it works? He dies and then you come back?"

Nothing but fog still, but I can feel her all the same as I turn towards the growing agitation of dogs in full cry, listening and hurrying my pace again. She climbs over me, ready to get to the kill, too, wrapping me in more thoughts of love and pulling me forward into the cacophony of sound that increases with each pace forward. They're so close to him, so close I can smell their heated scent coming from somewhere up front as I keep powering through the mud to reach them in time.

I round the last of the headland, and the sight of Madeline scrambling over the rocky ground catches me off guard. She notices me, her eyes frantic as she chases onwards, naked legs propelling her faster no matter the distance she's already run. I look to see what she's following, and find the feet of the small one half a field in front of her scurrying through the opaque ground below. She forges over to the left bank of tall trees, her fur coat still billowing out behind her as she goes as if pointing out where her husband is. Good, he's heading back to the bog. He can die in there, his bones swallowed down so that no one finds the evidence.

I swing that way, crossing the undulations of ploughed ground to punish my body with more sweat and vigour. This is all I have to give any of them. This power that I still hold ensures someone will die here. I have to get there and see this, see her transformation. The husband, the dogs, all of them can rot beneath this ground if I get to have my family back again because of it. I need them home now. I need to feel them all beneath my skin and let this guilt go.

"Stop them, Jack," she shouts, her breath panted as she turns and powers on again to try to get in front of me. "Please."

I'm not stopping a damn thing, and neither is she.

Fury pushes my limbs faster at the thought, and I crash through the brook again as I duck under the low hanging branches. Stop this? I'm so incensed by the thought that I turn at her instead, remembering the gun in her pocket, and jump the old stone boundaries to cut through the small wood to get to her. She's not stopping anything. Selma is nearly here now. All these dogs need to do is kill the one thing that threatens her return. Madeline will be locked here then. She'll know the point of all this, understand like I do.

The sound of gun fire from my left infuriates me further, and the squeal of a pained yelp following the noise makes me desperate to get to her before she kills my hopes.

"Madeline, stop shooting," I yell, crashing through more rough brambles.

She doesn't, and as I break out into open ground, the rapid fire of another two shots followed by the vision of her managing to make ground on the last dog makes me charge at her.

Her eyes widen as I storm towards her, fingers fumbling over the barrel as she tries to keep running and aim. His feet scuttle through the undergrowth, branches swinging back in her face as I strengthen everything I've got to get to her and cut across the outskirts of the bog.

"I've got to stop them. I've got to end this," she calls, her body disappearing behind the bank of trees.

My feet quicken until I'm within meters of her, mud sluicing the dirt she's already run through, and I grab out at her. She damn well swerves before I have a chance to get her in my hold. I snatch out at a trunk, levering myself over the boulders that she's managed to veer off around, and then scramble though the small brook passing along the bog's edge. She bolts right, jumping to gain distance and refusing to look at me as I keep calling her name.

"Stop, Madeline."

She doesn't stop. She runs with renewed vigour, somehow increasing her pace and steeling her resolve to help the bastard in front of us.

The next shot makes me sneer and reach for her swinging coat regardless of the distance between us, desperate to stop her before she gets to the lead dog. He's going mad with his howls, and the sounds of terror splay the darkness as I begin to hear the abuser pleading for his life up ahead somewhere. He cries out, pain evident in his tone, and then he begins begging as uselessly as he's probably lived. Snivelling and shouting. Whinging. Whining.

I snort and let the pained sounds of death mix with my images of Selma's prone body. It slows my pace as I blank out what's around us, choosing to see the bloody form of my wife rather than this insidious little hunt that's continued. Good dogs. They've paid their dues, given their all so our lives can entwine again.

My feet walk on, blind to where they're heading until all becomes still again. There's no sound at all for me, just the ground beneath me ghosting by gently, occasionally gifting whispers of Selma's voice. I've no interest in catching Madeline anymore. It's done. Finished. Over. She can find what's offered by her protectors and then we'll find our path together. Selma will show us. But first they can both see the chaos these dogs can cause. Let them see what they did to her on that fateful night.

Words whisper to me again, talking of harmony and love, passion and forgiveness. I can almost see her travelling through the mist to get to Madeline, sense her leaving the part of me she clung to through this chase. She looks beautiful as she walks slowly, her white dress layering out behind her and brightening this murky land we've run over.

I look to where Madeline was. Still she crashes onwards, and I watch her hurtle silently through the wooded space as if she's run it a thousand times before, intent on stopping what's already happened. She has. She's had me chase her through it. Walked it with me side by side, holding hands. We've even made love just over there on the far bank of headland, watched the moon rise above our bodies as we did.

She's known this space around us for longer than I have. *Selma.*

Charlotte E Hart

THE SPIRAL

Chapter 20

Madeline

I can't feel the cold that surrounds us as I keep pushing through the mud beneath my feet. I know it's here. It's been with me all the time, making me run faster and faster to get to them before they kill him. I'm not even sure why I don't want him to die. I should. I should want my revenge for him burning my home down like I did the morning after it happened. And I should want him dead for all those years of bruises, if nothing else to make sure it doesn't happen to anyone else, certainly not me again, but it's just not in me to kill. It's not who Maddy is inside me. And I want her back again so much. I want to feel her happiness, enjoy it. I want those moments with Jack, like Selma has. I want to find them with someone.

Charlotte E Hart

THE SPIRAL

Jack seems to have disappeared again. I check left and right, crashing through the next obstacle that this fog obscures but still not finding a trace of him anywhere. He must know this ground so well. I guess he might already be where they are because the noise they were making has petered out to near silence. I could focus on something when I heard Lewis' sickening shouting, find a path through all this to get to him, but there's nothing but calm and mist left.

My knee buckles as I slam into a boulder, left arm trying to push me over the damn thing as I carry on and peer into the gloom. There's nothing there, no sound to cling on to or run towards. I can't even feel Selma like I did earlier. She guided me, all the time trying to talk me out of this. I was arguing with myself as I ran, part of me wanting to let all this play out as she wanted and the other part desperate to reach Lewis before it ended. The gun I'm holding shot as I watched one of them baying into the night, animalistic as he kept charging after the others, and then it shot again. I'm not even sure who pulled the trigger, or who it was really aimed at, but those men were repulsive to watch, hideous, like they'd been turned into something they shouldn't be somehow.

Tears come at that thought, unsure whether they're mine or Selma's as I keep wondering about right and wrong, but my feet don't slow. They tear on through the brush, as if they don't belong to me, as if they're being forged forward by her energy inside. I, *we*, need to get there whatever the outcome. Some part of me is elated at the thought of death—any death—the other nauseated.

Freedom seems to come at a cost here.

Eventually I slow down, trying to listen closer in the hope of a sound to lead me in, but it's futile, regardless of my pace. There's nothing left for me to follow. Not even the sound of the men chasing him now. They were triumphant for a few moments with bays and cries of jubilation. I heard that, felt it in my guts as a gruesome image washed across me. There was so much blood, all of it slashed and gashed across Lewis' body as he lay in the bog. I shook it off, not allowing it to invade my mind, and kept racing to this spot I'm now in, but I know it's real. I can feel that now I've stopped trying to reach him.

It doesn't matter that flowers should grow beneath my feet in this tranquil glade. Or that we're not far from the treehouse Jack brought me to, the place filled with love and memories of Lenon. Those images I saw—the ones that came as the howling noise subsided around me, leaving me alone in this barren clearing of gloom—I'm going to find them soon. I'm going to find Lewis dead. Mauled.

The bog squelches as I edge around some rocky land, leaning on trees to hold me firm against the ground that wants to swallow me down. Anxiety comes racing though my skin, forcing the stability I seemed to hold while running to disappear and wrap me in fear. It's so dark, so cold and dark and full of images that creep into parts of me I haven't wanted to listen to. Jack is all I've seen lately. Jack and feelings of love and pleasure, irrespective of whether they're my thoughts or not.

Maybe I thought they were mine. Maybe I thought I could make this my new home, live with him and blend into her somehow, make us all one, but then Lewis came and showed me my real life beyond these grounds. I'm not her, am I? And this feeling crawling through me, the one that warns of something I'm not in control of, it makes me snatch glances nervously, hoping for something to lift me away from what's happened.

A shriek of sound comes from above me, making me duck and scramble through the undergrowth, looking upwards sharply. The crow's there, the one who gave me her ring. He flaps and claws across the branches, opening his wings and batting them against the branches, feathers falling from them as he jumps and thrashes.

Maddy.

Tears flare up in my eyes as her voice permeates the dense void of emptiness, her fog slithering over the course of my skin. It forces trembles and quivers to come with her, a warmth beginning to creep around my bare feet as I watch it swirl and swell. I don't know what she wants with me anymore, though. I don't understand what this is all for.

"What do you want, Selma?" I mumble, sidestepping another black pool of muddy ground beneath me, still hoping to find Lewis. "I don't understand."

The crow squawks again and flies low across my head, his wing glancing my hair and turning me to look towards his path. He lands on a piece of stone in the middle of the fog, continuing to caw and hop around on it, as if trying to show me something. I stare at him, holding onto the tree and gauging his route as the fog clears slightly. That's the bog. I know that much. I can tell by the way even the slightest deviation from these trees has me sinking, oily murk blackening my toes further.

Oh god, where's Jack? I can't go in there without him. He makes this normal somehow, gives me something to brace against when she comes.

"Jack?" Nothing comes back. "JACK?" I call out, louder and with a sense of urgency I hope he can hear.

I need his hand to hold onto, his skin to scrape at so I can feel something real in this. He's a part of all this with me. I want his stoic gaze, his smile when he sees her in me. It's the only way I can face it, be part of it. And I'm scared, I am. I'm alone out here with her and I can feel the nerves making me want to back track, find a route away from what she's about to show me.

The crow screeches again, the kafuffle of his inky wings making me gaze at him as he flaps and fidgets around the mist below his talons. My own toes curl against the root of the tree, heels digging in to the soil as I try to do what my body's screaming at me to do. I should run, back away and get to a car, or the road, anything so that I don't have to see Lewis' mutilated frame. I've seen it already, felt it in me as she pushed her visions through my mind.

Maddy.

My hands grab my shaking head, covering my ears as her voice comes again to haunt her way through whatever resolve I'm trying to achieve. No, I don't need to see this. I'll go, find my way back to the house. Maybe the old man will have my car fixed now and I can leave.

My feet scrunch deep into the sludge, pushing away from her suggestion as I turn and try to move back the way I came. I'm free now, aren't I? Free to make my own choices. Lewis is dead. These men have made that happen. They took away my threat, gave me a chance to live my life again for whatever purpose I see fit. I still don't know why, or why Jack had them in that cage other than what he told me, but it's not a part of him I want to know. I'll go and get on with that life I was after before all this happened.

Live free of worry.

A stun of freezing air comes at me suddenly, blasting a ray of light in my face and nearly knocking me off my feet. I stumble back, dazed and confused, as the ground flitters past my hands, wetness glancing off my fingertips before I reach for a large trunk to cling onto again.

"Madeline?" I spin to the sound of him, my body clawing onto all fours, desperate to see his face as I grip the tree.

"Jack? Where are you?"

"Over here."

I scramble to my feet, not daring to let go of the only support I have against her until he gets to me, and peer into the dankness to the right of me. I can't see anything other than the path clear of fog towards the crow. It's still as murky and blurred as it's always been.

"I can't move, Jack. She won't let me come to you." He chuckles, a cheery tone coming from him as I stare towards is the sound of his voice.

"Yes, you can. You can go wherever you want now, baby." Figures appear in the gloom, three of them, all lurched over slightly as they creep through the opaque smear. "Good dogs," Jack says from somewhere. "Good dogs."

I gasp, unsure what they're coming towards me for. Nerves pool again as I watch them getting closer, my own fear driving me into the tree I'm holding onto as I wonder if I can climb it. They're killers, these three. I know I haven't seen it with my own eyes, but I know they've done it. I saw it in my mind, watched it happen. They killed Selma and Lenon, and now they've killed Lewis. It's madness. All of it.

Maddy

The fog starts moving as I watch them come at me, the ebb of it churning over the ground they come through, and then pain explodes in my head. It's excruciating, enough that I grab at the side of my scalp trying to get it out of me. My knees crumple beneath me, shins knocking heavily against the ground as I tumble over and feel the mud sluice my lips. I try to gasp in breaths, but the pain intensifies with every pull. Visons erupt through the sensation—the three men, their faces blending together. Teeth and snarls, sinister laughter, the echo of screams in my mind. They're raping her, hitting her. Oh god, they're hurting her so much. The three of them holding her down, one of them smothering her mouth as she tries to screech Jack's name.

It replays over and over, to the point where I scream with her at the feel of it happening. She's so much like me. Her eyes, her face as it contorts in fear, the same way mine must have done every time Lewis held me down. And Lenon's body comes next, the sight of him asleep in his bed, soft eyes fluttering against the comforter he's wrapped in.

My head shakes again, knowing what's coming. I don't want to see it. I can't. I scrabble at the ground beneath me, trying to crawl away from the image she's making me see, but one of them comes into view in my mind, the tall one, followed by the other two dragging Selma with them. I prise my eyes open in hope, heaving my body to move away from them towards the clearing in the fog, but I'm knocked off my knees the moment a shot sounds.

My throat lurches, the blood splattering in my mind making bile race through me. I roll to my side, gasping in breaths as I watch Lenon's body convulse under the bullet, his tiny chest broken open. A sadness sweeps through me that's so profound the tears of fear that were coming halt me in my tracks, knees coming up to my chest for comfort against the pain. A child. Lenon, their son. *My* son. I can feel him inside me, feel his body moving as he grew. I can see him running, laughing. See Jack with him out here in the sunlight as they played.

"I'm so sorry," I whisper, unable to stop the words as I cradle my knees in and rock back and forth, tears spilling from me.

Kill them for me, Maddy. Let me kill them.

I do nothing more than keep reliving the visions in my mind, locked in them as I stare at his bedding and watch the blood drip down the white sheets to the floor. That's all I've got as I lie here, my body curling in on itself, lips smothered in mud. It's sickening, vile. I feel brutalised and exposed, my skin harbouring her pain as she keeps feeding me with more and more nauseating images, one after another. And the noise—oh god the noise keeps coming. Screams and wails, begging, the sound of her head hitting the floor, the throb of it in my own head more vibrant than any pain I've ever felt.

Kill them.

I'm barely breathing as I feel her make me move. She slides inside me, her fingers pushing me up from my position and making me rip the coat away from my skin. I'm not in control of my own movement anymore. I'm still hugging my knees, crying into the mud, unable to do a thing. It's all her. Her fingers tear at the fur on me, her thoughts propelling me to the pocket, my hands pulling the gun back out into the open.

"Selma, please," I slur, watching as my hand grips the metal regardless of my hatred of the thought. I only used it try to scare them off, to stop them. "I don't want..."

My head whips up, eyes targeting the three of them as they close in on the ground she's pushing me towards. They look humble as they move, reverent even, all of them with their eyes lowered as they stalk the lying mist slowly. "Please don't make me do this."

A shrill laughter follows, wicked and full of malicious intent as it echoes the gloom we're all in. I can't stop it resonating somewhere inside me, filling me with her cruelty and pain. She's so much stronger than me here, her power still flowing from her and flooding me with those images over and over again.

My guts coil, unable to stop the next wave of nausea as a flash of the tall one I'm watching comes crashing through my mind, his teeth biting into my neck as he pushes inside me and laughs.

"Get up, baby." *Jack.*

I peer into the sound, looking for him, and see his face coming through the fog behind these three. He looks so handsome, his face a picture of refined splendour in the middle of this carnage. There's nothing but his eyes for a moment, piercing me as he continues towards me. He seems to float through the space, his stride longer than theirs as his hands caress the swirling mist around him. They scamper at his feet, one of them banking right over to the stone the crow's on, the others following suit.

"Jack, I..."

He smiles, his hand reaching for me as he finally arrives at my side. I stare up at him, flicking my thoughts between his hand and the inevitably of what will happen if I do stand. I'll kill then; I know I will. I'll lift this gun and hold it out in front of me, pulling the trigger three times, regardless of whether or not I want to. These men will die because of me.

"I'm not her."

"Yes, you are. Let her come home," he replies, the softness in his voice mimicking the same love he has when he's inside of me.

He grasps onto my fingers, and a warm strength surges through me instantly lighting up all of this darkness. It's filled with honour and loyalty, love ebbing between us and causing all of Selma's venom to disintegrate. We hover here, me looking up at him as he continues smiling, him peering into recesses that don't belong to me.

"You know what to do, Madeline."

Tears come at the thought. Not because I'm scared of doing it, but because I'll lose me when I do. I'll be someone else, someone I never wanted to be. I don't maim and kill. I don't bruise or harm. I love. I love and I hope. That's what I am to me. I'm full of care and dreams, weaknesses too. And if I do this for them, if I let them have their way, I'll become a monster, no better than Lewis, or the animals I've just witnessed in my mind, the same ones standing here waiting for their end now.

Please, Maddy.

My knees push me without consent, his fingers pulling me into him the moment he's able. His lips come so quickly I barely notice the distance that's passed before I'm deep in his mind again, reliving images of them together. Their lives, their heat, and their smiles in this home she made for them, Lenon running around their ankles as he sings. And the sunshine pours down on them in here, darkness and fog obliterated as I watch them laughing and holding hands, his tongue reminding me of the way he loved her. So warm. So free of torment and pain. It's too much to stop, too much for me to deny or resist.

I back away before I lose the courage, knowing I have to do this, and lift my hand to point it towards the crow that still caws and scratches the stone he's on. I want them free. I do. And if that means I have to change, I will. I would rather that than see them in a moment's more pain because of their loss of each other.

The men cower, their bodies alert to the threat I'm aiming at them, but they know it's coming as they linger in the fog behind the crow. We all do. It's unavoidable now, something she's always wanted from me. Perhaps that's what this has all been for—these men killing my threat, me removing Jack and Selma's from them, too. I don't really know, but this feels right now that I've bathed in that sun with them again. Perhaps then we can all carry on, finding our way together.

Two shots come quicker than I expect from myself. No hesitation. No thought of harming or maiming involved. Just death.

The first one drops instantly, the second holding his arms out ready for the impact before I've shot, and the third, the tall one, he bows into the mist as he kneels and looks straight at me waiting for his turn. It's poetic in some ways, making me stare at the falling bodies as they disappear into the fog beneath them and hover over the trigger some more. She's here in me. I can feel her finger holding mine, guiding me, as if this is the one thing she needs to be free.

"What happens now?" I whisper out, allowing her to take the last shot from me.

Because this is it, isn't it? It'll be over when I've done this. What will come after, I don't know. Perhaps I'll die too in some way, be lost in them and unable to find a way home of my own. I'm here, naked and at their whims, held hostage in a ghost story that has no end. I look across at Jack, hoping beyond all hope that maybe I can keep a part of him just for me, that maybe if she lets me I can be part of them so I won't lose what they've given me. Such beauty and care, their world filled with a happiness I've only just begun to comprehend.

He smiles again and moves a step backwards, slowly receding into the fog as if he's never been here at all. My left arm reaches for him, but my head's whipped back to my target, Selma owning the last shred of me left as the trigger pulls.

Home.

Chapter 21

Jack

They're dead.

The issue troubles me as I wander backwards, towing the fog with me and watching as she stands above them. It irks me, as if my protégées have been taken from me without consent. I frown at the vision, a melancholy etching my bones that makes no sense. I should be elated, touched by her offering in this final stand, but I'm not. I feel deadened, as if the weight of loss has become unbearably heavy rather than the light I assumed would come.

And it's cold. Stone fucking cold. Selma's warmth around my legs is suddenly gone, her panted breath at my shoulder fragmented back into the night around us.

"Where are you, baby?" I ask, still looking at Madeline.

No glow or mystic apparition comes to eclipse the gloom. It hovers around the space still, Madeline slowly beginning to move through it towards the stone. She halts a step or two, looking around her as if searching for something, her lips moving. I can't hear her, though. There's no sound as she starts moving again, feet slowly trudging to the place they all lie, lifeless. There's nothing but silence, not even the sound of the sludge beneath her.

The crow jumps and clacks his wings, lifting from the stone and flying into the air as she approaches him, beady eyes focused on her. I watch him, wondering where the hell he's come from as he squawks at her. She looks sullenly at the stone, her colour turning pallid as she finally sees what she's achieved with her gun. I sneer at the thought, wrenching at memories of Selma's corpse again to prolong my disenchantment, her equally violated frame on show when I found it.

I scan the area and blow out a frustrated breath, looking for signs of my wife other than this fog, but there's nothing here. I thought she'd be here now, thought she'd come and show me what this has all meant, but it's just Madeline and the stone she eventually puts her hand on. Nothing to finish this. No miracle of my wife coming home. Just a woman who looks like her again.

Misery crawls over me, a deep seated and clawing desolation. It binds my guts with a sickness, swathes of it rising through me as I gaze at the woman who holds my wife inside her. I should have shot myself when I had the chance. I should have pulled that trigger, let the bullet kill me. I could have made my own way back to Selma and Lenon then. Instead, I've waited for this to end, only to be dissatisfied with the fucking result. I'm alone still, regardless of all that she's done. Desolate.

Even my damned dogs are dead. And for what? Nothing.

"Jack?"

Selma.

I turn slowly at the sound of her voice, not convinced of my own rationality, and look back into the trees behind me. She's there, her body encased in nothing but white silk that drifts out in a light breeze, framed by the woodland she adored. I smile at that and gaze, unsure if she's real or still a ghost, but at least she's here again. Mad or not I don't care.

"Are you real now?" I ask, ready to turn back for Madeline if she's not. Perhaps I could go reach for that gun, use it and finish this off the way I should have done.

The thought makes me wander towards Selma, hoping she might have something more than ghosts and blurred edges to bring to me before I kill myself for her. I will if I have to, happily. I'll put it in my mouth and watch her, let her take me through to wherever she is because I can't go on anymore. Not now. There isn't any point without my dogs to keep hurting.

She seems so still this time. No floating, no drifts of imaginary lines. I peer closer, observing her against the tree she softly fondles. She's sharper now, crisp, like she's part of reality rather than the cloudiness of feeling and sensation we had before. And the smile that breaches her lips as I watch causes a rush of heat to come at me, readying me for whatever she wants.

"You're home, Jack."

Me? I snort and glance back in the direction of the house, not knowing what she means as I notice Madeline lower herself to the floor, a choked sob retching her throat as her hand scrubs the stonework. I've always been here. Always been here harbouring these thugs, turning them into their worst nightmares, waiting for my next chance at revenge and using my memories to inflict retribution for her. She's the one who's come home. Finally.

Madeline hunches down to her knees, her fingers running over something beneath the fog. She just stares, a flitter of tears coming down her cheeks at whatever she's found. I smile at that, too, knowing she'll be free regardless of whatever atrocities she's looking at now. The abuser is no more. She'll move on with her life without him to threaten her existence, whether here or not, but that sadness etches back into me as I watch on, some part of me remorseful at the thought of not dancing with her again now my wife is back, not feeling her between us.

"We did it, Jack," Selma says.

I'm not sure what we did, but I smirk as I keep watching Madeline and wait for Selma to come to me, wrap her skin around me again. She does after a minute or two, her hand slotting so easily into mine just as it always did. I squeeze at it, feeling the flesh of her in my hold, and pull her into my back so we can watch together, know what we've done and remember this moment. She links her arms around me and rests her chin on my shoulder, her scent coming so quickly it nearly cripples any sentiment for Madeline I might have sheltered inside.

"You after a fucking?" I ask, remembering the first time I saw her in that dead-end town, her eyes watching me like a hawk as I entered the bar. She just sat in the corner, her nose in her book as a ruck of us walked in drunk. She giggles softly and cuddles tighter in, filling me with more memories of our son and the way they laughed with each other, clung on. "Will he come home, too?"

"Soon, Jack," she says, brushing her lips over my neck. The feel of them sends shivers over me, riling my dick up into thinking about anything but our son, but she loosens her grip and walks past me before I get the chance to think anymore. I frown and follow her, gazing at the way her bare feet leave no impressions in the wet ground beneath. "We need Maddy home for that. In love."

Both the statement and the lack of prints confuse me as I gaze over her frame again, watching the way it glides and glitters against the slow light that's beginning to return around us. She's so beautiful I almost don't care, part of me wanting nothing more than to touch her again and feel the reality of her against me, but if she's real there should be footprints, just like mine. There should be a presence of her against this earth, a weight in her balance as she lands on it.

"We just have to be patient, Jack." I don't know what that means as I keep following her, waiting for her to give me more answers to the thousand questions I have. "She really does look like me," she says, standing feet from Madeline and casting her hand out to the right.

The fog starts clearing with her movement, ribbons of it reaching out onto the horizon before my eyes, creating pathways. I frown and survey its touch across the headland, watching as the flow of it bobs and dances, clearing further, wondering how she's still doing it if she's really here.

"Selma?"

"Mmm."

I wave my hand to her, reaching for the back of her dress to ensure she's real, but then notice the body Madeline's leaning over for the first time. The abuser lies there, his body clear of my dog's mutilation, just three bullet holes in his chest, blood seeping from them. I scowl and look for my dogs, needing to see them for clarification. They're nowhere to be seen. There's just his lifeless body becoming encased in mud and soil, the ground around them both coated with Selma's mist as it bubbles below them.

Madeline's crying as she clings to him, her naked frame shuddering in the dank air around us. Rivers of tears pour down her face as she mouths words, screams them in fact, as I gaze on, but still I hear nothing other than Selma's soft breaths. I stand closer to them, still scanning for my dogs and wondering where they are.

"I can't hear her," I mutter, scowling. "Why can't I hear her?"

I swing my eyes to the crow, wondering why I can't hear him either anymore. He jumps and flaps silently, pecking the stone, and then suddenly lifts as Selma throws her hands upwards and laughs. I watch as he flies higher, wings stretching up towards the sky with each laugh she delivers.

"Because you're home, Jack. You're here now, finally with me."

I still don't understand, but the words make me look back at Madeline, questioning where *here* actually is. Her here, or my here? Here has become a jumble of light and dark lately. Fog and daylight, warmth and freeze. Perhaps here isn't even here anymore. Perhaps it's somewhere else, somewhere we haven't all found yet. "You wouldn't let go, would you? My tenacious husband. Never one to be beaten. All of this to get you home."

I chuckle at the sound of her laughter, unsure what the fuck to think, but the ground seems to weaken as she carries on laughing, bubbles of slathered soil inching along Madeline's legs. She barely notices in her misguided grief, too absorbed in whatever pain she's feeling to see what's happening in the ground she rests on. Stupid girl. She'll sink here if she doesn't move. She'll die as she wails incoherently over something that deserves nothing but hatred from her.

I barge around the tall stone lying between us, ready to lift her from the ground before she gets sucked under the bog. She doesn't falter one bit as I get in her sights. She just lays her head on his chest and weeps more, bestowing some chant from her lips that I still can't damn well hear.

"Madeline, get up." Nothing, no movement other than continued heaves of her back as she sobs out absurd anguish, one hand still scratching the stone. "Madeline?"

She doesn't flinch at my forthright tone. There's nothing but Selma's laughter carrying on, her dress fluttering in my eye-line as I try to get Madeline to move. And where the fuck are the gashes and gnarls my dogs would have left on this body she cries for? Where?

I stand again, irritated at my sudden confusion. Why are there shots in his body at all? She didn't shoot him; she shot my dogs so Selma could come home. I watched it happening in front of me, saw her fire the gun at them and walk over, triumphant in a job well done. She was so damn fierce, Selma's face haunting her own as she took those steps.

"I don't understand," I spit out, annoyed at whatever the hell this is. "Selma, make her get up." The bog slathers again, making me more anxious of the ground that begins sucking the body she's resting on downwards. "It'll swallow them both. Why won't she get up?"

She only smiles at me and begins walking backwards away from the situation, a peaceful look on her brow as she reaches out a hand and beckons me back to her.

"Don't worry, Jack. It's not our concern anymore," she whispers, mist starting to form around her again. I stare, bemused at what the fuck she's playing at. Madeline will die here if I leave her. She won't make it out of this bog. The fact that Selma's so cold towards her turns my stomach, making me question the bitch I know she can be. "Come on, Jack. We've got some catching up to do." She winks, her hands pulling her dress higher as she continues backwards.

"The hell is wrong with you?" I spit, circling in front of Madeline and reaching down to drag her from the bog if need be. "Madeline, get up. The bog. Hold onto me."

"He's coming, Jack. Leave her now. You're mine. Come remind me what I've been missing."

I growl at her, aroused in a flat fucking second and yet unable to leave Madeline alone here to die. She'll get her fucking. She'll get it and moan my damned name for days because of it, but not until I've got the woman who made this possible away from her own demise. She deserves more from me, more from us. Life is what she deserves.

A life free of concern.

"Mrs. Blisedy?" The words come from behind me somewhere. I swing round, searching the ground for the voice as it climbs the headland behind me. It's distant, the tone of it muffled by the bank hiding us. I stare into the distance, waiting for a sight of whoever it is on my land. No one should be here other than Bob. It's not Bob, and the thought of someone seeing her naked pisses me off, some latent part of me clinging to the memory of touching her even though Selma stands ten feet from where I am. "Madeline Blisedy, are you up here?"

Chapter 22

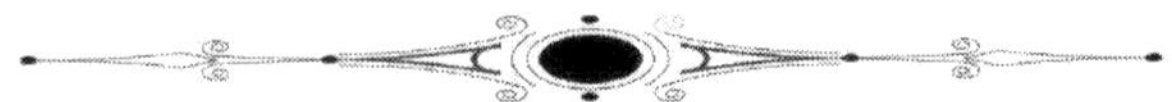

Madeline

I can't breathe, don't want to. I've lain here for so long, nothing but tears coming to choke whatever breath I had left when I saw him, that I've run out of air to pull in. He's dead. Here beneath my body. Killed by my hand, the bullet holes trickling out the blood I'm lying in. I don't know how, and no matter how much I've screamed out her name, or screamed out Jack's name, no one's come to help. I'm alone with him on this ground.

Guilt racks through me with every passing second. It courses through every fibre I've got, filling me with dread and torment as I try to will him back to life under my hands. He might have been a monster, might even have been the man who abused me to the point of near death, but he didn't have to die.

Charlotte E Hart

THE SPIRAL

He didn't have to die.

"Why?" mumbles out of me. "WHY?"

I don't even understand what happened. Selma wanted the men dead. She made me do it somehow, made me stand and point that gun at them. I felt her inside me, twisting my hand, forcing me into it because of her pain. And I did it for her. I did. I looked at all three of them, looked at the fear wide in their feral eyes, and pulled the trigger anyway.

Bang, bang, bang.

She said she wanted to be free of them, that she wanted to kill them. I didn't even flinch, somehow strengthened by her push behind me and the chill from her touch, but not this. I didn't shoot Lewis. I didn't. Oh god please tell me I didn't. Someone tell me this isn't real.

My fingers rough the stone in my grasp, as if it's the only thing that's grounding me. He's still warm beneath me, and I can almost feel his chest rising and falling if I close my eyes tightly enough, hear his heart thundering away. *Bang, bang, bang.* The noise keeps rumbling through me, shot after shot, the sound of their bodies hitting the ground as they fell coming, too. It's never-ending, filling me with hatred for myself, hatred for her, and even hatred for a man I thought I loved in some way—Jack.

Charlotte E Hart

THE SPIRAL

What was the point if they're not here with me now? Why? Why make me do all this if only to leave me alone and lost again.

A distant sound comes at me from somewhere in my mind. I let it wash through me, not caring for anything but lying here some more, trying to find some explanation for my actions. There's nothing, though, no matter how long I lie here. I killed my husband, the smoking gun still on the ground beside me showing the truth for all to see. It makes me curl in on myself, coiling tighter to shield myself against anything in the tangible world they've plunged me back towards.

"Madeline?"

My eyes crack open slightly, the sound of a man's voice taunting me with that real life. I don't want it. I don't. I don't deserve it now. I'm no better than the body I'm lying on, worse actually. It makes me spiral inwards further, knees pulling up to my chest as I stare at the grey stone in my grasp and try to keep listening for a heartbeat in this soaking chest I'm on. None. Dead. Nothing but ooze and gore, his blood still warm and wet against my ear.

"Can you move? Jesus."

Move? Why would I move anywhere? I can't remember doing anything of my own volition lately. It's all been about them and what they want, what they need. It's never been about what Madeline wants, what Maddy needs.

He never even saw me, did he? It was always her he saw when he looked at me, always her he felt when he held me. And now they've gone. They've gone and left me to deal with the aftermath of their actions on my own.

"Hold still. Don't move a muscle."

I'm not moving any muscle. I'm staying right here with Lewis, hoping to cling to what memories I have of the Seine and his smile. Why did he have to turn into that monster he became? Why? None of this would have happened if he'd just been the man I fell in love with. We should be in our garden now. In love. Happy. Instead he's here, his body decomposing with every breath I pull in and out. I can't even blame them. This was me. My hand. My body.

I sigh into him, a passive lull settling as the weight of my actions finally begins to find a home inside me. It's getting colder with each passing minute, my bones sensing the loss of heat from him. Maybe when he's as icy as Selma's fog I can figure a way out of what I've done, find something to tell the police when they come for me.

A sharp shriek catches my strained attention, pulling me from my blurry haze. It's my crow. He's there, hopping about in the fog, wings batting the mist towards me and clearing the view in front. I smile a little at him, my hand relaxing its grip on the stone, not knowing if he's real or not but finding comfort in something familiar. He reminds me of Selma's ring, of the love they shared and the warmth I felt with them. I hope they're happy now, I do. I hope they've found each other again somehow, even if it does mean I'm alone.

He jumps, gliding over the murk to land by my side, his sharp beak nipping by my hand on the stone.

"What do you want now?" I mumble, my throat scratching. He pecks again, furiously flapping and fidgeting to rouse my attention further.

"Just hold onto him. I'm nearly there."

I shake my head at the sound of the man's voice behind me again, not giving a damn if he's nearly here or not. I don't even know if he's real or not, let alone what he's coming for. And if he's coming to help me, he can turn back around and go home. I don't deserve help. I'm as damned as Jack was with his dogs, as loathsome in my vengeance.

The crow shrieks again, louder and more intent. I squint, trying to shield myself from his wings as he keeps up his unrelenting tantrum.

"What?" He pecks again, feet jumping in front of me, then moves to the side and pecks again.

"Don't let go of him 'til I get there."

Who? The crow?

Something grabs at my ankle, grasping it tightly and beginning to pull. I slide backwards a little, causing reality to come crashing in around me as wet ground sluices my lips. My leg kicks out, fear tearing through my body as I haul on the stone to pull myself away from whatever it is. The crow flies up, his wings flapping, talons reaching towards my face and then over my head.

"What the fuck?" the voice shouts behind me, a sudden aggressive lilt to his voice. I spin sluggishly to the sound, watching as the man tries to bat my crow away. "Just hold onto that damn stone until I can get to you."

His tone makes me peer at him through the cacophony of wings and arms. It's so familiar, like an embedded resonance from my past. I can't pinpoint it, though. It's suppressed somewhere inside me, a memory carved into my mind that I can't see. I grab the stone again, heaving my tired limbs forward to cling to it rather than have another man ever touch me again. Ghosts and guns are all I have left for men now. That and the reality of my life without anyone in it.

I feel dormant as I watch the silhouettes fight with each other, the crow bouncing between the light of the sky and the pitch black soil beneath them both. The man defends his position as he tries to get across the bog, arms striking at the crow as he keeps coming for me. The bog? I scan the ground, suddenly realizing where I am, and watch as the earth lathers and quivers around me, nothing but this stone somehow standing firm in the middle of it. There's nothing else. Not even Lewis.

I frown, my hand reaching for the ground he was on a minute ago.

"Lewis?" I whisper, unsure what's happening. Where's he gone? I stretch further out, testing the sodden ooze of oily blackness, only to find nothing but more of it below the surface. "But he was here. He was. Where..." My eyes tear around the area, both hands reaching around me, searching for his body. I was lying on it. I was. I saw the bullet holes, felt the heat of his skin against mine. It was here. It happened. And where's the gun gone? "Selma." Her name whispers out of me quietly as I slowly move out into the bog, still searching for Lewis, fear I've lost my mind completely pushing me towards the only image of reality I have. "Are you still here?"

"Jesus. Don't let go of that. Fuck." His voice startles me back to the present as he latches onto my wrist and starts tugging. I stare straight up into blackness, his looming shadow casting into my face. "Just stay down. I'll have to drag you out. Hold onto me."

Hold onto him.

Time seems stagnant as I hear those words. Hold onto him. Just hold onto him.

I've heard that before. Moments ago, or perhaps years ago. I don't know. I frown into the shadows around me, trying to remember when I heard it, or who I heard it from. It's familiar again, like this man's tone. He hauls me, my body sliding over the mud and ooze underneath us, powerful arms seeming to pull me along without any fear of this bottomless ground.

"Nearly there, just hold on. Can you push through with me?"

My free arm reaches for him weakly, my feet trying to propel me against the slippery surface, but I haven't got anything left to push with. And why should I anyway? I probably deserve to die in here with Lewis. I should let this bog suck me under, let it drown out the last memories I have of a life lived inadequately.

Just hold onto him.

Get up, Maddy.

Real time comes racing back before I've taken another breath, her voice exploding in my ears. My vision swims round, bright colours erupting from the grey shadows I've been in, making me squint and hold my arm up to stop the brightness. I can't move, though. I can't. It's pulling me back down, the pressure dragging me. I claw at him feebly, fingers trying to hold on as I feel my legs sinking back into the bog. It sucks at me, trying to yank me back regardless of his heavy pull on my arms and my pathetic fight against it. It doesn't matter how often I push, or how hard I seem to try, I've got nothing left to try with.

I'm done.

Get up, Maddy. We need you. The future.

Something lifts my hips. I feel it, and the abrupt forward surge of my body has me clambering onto firm ground, looking back for whatever pushed me here. Nothing's there. Nothing but the stone a few metres out and the sluice of bog I've come through.

I pant, weary limbs heavy against the grassy bank I'm on, and curl up into a ball again to stare into daylight, searching.

"Are you alright?"

Warmth dowses me, something soft landing against my skin and blanketing me. I shake under it, still staring back towards that stone and wondering what the hell just happened. There's no Lewis to see. No gun. No sign of the men I thought I'd shot either. There's only daylight, a bright spring day casting nothing but sun onto what was gloom and shadows a minute ago, birds chirping in the trees around me.

"Madeline?" The voice moves in front of me quietly, his tone lighter now he's stopped shouting and yelling. "Are you hurt?" I don't know if I'm hurt or not, nor do I care. I'm just a ball of nerves and sensations, barely registering anything but this daylight I'm in as I stare at the stone and finally see some reason for it. My fingers reach forward a little, unsure what I'm trying to reach for until something small lands in my hand. I bring it closer, suddenly understanding what it is and looking at the glass screen caked in mud. My phone. "Come on, let's get you warm. Just hold on."

I feel his arms pick me up, feel him shrug me into him and move, but I can't take my eyes off the stone behind me. It's the words I've just seen carved in. They're words I didn't see before in the gloom. Words I wish I wasn't seeing now. And tears I thought had run dry come as I keep reading them over his shoulder, my head bobbing with his movement. They're tears that threaten to spiral me into a madness of a loss I didn't know I'd feel. Didn't realize I'd have too.

Three names and dates. All of them together on a blackening stone.

The last one a man I loved.

Chapter 23

Madeline

Soft hands put me down at the front of the main house, gently lowering me onto the steps. I stare out towards the gravel, barely holding the covering around me. I haven't looked at him yet. I chose to close my eyes and imagine Jack as we came back, remember him. And now I feel bruised somehow, my limbs all but exhausted as I gaze onto the parkland we've just come across. It's all so bright, sunshine pouring onto the fields and valleys, the tall redwoods bathed in a sprinkling of glittering gold, but I feel empty of the warmth I should feel because of it. Lost.

"Wait there. I'll just unlock the door."

"It's open," I mumble, searching the skyline for him. "It's always open."

"What?"

Shoes walk around into my view, mud still covering them from his heroics as a tall frame blocks my view. Not that he pulled me out entirely. I know that now. I knew it the moment I saw their names on that stone, the dates of their deaths engraved next to them. It was Jack who lifted me out. Jack who offered that final shove to get me free as my own will faded.

"I think we need to get you to a doctor," he says, alarm in his voice.

I smile at that and look past his legs, the curve of my lips creeping up from somewhere deep inside me. A doctor couldn't tell me what's happened here. No one can. I'm not even sure I know, or if *they* even do, but it has happened. I can feel it all as I look around for Lewis' car, knowing it won't be here. She'll have made that disappear along with him, leaving me free to go on as I please without his menace controlling my life.

"Do you think they're happy now?" I ask, slowly climbing to my feet and bypassing him to aim for the old redwoods, perhaps hoping I might get a glimpse of them together.

"What are you talking about?" he says behind me, feet crunching the gravel to catch up.

My own bare feet hardly feel the sharp indents as I peer into the glade, smiling at the bluebells and lush green grass. It all seems so alive here now, as if the last however long was held under a cloud, waiting for spring to bring the sun and start life again.

"Jack and Selma. You think they're together again now?" He slides to a stop, grabbing my arm harshly and swinging me back to him. I shrug him off and keep walking, intent on my destination and refusing to see anything other than my thoughts. I want to see them, thank them maybe. I don't know how, or even if I should, given me killing my husband, but I need to tell them it's okay now, that all of this is okay. "Maybe they've found Lenon, too."

There's an infuriated huff behind me, one that reminds me of a man I made love to. It's the type of sound that would have once had Maddy shaking in fear, her limbs shivering under the thought of malice and bruises, but it's not enough to stop me walking away anymore. I'll walk where I damn well please, certain in the knowledge that they did all this for me. And I want to find them because of that, thank them and see something I helped make happen. They're alive to me, still here somewhere, maybe inside of me or really out there, running free. Perhaps if I go up to the treehouse again I'll see her fog, find her in it.

"Mrs. Blisedy, my brother's dead. What are you talking about?"

Brother?

The thought piques my interest back to him, a sneer touching my lips at the thought of that name. Blisedy. I'm no longer Blisedy. I'm Cavanngh again now. Fully. The death of my husband proves it. How and when I'll explain that to the world I don't know, but I will. Somehow.

I turn slowly and hope beyond all hope that I can see Jack hiding in him somehow, see his smile coming for me to remind me what all this has been about.

My stomach convulses at the first glimpse, part of me wanting to run into his arms, the other needing to sit down and take him in. Tall, dark, the frown I know so well covering heavy set eyes. He quirks a lip at my stare, hands faltering at his sides under my scrutiny until he pockets them and lowers his gaze a little. I keep staring, suddenly unsure if I should keep walking away from him towards Jack and Selma, or stay here and let whatever they've both been playing at carry on interfering with my life.

"Twins," I murmur, still musing over every identical feature on show. My legs inch me closer, the long Mackintosh I'm wearing hugging my frame in a show of decency. "Or maybe you're not you at all. Maybe you're him." He raises a brow, brightening his dower look into the mischievous man who smiled at me when ghosts starting appearing in my life. "Who are you?"

"I'm pretty certain I'm not my brother, Mrs. Blisedy. You definitely need a doctor."

"Really? You look like him." I edge closer again, noticing every line that seems to make him more like Jack the nearer I get.

"I don't see how you'd know that," he says, his brow folding again as he stares me down.

It's a fair point, one I'm struggling to explain other than simply blurting out the truth. He's been dead for two years apparently. That's what the dates said. Selma and Lenon a little over a year before that.

"You recognize me, too, don't you?" He shakes his head and reaches for me, beckoning me back towards the house, his hand outstretched as if wanting to guide me. Oh, he's so like him. Handsome, that slight look of superiority waiting in his features, showing the world he will not be pushed into conversations he's not ready to acknowledge.

"Please, if I get you inside I might be able to find you some clothes."

Clothes? I'm not sure I want any. I tug the coat a little tighter, still able to feel Jack's last touch on my skin in the treehouse, some element of me desperate to leave any trace of it on me that I can. I look back to the headland, missing the sensation now I know it's gone, and search the ground for any kick of spring leaves that might flutter up. There's nothing, though. Nothing but a tranquil landscape stretching on for miles and miles, the air as clear as they've made it become.

"How did he die?" I eventually mumble, sighing as I turn back towards the steps and wander past him into the house.

He catches up as I weave along the hall, my fingers running through the dust on the surfaces in the hope of feeling them somehow. It's all so familiar, all so engrained in me, just like it was when they were here. I stop by the bottom of the spiral, eyes flicking to the rug we made love on, and then stare up the black steps. They turn as elegantly as they always have, the carvings of the bannister flowing upwards like a temptation, but this time they seem brighter, as if the darkness has left.

"Are you alright? You sure we don't need a doctor?" I swing back, irritated with his concern, and peer into his face.

"I asked how he died." He sighs and runs a hand through his hair, another Jack scowl descending, which makes me giggle slightly and look back at the spiral again.

"Look, I don't know what's happened here, or why you're naked for god's sake, or even what the hell you were doing up there in the bog, but can I suggest we get you some clothes and then get you home?" he says, walking away from me through to the kitchen. "I'm sure there must be some of Selma's clothes here somewhere that you can wear." Clanking and banging reverberates back from him as I keep looking up the stairs, wondering what's up there now that the men are gone. My foot inches onto the first step, then the next, ready to go look for cages and work out what was real and what was not. "The buyers will be here soon, and if you're okay I'd really rather you weren't naked when they arrive."

My head whips back towards his voice coming from the kitchen.

"What buyers?"

"Blandenhyme is being auctioned off this afternoon." Every nerve I have rushes through me at the thought, violently tingling and telling me something I don't understand. He walks back into the circle around us and holds out some clothes "That's the reason you're supposed to be here, to value the antiques before it's gone so we can empty the place." Anger suddenly explodes inside me, the image of any of this being removed sending shivers of disgust across me in waves.

"How much?" I snap out, feet storming back to him as I reach for the clothes in his hands and snatch them from him.

"What?" he says, confused at my abrupt hostility I'm sure.

"How much is it being sold for?"

"A lot." My eyes narrow, unsure how much I have in my bank accounts.

"How much is a lot?"

"Look, Mrs. Blisedy, I'm–"

"HOW MUCH?" He startles, his hands coming up as he backs away and crunches over the very rug I made love to him on. What the hell was that thought? I shake my head, snorting. Not him. Jack. His brother. He glowers at me, clearly infuriated he's not in on whatever joke I'm thinking about, his mouth clamped into a line of unamused consideration. "I'm sorry. Just, how much do you want for the house and land?"

"One point three million, at least. It's a substantial property. Now, please. If you could…"

My shoulders slump, his words trailing off as I think about that much money, and my legs reel back towards the stairs. Any thought I had of being able to get the place falls away as quickly as my shoulders. I might be wealthy in my own right, but that much is out of reach without Lewis' backing, no matter how well my business does. And he's gone now, no help available to save this house from whatever development will ensue.

The dust in the air flickers past as I quietly pull my legs into the trousers, blanketing the area with visons of what I've been involved in here. I smile weakly and shrug into the loose fitting jumper, wondering if they're Selma and Jack, the particles little flecks of them still wandering around their home.

"What's your name?" I ask as I get up, melancholy flooding me with memories that still aren't mine to remember.

"Toby Caldwell."

I nod at that and walk towards the hall, remembering Lenon in this very room, fire trucks scraping the wooden floor. I can almost hear Jack's voice from the other end of the building, too. He's calling out for him, telling him he's home and ready to play. They both make me smile and giggle slightly, the sentiment as vibrant in my heart as it was when I first felt them.

"And you're positive you're you, Toby?" He laughs at me, his hand reaching around me to open the main door.

"As much as you're sure of who you are." I snort at that, not sure who any of us are anymore, but knowing there's nothing left I can do now regardless. I suppose at least they're together now. And Lewis is dead. They've done that for me, helped me pull a trigger I never would have pulled on my own. "As I was saying, Bob's fixed your car now. I'm sorry I was late—traffic, you know? Perhaps you wouldn't have been wandering around in the bog if I was on time. Might have kept your clothes on. Not that that was too much of a hardship for me to witness. What happened to them by the way?"

"Late?" He frowns and hovers, his hand on the door.

"You're more bothered about me being late than the loss of your clothes?" He chuckles. I stare, focusing my point. What does he mean late? "It's three o'clock. My secretary told you one, didn't she?"

"But I've been here for days." I gaze at the hall table, trying to work out what he's talking about and find some sense in it. "I met Jack here at the door and he took me to the ballroom first." The thought hovers, searching for reasons even though I know I must sound idiotic. It's just the timing's not right, regardless of if he was alive or not. Too much has happened for only a few hours. "The Hopper sketches. They're in the study. I saw them. And then we danced after that. He held on too tight, frightened me." A hand rubs my back, seemingly trying to soothe my ramble. I snatch away from it, hands grabbing onto the table to focus me into sane thought and search for answers.

"No, you arrived around one, via the lower bog according to Bob, and you were meant to meet me here. Toby Caldwell? Bob said you wandered off when he started fixing the car." No, that's not what happened here. It isn't. I hold up a finger at him, remembering the drive back home, the smoke that filled my lungs as my house burnt down around us.

"And my house. He took me there. He did. We went in the Porsche. The green one. Lewis burnt it down and then he came here looking for me. Jack showed me those men upstairs in the cage, told me they would protect me." And they did, they chased Lewis up into the woods, and Selma helped me, made me kill him. "That's why I was up there, Toby. Because of Jack." Toby looks confused as I ramble on with my thoughts, trying to piece it all together.

I look back into the main house, peering for the stained glass window Jack stood under with a gun aimed at himself. I can still smell him. I'm right. I know I am. And I know he's dead because I saw the gravestone but…

Both hands fly to my mouth, a gasp escaping before I've controlled it. "He killed himself, didn't he?" Oh god, I saw him do it. I never took the gun off him, did I? I thought I did, but maybe I didn't and all this is twisted somehow.

I look at my hand, the other grasping around on the table for some support against the image of him firing that gun into his mouth. I remember him holding me, remember the kiss that came from his lips as we hovered there in that strange light, remember his fingers entwined with mine as we made love.

"How do you know about the cage?" Toby asks.

I snap my gaze to him, back to the present with just the sound of him. He peers, aggression suddenly all over his face regardless of his cool demeanour. I watch the change, see the scowl develop to show Jack shining back at me.

"That's where he kept them, after they'd…" I swallow the words, barely able to utter them as I remember the vile images Selma forced through me. "After Selma and Lenon." His eyes narrow, the door quietly shutting under the weight of his hand. I grit my teeth, ready to defend myself against whatever taunt he might try for. Someone has to believe something. If they don't then maybe I have to admit Lewis isn't gone either, and I need him gone. I do. "This was real, Toby. It was. I'm not mad and you're not telling me I am. I'll show you if I have to." How, I don't know, but I'm not delusional. I saw all this, was part of it with them.

"I'd say you're quite mad, but keep talking, Mrs. Blisedy."

My hand flusters on the table, unsure how I prove any of it, and something flicks under my finger and bounces to the floor, metal clattering the tiles in the large porch. The sunlight glints off it as it tumbles, making me squint into the corner as I see it stop. It's Selma's ring. It lies there naked of anything. She should have that. Why hasn't she got that? I reach to pick it up, but Toby's hand gets there before mine.

"What's this?" he asks, bringing it to his face.

"Selma's wedding ring. The crow brought it to me." I frown. That even sounds ridiculous to my own ears. He raises a brow at me in disbelief. I don't blame him, but this is true. "It did, Toby. I promise. It was stuck around his leg and I helped get it off. Jack snatched it from me. He was so angry with me for having it. He said he'd never found it, and then Selma came for the first time and I started to understand. Sort of." He keeps staring at me, seemingly interested, eyes like slits. "I wish I could make you see. The ballroom was covered in fog and the curtains billowed." My hands flap, mimicking curtains. "It was cold when she came. God he was grouchy with me about that ring."

He smiles slightly, I don't know what at. I'm rambling, barely coherently, about billowing curtains and ghosts. I stare through him, trying to find something real to help in my quest.

"Hmm." He abruptly walks away into the house again, leaving me standing there not knowing what to do as he disappears. I don't know how to explain this, or even if I should. Maybe I should just go, remember this on my own somehow and go see if Lewis really is dead. "You want a drink?" he calls back. Oh god, yes please.

By the time I'm back to the spiral, he's in front of me with a bottle of something brown and two glasses, one handed in my direction.

"Up you go then," he says, tipping his drink to his mouth and pointing up the stairs.

"What?"

"Show me the cage." I gape, unsure what he wants to see that for. I'm not even sure if I want to see it again in all honesty. How's that going to help anything? "Let's see what you think you know about my brother, Madeline." He sips again and runs his tongue over his lips, the wry smile lingering making him so much more than simply Jack's twin. "You've got fifteen minutes to convince me about ghosts and ghouls before I call the loony bin for your ass. Cute as it is."

Fifteen minutes.

Chapter 24

Toby

Jesus. If my dick wasn't straining at my pants so hard I'd probably think I was on the same planet she resides on. Jack still here? It's irrational as hell, but whether it is or not I'm still intrigued. The fact that she's the image of Selma really isn't helping me. How my bastard brother ever snagged her is still beyond me, even to this day. He did, though, regardless of the fact that I went for her across that bar first. Drunk.

"Go on then," I say, pointing again. She frowns at me still, her hands tightening, fidgeting as she looks at the spiral. "Tick tock."

"Why?" she snaps with a haughty lift of her chin.

My dick strains again at the image of it. Any woman who can stand there wittering on about fucking ghosts, all the time covered in mud with twigs in her hair, and then dare lift her chin at me like I'm the fool deserves the smirk that comes across my face.

I walk closer, licking my damn lips again like I've got no control over anything.

"For a start, no one knows about the cage. I dismantled it myself." It took me two fucking days, but no way was the rest of the world knowing what he'd done. "You do, apparently." It's damn well concerning. He might have gone mad after Selma and Lenon, and I don't fucking blame him after what they did to them, but I wasn't having anyone vilify his body for it. I'm still not. "And secondly, look at you." She scans her body, filthy feet turning in on themselves, and yet still she manages to raise that damn chin like she's got every right to be covered in dirt.

I flatten my infatuated smirk as I think about that, and sip my drink instead, trying to hold onto some amount of superiority in this situation. The fact that I own, run, and mediate the biggest construction company this side of Canada apparently means fuck all in her presence. I'm like a child again as she sneers a little.

Doesn't stop her looking at my dick, though.

"I want some answers, Madeline."

She nods after that and starts climbing the stairs, determination setting in, as if she's looking for answers, too. I'm not surprised with the crap that's been pouring from her mouth, but she knows things—things she shouldn't fucking know.

"It's on the third floor," she says quietly, her hand holding the bannister gently as she turns.

See? Things like that. No fucker knows that.

I follow, pouring another damn drink. It's not just everything she's saying that makes me need another. It's the memories of what I did. I dragged those three bodies up to the bog with Bob, burying them so that no one would ever find out what Jack had become. Bob had always known they were there and called me two days after the suicide to ask me what to do. How the hell I'd never noticed what he was up to, I don't know. So much for twin intuition.

And that's where I found her, right on top of where we buried them. Naked.

She spins on me suddenly, still narrowing her eyes and scanning me constantly like I'm a damn conundrum she can't fathom. I know the fucking feeling well. Her mouth opens, and I wait for another dramatic outburst about my brother.

"Why are you selling up?"

"Keep climbing, Madeline. Or are you a Maddy?" She chuckles instantly, laughing at me as if I've said the funniest thing she's ever heard.

"You can't sell up, Toby. They still need it."

She trails off after that, begins mumbling and muttering to herself about something as she hangs on the bannister, feet lightly tripping around the stairs. "You look so much like him. It's eerie really," she suddenly says, tipping her head back to look at me and stopping. Of course I do. She said it herself—twins. Although I still don't understand how the fuck she knows that either.

I stare at her over the rim of my glass, half wanting to lay her down and burrow into something I never got the chance at. She looks like she owns the place, and I half smile as I remember Christmases here—Selma standing on the stairs with Lenon on her hip and Jack berating me for staring at his wife too long.

"You want lifting to the top," I mutter, unsure what the fuck is going on. "Or can you get there without opening that mouth of yours again?" She fucking sounds like her, too. Different, she's got more American going on than Selma ever had, but it's there nonetheless.

"I thought I had fifteen minutes," she says, a hand resting on her hip.

"Ten now with all the time you've wasted climbing fucking stairs, Madeline." She smiles, lighting up this tired old house exactly the same way Selma did, then spins away again giggling to herself and beginning to dance her way up the stairs.

"Very Jack like, Toby. Grouchy." I watch her go, bemused as she begins humming and bouncing slightly, arms out as if she's balancing on eggshells. "Are you positive you're not him? Because anything's possible in this house, they've shown me that." I'm so close to showing her how different I am from my brother. I'm barely restraining the need to grab at her and do things I have no business doing. "Strange things happen here, Toby." She's damn right.

I watch as she turns onto the third level, tiptoeing across the floor and heading straight for the door the cage used to be in. She doesn't even look anywhere else, like she knows exactly where she's going. She's right in some respects. This old mansion has been odd since the day I found him here, brains blown all over the damn wall. It wasn't when they moved in. It was just old, ready to fill with furniture and dreams, but then after Selma and Lenon died he let it rot around him, and after I found him dead a year later, it seemed cold constantly.

"What do you want to know?"

The question catches me off guard. I don't know what I want to know. I just know that this woman is the closest I've got to seeing my brother for a long time. I miss him, miss his dry sense of humour and his ability to push me harder than I thought possible. I felt like a part of me died that night along with him. Twins are like that, bound by something that other siblings don't have access to.

"What did you see in here?" I ask, nodding at the door.

"Three men in a cage," she replies whimsically, walking closer to it and running her fingers over the chopped up handle. "They moved like dogs." Dogs? "I did that." My eyes narrow. "With an axe." The thought of her with anything close to an axe has me snorting in derision.

"Madeline, that's been like that since I found him. I don't know what you think has happened here, but–" She swings back to me, her finger pointing as she walks up to me and pokes me in the chest, hard.

"No, Toby. I did that a few hours ago." She pokes again. "I did it before he took me to that room up there." She waves her hand along the corridor towards the room I found all Selma's belongings in. "And then I found a picture of Selma in this drawer, realised how much I look like her," she says, walking to the old bureau and running her fingers over it. She smiles at something, eyes directed at the staircase. "And then we went to Lenon's treehouse and she came again, showed me what they needed me for."

There's no way she should know shit like this. It's weird.

I watch as she turns back to the doorway, pushing on it and walking in. She stops immediately, eyes scanning for whatever she can't see, and then wanders straight for the marks on the wall where I detached the bolts.

"Here," she says, fingers running over the holes. "And the keys were here," she continues, wandering those fingers back to the old hook. "Jack stood behind me." She looks back towards the small table. "There was a picture of Selma in a sliver frame, taken on the terrace outside." All true. I can't even find a reason to tell her she's wrong. "I can still smell them." My stomach rolls with the thought. I can, too, but if she thinks they were alive then I'm damn glad she didn't see what I found after Bob called me.

I find myself leaning against the wall, some part of me falling into a damn trance as she carries on around the room, reciting everything in exact order. The lines of the cage floor. The shackles that were hanging. The curtains that were heavy against the back wall, ones I eventually pulled down to let some fucking light and fresh air into the cesspool of filth and blood that was here.

She turns abruptly, scanning the walls in the corner. "The gun." What? She flusters her hands around the woodwork, skimming the wallpaper lightly. "The bullet must be here somewhere. That'll prove this is true." I didn't find any guns, apart from the one in Jack's hand, and that's still under this suit to this day. "I shot at Lewis here. Well, not at him. I only wanted to scare him off really." She glances back at me. “And they were in the way so I couldn’t see straight anyway.”

“Who?”

“The men. They were in front of me after I let them out, protecting me,” she mumbles, still searching. My brow creeps up, wondering what fucking planet she’s on. I can’t damn well deny any of this truth, though. No matter how much I want to. “Oh, for god’s sake. It must be here.” She inches down the wall, peering, and still not finding what’s she’s after. Her head swings back again, looking at me. “I was right where you are, Toby.” She storms over. “Do you have a gun? Of course you do. All Americans have a gun. Give it to me.”

“You think I’m giving you my fucking gun? In your state of mind?” She frowns.

“Okay then, hold it yourself and point it over there.” My eyes roll at the suggestion, making me sip another damn drink and huff. She quirks her head at me, somehow steamrolling me into doing what she says. “Scared, Toby? Not so much like Jack then, hey?”

Perhaps it’s intrigue, or perhaps it’s just the suggestion that he was braver than I am, but I’m pushing of the wall, putting my drink down, and getting the fucking thing out before I’ve over thought it. She gasps, reaching for it. I snatch it back to my side.

“Not likely, Madeline.”

"That's Jack's." Fuck.

"How the hell do you know that?"

She shakes her head and smiles, disregarding whatever thought she's had. "It's the one I used, Toby. He opened the panel and let me have it." How the hell does she know about that? "Hold it up." She trails off again as I slowly raise it at her, and walks to the wall, inspecting it until eventually she turns and points at a small indent in the shadow of the door frame, a triumphant smile gracing her face. "See. Bullet." And then she's off out of the room, determination in every step. "Not mad, Toby." I follow again, noting the small hole she pointed out and peering into it to find exactly that. Damn, she's right. "Come help me find the other one," she calls.

"What other one?" I pick up my drink and slowly exit the room, wondering what else she's about to tell me.

"Well, he was trying to shoot himself and I stopped him." That is mad. He's dead.

"Gravestone?"

"Yes, but not then. I mean, he is dead, you're right, but he wasn't a few hours ago. Well, not to me anyway." I turn onto the second floor and find her skimming her hands over the steps, searching again. "We wrangled the gun. Fought. I stopped him, but the gun shot around here somewhere and he was desperate to find the bullet." She moves again, glancing around. "Now I think about it, he said he didn't want to let another woman down. Muttered it beneath his breath."

Stupidity, or intrigue, has me searching with her, because that is just what he would have said. He was so angry at himself for allowing their deaths. He blamed himself for it all, no matter how many times I tried to tell him there was nothing he could have done. Weeks and weeks passed and all he did was drink himself into a stupor, barely existing but for these old walls around him. He revered them, said they were all that was left of Selma and Lenon. And then he seemed to change, became someone I barely knew at all. It happened overnight. I eventually knew why two days after I found him dead. He'd found the fuckers, made them pay.

I smile at the thought, part disgusted by what he became and yet still in awe of him because of it. My brother, never one to let something go until he'd got the better of it, beaten it.

"Why can't I find it, Toby?" she says, scrabbling around on her hands and knees. I watch her and slow my searching until I can't be bothered and just watch her move. "I've got to find it. Prove this somehow." I'm not that sure she needs to anymore. Not for my benefit anyway. For some reason, and maybe because of those earlier words, I believe her. Or at least I believe she believes it.

"It doesn't matter."

"It does," she snaps, her face flying to mine as I look down at her and sit on a step. "It does to me. I need to know why. Why did they make me kill him?"

"Who?"

"My husband." Her fingers fly to her mouth the moment she says it, her body halting its erratic movements. "Madeline Blisedy." She chuckles a little and looks back at the stained glass window, musing the patterns of light that come in. "How much did you say you wanted for the house?"

"What?" She laughs. She laughs out loud and all but falls onto the step behind her until she's almost hysterical.

"Oh god. I'm free, Toby." Where the fuck is this going now?

She clambers up and runs down the last of the stairs, swinging to the right and heading for the back of the house as fast as she can. I shake my head at her absurdity and check my watch, wondering what the hell I'm going to do with her when the buyers start arriving. I'm not even sure I want to do anything with her other than listen to her as she keeps talking about Jack. It's comforting, warming. Enough so that I pull Selma's ring out of my pocket and wonder what it's trying to tell me, let alone why it was just lying there on the hall table.

I stand and follow her slowly, scanning my eyes over the interior, desperate to see him walk around the corner and berate me for looking at his wife again. But she isn't his wife, is she? Not this time. I chuckle a little at that and try to clean the old ring up, my thumb pushing against the dirt ground in. It comes loose easily enough, the engraved letters muddied but still legible. They make me smile as much as the day I stood by his side as his best man, handing the platinum over to him when the time came.

Love Eternal.

"I'll have it," she screams as I wander along the hall towards the ballroom, her voice filled with joy. I look up, wondering what the hell she's talking about now. "Home, Toby. That's what she meant all those times she said it. Home."

She's spinning around by the time I get to her, arms wide as she twirls in the middle of the room. I stare and back towards the sidewall of mirrors, a smile on my own face as I remember their wedding day in here.

"Whatever price," she says. "I've got the money now he's dead." She twirls and glides again, barely a breath coming from her as she sweeps the circumference of the room in my coat, mud coating limbs that need bathing and caressing. My own throat tightens, my dick still struggling to contain inappropriate reactions to this insanity as I watch on. So beautiful. Insane, but beautiful nonetheless and dragging me onto whatever fucking planet she's from. "I'm home."

She suddenly pulls to a stop in front of me, a slight frown glancing her brow. "As long as he *is* dead. I'm very rich if he's dead. You think he is? I shot him. I think I did anyway. With that gun under your suit jacket. Jack's gun. Not that you can tell anyone that if I did. You won't, will you?" She looks at the window then the door. "Selma?" I frown at that, unsure if talking to the dead makes this more plausible or less. She nods, then giggles, apparently happy with whatever answer she might or might not have got. "Do you dance, Toby?" What the actual fuck?

"No."

"He said that, too." She smirks. "He did, though. He was very good at it. Are you? Come on." She holds her hands out, wafting them at me. "We have to dance. It'll make it all real. Give it reason. I'm not wasting this house away not I've got it." I tentatively step forward, scarcely sure any of this is real. Real would mean none of this came from her mouth, but then if it's not real, how does she know? And she feels real as I take hold of her. Perhaps it's the way she tilts her head, or maybe it's the way her fingers lie softly in mine, hesitancy making me squeeze for more contact to make this as real as she wants it to be.

She smiles at me, and waits for me to lead her, her body swaying slightly to music that isn't here. So I tighten my hold again and grab her into me until she's up on her toes and a breath away from my lips. She's prettier than Selma this close up, a softness in her face that Selma never held seeming to radiate in the glow between us. Even filthy and insane, she captivates every thought I'm having, tempting me towards her with every exhale for some goddamn reason.

My tongue licks over my lips in an attempt to keep them away from her, but then why fucking bother? As she said, strange things happen in this house, and if it's all true then maybe this is meant to be somehow.

"You want to dance then you dance with me, Madeline," I mutter out, barely able to form sentences with her features clouding rational judgement. "I'm not like my brother."

She widens her smile, eyes flicking down to my lips and then back to me again, as she moves her hips onto mine. It's enough that my dick forges me closer, too, my own hips beginning to sway to music that neither of us can hear.

"Prove it," she says, tightening her hold on me, eyes locked. "To them as well as me." She's mad. Perhaps I am, too, but my feet are damn well moving before I know it, some rhythm coming from the way we move together creating sound. "Because they're here, Toby," she says, her head tipping backwards so she can stare at the ceiling as we turn. "Watching. Being part of us." She smiles and leans further back, letting me take all of her weight to keep us spinning. "They always will be."

The End

Acknowledgements

As always I'd like to send out love and thanks to:

My PA - Leanne Cook, without whom I wouldn't survive this booky world. I always write that, but this time, and especially given this genre swap, I love her more than any of my words can say.

My beta Readers – Jodie Scott and Katie Matthews. Amazeballs. You helped remind that I should believe in myself.

My Editor – Heather at Heathers Red Pen Editing. As usual, love you. Thanks for everything. You're still a star.

My other half – Who is my world and gives me this chance. You don't know how much you mean to me or my words. I love you.

And, of course, all of my readers.

You all amaze me with your kind words and encouragement. There will always be a story in me ready to come out, but it's you lovely readers that help me believe the words are worth reading.
I can only hope that I continue to provoke thought with every novel and encourage your minds to search horizons new.

Also Available by the Author at Amazon

Innocent Eyes

A Cane Novel (Book1)

Hart De Lune

****

"If he's gross, I'm bailing."
That's what I said to my supposed best friend when she asked me to take her place. A blind date, she said. What harm could it do?
He was charming. Beautiful. God's finest creation. He wined me and dined me. Made me do things I'd never before dreamt of in the bedroom. It was perfect. Dangerous. Arousing.
But Jenny didn't tell me the full story. She didn't tell me about the debt she owed. And now Quinn Cane wants his money's worth, and he's going to make me pay whatever way he can.

"A debt needs to be paid."
The woman who came to meet me didn't owe me money. I could tell by her innocent eyes. Still, the debt will be paid either way.
She was something to play with and use as I saw fit, but something about Emily Brooks made me want to keep her.
So she became my dirty girl. Pure. Innocent. Mine.
Then she whispered my damned name and invaded my world, changing its reasoning.
She wasn't meant to break the rules. But she rolled my dice and won.

Charlotte E Hart
THE SPIRAL

The Stained Duet

Once Upon A (Book 1)

Alana Williams is three published authors. She has been for years, but now she wants to add another voice to her whirlwind of deadlines and unachievable targets. Trouble is, she knows nothing of her latest literary undertaking.

*****

Alana

It began as research. Just research. The technical approach. One that delivers the content necessary for a hidden culture to seem plausible, even if it's not. Readers expect perfection from me. They want the experience. They need to be taken on a journey. That's my job as a writer.
Blaine Jacobs is his name. He's my research. A man who seems as logical and focused as me. A man who agrees to help. A man who, regardless of his stature in the community, seems to offer a sense of realism to this strange section of society. And even if he does occasionally interrupt my data with dark brooding eyes and a questionably filthy mouth, what does it matter? It's just research, isn't it? It's not real. None of this is. Nothing will come of it or change my mind.

So why am I confused?
I'm becoming lost.
Falling apart.

And Blaine Jacobs, no matter how calm he might have seemed at first, now appears to linger on the edges of sanity, pushing my boundaries with every whispered word.

Charlotte E Hart
THE SPIRAL

18+ ONLY. Intended for mature audiences.

This book is followed by The End (Stained Duet Book 2)

The White Trilogy Nominated for best BDSM Series of the Year

Seeing White
(Book 1)

"OMG. Amazing writer, amazing books. Deliciously dark and tantalising."

****

Alexander White, the wealthy business man with looks to die for. Just like the other colours you'd think.......but no. He came from a very different place and made some of his money a very different way.
And he keeps it well hidden because the truth would destroy everything he has. All that he's worked for would be gone in an instant if they ever found out what he's capable of, or what he really did and who he did it for. So he keeps people far away with metaphorical games and walls to deceive and confuse.
Three people shaped who he is today. One damaged him beyond repair, another taught him to control the rage, and a decent one helps him to consider his options more appropriately.
But be under no illusions ladies, Mr White has not been a nice man, and he will probably never be a decent man, but as long as he keeps up his image, and nothing gets through his barriers, no one will ever see the truth.

Life's good for Elizabeth Scott, successful business, happy

Charlotte E Hart
THE SPIRAL

kitchen and a great sister who deals with all the expensive people so she doesn't have to. She just cooks, bakes and smiles her way through each day......well most of the time, anyway, that is when her great sister isn't pushing her to, "get out there a bit more," or "sort her shit out."
Then the biggest contract of their lives comes up..... And the ever useless London tube, with her sister in it, catastrophically breaks down. Unfortunately, that means only one thing. She'll have to deal with some of that wealth herself, and that means the devastating Mr Alexander White in all his glory.
Life suddenly couldn't get worse, regardless of his unfairly gorgeous backside.
She has no idea what the hell she's doing.

******

This book is followed by:

Feeling White (Book 2)
Absorbing White (Book 3)

The VDB Trilogy

(Best read after The White Trilogy)

The VDB Trilogy begins a week after the end of The White Trilogy and is told from new POV's. It is, in some ways, a continuation.

****

The Parlour

(Book 1)

Above all else Pascal Van Der Braak is a gentleman. Devastatingly debonair and seductively charming. Always styled and perfected.
He is also a cad, scoundrel, rouge and kink empire founder. Tutored in the highest of society, having been born of royalty only to deny it, he found his solace in a world where rules need not apply. Where he chooses to ensure rules and duty do not apply.
Some call him Sir, others call him master, and no one would dare risk his wrath unless they required the punishment he favourably delivers. Except one, who has just strapped a collar around his throat, one he asked for. So, now he needs to appropriate his businesses correctly for peace to ensue. He needs to find the correct path forward for everyone concerned, so he can relax, enjoy, and finally hand over the responsibility to someone else.
Simple.
But where comfort and a safety of sorts once dwelled, there is now uncertainty, and a feeling of longing he no longer understands. A need unfulfilled. And as problems arise, and allies scheme, he finds himself searching for answers in the most unlikely of places.

Charlotte E Hart

THE SPIRAL

Lilah

It's the same every day. I'd found it odd at first, but I'm used to it now. I was so tired and weak when I got here that it was helpful really. That small woman comes in to help me wash and get dressed. I don't know where the clothes come from, but they're nice enough, and at least they're clean and dry. Not like the rags I arrived in. They were taken from me the moment I took them off to get into the shower, the first shower I'd had in god knows how long. Nearly a year I'd been running the streets, a year without a real bed or a home of any sort. There isn't a long and awful story to tell about an abusive family member, or a broken home. I suppose I just slipped through the cracks and got lost at some point. I lost my job first, and then I couldn't afford the bills on my apartment, so the landlord threw me out. I don't blame him, he did the right thing by himself. And then it was just a long and never-ending road to nothingness.

So now I'm here, wherever here is.

And I don't know why.

****

This book is followed by:

Eden's Gate (VDB 2)
Serenity's Key (VDB 3)

Printed in Poland
by Amazon Fulfillment
Poland Sp. z o.o., Wrocław